The Bloo

Morgan Greene is the pen name of British author Daniel Morgan. He studied Creative Writing and English Literature at Swansea University with a focus on narrative structure and theory. Author of the bestselling Detective Jamie Johansson series, Daniel currently lives in South Wales with his partner and snow-loving collie.

Also by Morgan Greene

Savage Ridge
A Place Called Hope
The Blood We Share

MORGAN GREENE

THE BLOOD WE SHARE

CANELOCRIME

DK | Penguin
Random
House

First published in the United Kingdom in 2025 by

Canelo Crime, an imprint of
Canelo Digital Publishing Limited,
20 Vauxhall Bridge Road,
London SW1V 2SA
United Kingdom

A Penguin Random House Company
The authorised representative in the EEA is Dorling Kindersley Verlag GmbH.
Arnulfstr. 124, 80636 Munich, Germany

A CIP catalogue record for this book is available from the British Library.

Print ISBN 978 1 80436 975 3
Ebook ISBN 978 1 80436 980 7

Cover design by Lisa Brewster

Cover images © Shutterstock

Printed and bound in Great Britain by Clays Ltd, Elcograf S.p.A.

Look for more great books at
www.canelo.co | www.dk.com

Chapter 1

It was well past midnight when Jacob Taylor stumbled out of the Silver Spur, a run-down roadside bar with a humming neon sign plagued by moths and drunks all huddled underneath, trying to keep upright as they fumbled with their lighters and their roll-ups, all fat-thumbed and cock-eyed.

The drawling tones of Lynyrd Skynyrd died behind him as the door creaked closed, 'Simple Man' playing through the jukebox for the fifth time in a row. He glanced back, catching an after-image of the two soaks clinging to each other in the middle of the dancefloor for support, shuffling back and forth, drunk, in love, and with one foot in a nursing home.

Average fare for a Tuesday night, Jacob thought, jostling past the lifers under the sign and finding his footing in the potholed car park.

He stumbled and then found his way towards his truck, walking with one eye closed, the fresh air telling him just how drunk he was. He let out a low whistle, the word 'Fuuuuck' dripping from his lips as he got his keys from his pocket on the second try and bumped right into the door of his Chevy. It took him a few seconds of trying to get the key in the lock before he realised there wasn't one, and that this wasn't his truck.

He pushed himself back off the fender of the Ram and turned around, finding that this *was* his truck. 1982 K10. He scratched up the paint a little getting it open, not thinking at all about how over the limit he was. Hell, if staring at those two drunks on the floor wasn't so depressing, he'd have thrown down at least one more shot and another beer, and then still have driven home. It was a straight road back to his rancher – like every road in South Dakota – and he made it his policy – a responsible policy, he thought – to drive ten-under the posted speed limit. Just in case.

And hell, if he did drop into the verge, it was nothing this old bitch couldn't handle. He slapped the dash proudly, cranking the key in the ignition, the battered and rust-bitten truck firing to life, its V8 coughing, spitting out some shit, and then settling into a satisfied burble.

'Good girl,' he said, patting the wheel and shoving the vehicle into reverse. He jostled into the potholes behind him and then put it into drive, swinging lazily out of the parking lot and onto the dark highway.

The light faded behind him and then it was just his headlights and the night ahead. He hunched forwards, squinting into the darkness, the beams cutting out into nothingness. Which meant he couldn't really see shit. Especially since the headlights were original and the bulbs might as well have been candles.

His eyelids grew heavy as he sailed along. Devils Lake wasn't a big town, and what there was of it was huddled on the shore of its namesake. This highway all but flashed right by it, and if you weren't paying attention – like Jacob wasn't – you'd go right by the turn-off sign.

He blinked a few times as the headlights lit it and then it sailed over his shoulder and shrank in the wing mirror.

Jacob watched it go, hanging on the wheel as he leaned into the door, and pulled the truck off the road and onto the verge.

The sudden step down into the gravel startled him and he swore, wrestling it back straight, just in time to see the headlights catch something else.

He stamped on the brake and all four wheels locked up, sending him into a juddering slide.

The truck came to a halt, the lights shining on the roadway ahead, outlining a figure.

A woman, he thought, walking in the fucking road in the middle of the night? He rubbed his eyes with his knuckles to make sure he wasn't seeing things, and once they were good and kneaded, he refocused, deciding he wasn't going crazy.

He let off the brake and eased forwards, his heart beating a little harder. On instinct he checked the rear-view and wing mirrors again, looking for other headlights this time, for a cop. He didn't want to get caught out stopped on the road.

Jacob didn't have any intention of stopping for this looney bitch. She was asking to get mowed down.

But as he got closer, a prickle struck the back of his neck. He didn't think he realised what he was looking at until he was right on top of her.

As he got up next to the woman, he realised she wasn't a woman at all, just a girl, probably scarcely eighteen, he figured. She was scrawny, barefoot, her heels and calves black with mud and asphalt. Her thin legs spiked up into the bottom of a white dress, the kind they make little girls wear at Christenings. Only it wasn't all white, it was red.

He could feel sweat beading under his jaw, on his temples.

She stopped and turned to look at him, the breath leaving his chest as her eyes met his, sky-blue, on fire in the darkness. He swallowed, seeing the red, knowing it was blood, and leaned across the bench seat, reaching for the handle to roll down the window.

But before he even touched it, she was at the door, pulling it open.

She stood in the gap, no more than three feet of cold night air between them.

'Y-you alright?' Jacob stammered, suddenly aware of how hammered he was.

Wordlessly she climbed into the cab and closed the door. She clamped her knees together, perching on more than sitting in the seat, and clasped her hands in her lap, wringing them forcefully.

His eyes moved up and down her legs, her arms, her dress. Looking for the source of the blood. He could see her hands were caked in it too, the stuff covering her to the elbows. What the hell had happened?

'You want me to call someone?' Jacob asked, his voice barely above a whisper. 'You need a hospital, or...' He trailed off. Police station is what he wanted to say. But he was shit-faced, and not in any frame of mind to explain any of this.

'No,' she said quietly, eyes facing ahead, unflinching.

She was shivering softly. Just a kid. Goddamn it, what happened to her? Who did this to her?

'Where do you want to go?'

'Anywhere,' she said. 'Anywhere safe.'

Jacob clenched his teeth and let off the brake once more. Home, he thought. The girl needed help. She needed to be safe. Once he'd sobered up, thought up some excuse for how he ran into her – one that didn't involve driving drunk – they'd head to the station and get this straightened out. But right now, dog-tired and piss-drunk, he wasn't in any position to be playing hero.

He eased the Chevy up to ten-under the limit, both hands on the wheel, and drove on, more carefully than ever before.

Every few seconds he stole a glance at his passenger.

But she never looked back at him; she just looked straight ahead, her eyes empty, cold, and telling Jacob she'd seen something no one ever should.

And he wasn't entirely sure he wanted to know what that was.

Chapter 2

They drove in silence. Jacob kept casting his eyes across to his passenger, watching as she kneaded the hem of her dress against her thighs. Her skin was pale, smooth, and with the drinks in him, he had to keep reminding himself of the situation, pulling his eyes back to the road instead.

As he slowed and turned onto the dirt road that cut between the modest, boxy ranchers lining the highway, he shifted in his seat, acutely aware that he was driving home. She'd said to go somewhere safe, and other than his house, he didn't know of any such place. He just needed some time to sober up, to think about this. To talk to her and find out what the hell had happened to her. He noticed she was looking around then, at the single-storey houses as they passed, most dark, and realised that if he was in her shoes – or lack thereof, currently, barefooted as she was – he'd probably wonder if he'd jumped out of the frying pan and into the fire. Where was he taking her? And what did he intend to do with her when they arrived? She must be thinking that.

Shit.

He cleared his throat, loudly. 'I, uh, I live here,' he announced, pointing off ahead, into the darkness.

'Oh,' she said, a little surprised by his outburst. 'Okay.'

The answer was subdued. Fearful?

'It's just, I've, uh, I've had a few… drinks – not many, like, I'm safe to drive.' He laughed nervously. 'I just mean that I wasn't sure where else to go, and—'

'It's okay,' she said, cutting him off. The briefest of smiles flickered on her face before her expression changed back to apprehension.

His mouth stayed open, but he didn't know what else to say. Everything else seemed like it might make it worse.

They arrived quickly at the house and Jacob pulled in underneath the attached car port, killing the engine. They were plunged into darkness, the meagre light from the dash disappearing.

The engine ticked softly.

'I live alone,' he said then, feeling like he had to say it. 'If you want to call someone…' He fished his phone from his jacket pocket and held it out to her.

The girl just looked at it.

'A friend?' He stared at her. She looked young. 'Your mom? Your dad?'

She looked at her knees, kneaded her dress again.

Okay, no parents in the frame, Jacob surmised. Shit. What now? What about his name? 'I'm Jacob,' he said, after a few seconds, and then looked up through the windscreen at his house. 'If you want to get cleaned up, take some time…'

'That'd be good,' she all but whispered, still pulling at the bloodied dress. Her hand lifted towards the handle and then paused, as though waiting for him to get out first.

Jacob's heart was beating hard, the cool sweat on his neck and temples chilling him. Who was this girl? She needed help, and though he'd given his name, she hadn't given hers. She was terrified. So terrified she'd gotten into a stranger's car and gone to his home without a word. But what in the world could drive her to that?

She was barefoot, so she'd run from somewhere without taking the time to get her shoes – escaped, Jacob thought. And she was covered in blood – but not hers.

A thought crossed his mind; one that frightened *him*. Who was he letting into his house?

He swallowed. There was a baseball bat leaning against the wall next to his bed and an old Beretta 1911 pistol in the nightstand – his dad's, from Vietnam. And the girl was probably half his bodyweight. So even if she was some psycho escaped from a mental ward hell-bent on wearing his skin like a fur coat, he thought he had a pretty good chance of fending her off.

Or maybe, in the sober light of morning, she'd tell him all about it. The funny, completely innocent story of how she got on that road. Of how she was cooking and managed to throw tomato sauce all over herself. That it wasn't blood at all?

But as he opened his door and climbed from the cab, he didn't really believe that.

She got out after him, walking softly on the gravel as they circled the truck and stepped up onto his rickety porch.

Jacob was a big guy, broad. Probably a little overweight, but he carried it well. He'd played football in college, bulked up for it, and kept his size all this time. And in his thick, wool-lined jacket, he was even bigger. As he fiddled with the key, hands shaking, he realised how small the girl was next to him. The hall light was on inside, casting a glow through the diamond-shaped frosted glass panel in the door, so as he slid the key into the lock, finally, he turned his head and got his first good look at her.

8

She wasn't quite as young as he thought — older than eighteen, but no more than in her early twenties, with soft features. Not quite a woman yet. Delicate. Pretty, even, despite the dark spatter of what might or might not be blood.

She looked back at him, holding his gaze. Her blue eyes the colour the ice on the lake went every winter at its thickest.

'Okay?' he asked, the word catching in his throat. One final confirmation that this was the right thing to do, even though he knew that it wasn't. That it wasn't even close.

She gave an almost imperceptible nod and Jacob's grip tightened on the key.

He let out a shaky breath, turned the key, and then opened the door.

Chapter 3

They stepped inside and the girl moved forwards, her steps unsteady on the soft carpet, as though she'd grown used to the sharp stones of the road.

She picked her way forwards, down the narrow corridor that hadn't been redecorated since the house was first put here in the Seventies. The wood-panelled walls were lined with photos of Jacob's father and his mother. They were both dead, his dad a war veteran that drank himself into an early grave. His mother... Jacob didn't know. She disappeared when he was seventeen.

In the photos, though, they looked happy. Locked in time. Jacob inherited the place when he was just eighteen, the day his mother was declared legally dead. And it'd been a time capsule since.

He hovered by the door, watching the waifish girl move forwards, running her eyes over the photographs, inspecting them slowly.

Jacob turned the keys in his hands, unsure what to do. His eyes drifted past her to his living room, seeing the empty pizza boxes, the dirty laundry, the beer bottles, and cans littered around.

'The place is a mess,' he called after her. 'Sorry, I didn't have time to clean up, and—'

She turned to look at him, her dark, near-black hair a stark contrast to her pale skin. 'It's fine,' she said, just standing there at the end of the corridor.

He took her in, the bloodied skin and dress, the filthy legs. She'd even left dark footprints on the carpet, dirty as it already was.

'Do you want to get cleaned up?' he asked then, a sudden pang of sympathy coming over him. He didn't have any kids of his own, but this was someone's kid. Someone's little girl who'd gone out into the world and got herself into who knew what kind of trouble. 'There's a bathroom,' he said, gesturing to the door behind her. 'There's a towel on the shelf in there, some soap and whatever – not girl stuff, but you know...'

She looked down at herself, as though realising just how soiled her clothes were for the first time.

'I have some old clothes, then,' he said. 'Something of my sister's, somewhere, I think...' He turned his head to the right, looking at the closet next to him, trying to think where some of Steph's stuff might be, but when he looked back, she was gone.

He blinked a few times, wondering if he'd imagined her all along, if he was just that drunk?

The water heater kicked to life then, the hum of the motor running the shower filtering back to him.

He took that as a yes.

Okay, clothes, he thought, reaching for the closet.

He stopped himself. No, they were in a box in the bottom of *his* closet. Right. He started forwards, kicking his boots off as he went, a little wayward from the drink, and neared the bathroom door.

It was a little open.

He willed himself not to look, but couldn't help it.

He slowed a little, looked through the gap into the bathroom, saw a sliver of pale skin.

An arm, a shoulder.

The girl had her back to him, standing in front of the shower, the room slowly filling with steam.

She was looking at herself in the mirror, the angle meaning she couldn't see Jacob.

He should look away. He should walk away, he knew that.

But as she reached up and slipped the strap of her dress over her shoulder and down her arm, guiding it with a delicate, bloodied hand, he held his breath and watched.

She moved softly, like water, her small frame moving and swaying as she guided the other strap off and wiggled out of the dress.

It fell to the floor, pooling at her ankles, revealing her naked back, narrow at the waist, the ridges of her spine showing through her skin, the faint outline of her ribs too, the small, gentle curve of her breast visible under her arm.

Jacob swallowed, his mouth dry as his eyes moved forwards to the dimples in her lower back, lingering there before he took in the rounded, womanly shape of her toned buttocks, her slim, almost muscular thighs, her triangular calves. Not the legs of a girl, no.

She moved then, and Jacob almost fell over.

The girl finished inspecting herself in the mirror and reached out for the door to the shower.

Jacob quickly pointed his gaze at the floor and nearly jumped towards the bedroom, moving in a haze, ignoring the seed of warmth in the pit of his belly. He got into his bedroom and closed the door behind him, falling back against it and closing his eyes. 'What the fuck are you doing?' he muttered to himself.

He shook his head to get some sense to take root, and then drew three deep breaths.

'One night,' he said. 'That's it. She's crashing on the couch and then first thing tomorrow… she's out. Doesn't matter where. Call the cops if you have to. You are *not* getting wrapped up in whatever the fuck is going on here. And you're definitely not getting caught with a twenty-year-old in your house. You're forty, you dumb fuck.' He knocked his head against the door a few times and then went towards the closet, hoping that Steph's clothes were there, that they were clean, and that, if there was any God in the universe, they were baggy.

Chapter 4

By the time the girl finished her shower and stepped out of the bathroom wrapped in a cleanish towel, Jacob had managed to find something for her to wear, and also clear the couch of crumbs and debris.

He stood straight, holding the clothes – an old sweat-shirt and a pair of elastic-waisted cargo pants that had been in his closet since Steph stayed with him two years prior when her roof was leaking and she came to crash for a few nights, leaving some of her clothes behind.

Jacob tried to say 'Hi', but his mouth seemed to be out of his control. His buzz was quickly fading, but he still seemed drunk enough to not be in full control of his mind or body. He'd been racking his brain for some sort of logic, some sort of explanation to all this, to any of this, and though he'd run through what he'd say, what he'd ask – what he'd all but demand to know before the night was out – he lost all sense of it.

The girl stood there in the doorway, arms wrapped around herself, hair wet, skin clean and bright, glowing pink, almost. Like she'd scrubbed herself almost raw. The blood, the dirt, it was gone. But what lingered couldn't be seen, only felt.

Jacob looked away, holding the clothes up. 'Clothes,' he said. 'I, uh…' And then he just put them on the arm of the sofa and took two steps back, keeping his head lowered, trying not to look at any more of her exposed skin than he already had.

She came forwards slowly and laid a hand on the sweater, running her thumb over the frayed collar.

'You can have the couch,' Jacob said then. What is your name? He willed himself to ask, but he couldn't. It felt too much, too pressing. She was standing there in a towel, in a stranger's house. She was trusting him, the least he could do was trust her, right? In the morning, they'd get all this sorted out. Call the cops; hell, call Steph. She'd know what to do. She always did. But right now? Pushing one in the morning, and— shit, with work tomorrow?

He let out a long, shaky breath and ran his hands over his head.

'I have work in the morning, so, uh… yeah. I'm gonna…' He hooked a thumb towards his bedroom and she turned her head to look where he was pointing. 'If you need water or… whatever… Kitchen is—' He gestured to the little kitchen in the corner, the plates stacked high in the sink, the cupboards and refrigerator decidedly bare. 'Just help yourself to… yeah.' He clapped, awkwardly, and she jolted a little. 'Okay.' He put on a strange smile that likely had the opposite effect from dissuading her that he was some weirdo, and then started towards the bedroom.

Usually he'd head into the bathroom, brush his teeth, shed his clothes, shower after a long day at work at the plant – he was a slob, not an animal. But tonight? No, straight to bed. He needed the morning and the clear head that came with it.

He turned to the door to close it behind him and found the girl watching him, still standing next to the couch, hand still on the sweater. Jacob dipped his chin, a singular nod to her.

She returned it, slowly, almost as though it were a reflexive mirroring of the action and nothing more.

God, let this be some fucked-up dream, he thought, before closing the door and kicking off his boots.

He knocked off the light, peeled off his clothes and threw them into the corner, and fell face first into bed, the thin mattress squeaking and bouncing under him.

This was his old room – his and Steph's, at least. He'd lived in this house his whole life. It was two bedrooms, but the other had been his parents', and when his mom disappeared, he left it, hoping she'd come back one day. And then... it just sort of became a time capsule, and then a storeroom. The bedroom wasn't bigger, wasn't nicer. So there was no reason to move in there.

If Steph came by, she'd sleep in there sometimes, but rarely. Jacob didn't like it, and she didn't either. It was Mom and Dad's room. Always would be. Which was why his mystery guest was sleeping on the couch. No way he was putting her in there. No way.

There was a noise beyond the door and Jacob turned over, looking up in the darkness towards it.

He breathed softly, listening. She was just moving around in the living room. Getting dressed, probably. Robbing him, probably. Good luck, he thought. Nothing out there worth stealing.

Another noise then, closer this time. At the door?

He held his breath. Was she looking around? Listening at the jamb to see if he was asleep?

A quiet creak reached him, the tired twist of the door knob, the ancient spring inside.

The door cracked, just an inch, light spilling inwards.

Jacob didn't move. He lay perfectly still, the covers rumpled and strewn on the bed next to him, his skin thinly sheened with sweat. He could feel it, cool and prickling suddenly.

She was right there, but what was she doing?

The door opened slowly, steadily, until he saw her, standing there, silhouetted, her face in shadow, her back to the light in the living room. She was in Steph's old sweater, the thing drowning her, falling to the mid-thigh, the sleeves covering her hands entirely.

She wasn't wearing anything else.

'Is— Is everything alright?' he stammered.

Her hand left the door and she hovered there for a second before entering, her blue eyes glinting in the half-light.

She said nothing as she walked towards him, coming up to the side of the bed until she was level with his head, standing right beside him.

Jacob was lying on his side, one hand under his pillow, the other clutching the bedsheet, fingers dug into the fabric. The only sound in the room was the heavy drumming of his heart.

The girl stood over him, her breath quiet and steady. He looked up at her, willing himself not to look at her naked thighs just twelve inches from his face.

'What are you doing?' he asked, his voice all but strangled in his throat.

Wordlessly she reached down, bending slightly, the sweater pulling itself further up her legs. Almost all the way.

Jacob swallowed hard, watching as her hand reached out, delicate and sure, and settled around his wrist. She tugged a little and he resisted at first, holding on to the sheet. But as she pulled harder, just a flicker of strain passing across her fine features, Jacob let go.

She held his arm, his hand opening, facing the ceiling, unsure what it was she was going to do with it.

And then she began guiding it, away from his body, away from the bed, towards the hem of her sweatshirt, towards what hid beneath.

He stopped her, pulling against her grasp.

'No,' he said, staring up at her in the darkness.

She just nodded.

'No,' he repeated, shaking his head. 'I can't. You can't.' He whispered it, afraid to speak with any kind of volume. This felt wrong. In every sense.

But she didn't relent, taking his wrist with her other hand now, too, digging into his rough skin, hers small enough that the tips of her fingers didn't reach the tip of his thumb. She pulled harder.

'It's okay,' she said, nodding again.

He opened his mouth to protest, but no words came out.

And then, as though to perfectly assuage him of any doubt, she said it again. 'It's okay,' and added the part he needed to hear. 'I know what I'm doing.'

Jacob closed his eyes and let her take his hand, lowering it, passing it under the hem of the sweatshirt. Guiding it upwards, his fingers brushing her inner thighs.

She moaned softly in the darkness, parting her feet slightly, making just enough space for him to touch her, to feel the warmth there, the wetness.

The girl moved his hand, using it as she came forwards, lifting one knee onto the mattress, then the other.

The bed rocked beneath her as she climbed, passing her leg over Jacob's stomach and settling on top of him, lowering herself so her body was pressed against his.

He was on his back, her hair spilling from her head, pooling around his. She smelled like him, like his shampoo, his soap.

Her eyes twitched, searching his face, looking for something.

Jacob didn't know what.

Without looking, she reached down, taking his hands once more and placing them on her hips, dragging them up her back, moving the sweatshirt upwards, undressing her.

He stared at her, at this stranger in his bed, the feel of her against him more intoxicating than any drink he'd ever had.

'Who are you?' he asked, finally mustering the courage.

But she didn't answer. She just silenced him with a kiss. Gentle, tentative, her lips quivering as she did.

Chapter 5

The sun was blaring through the windows when Jacob came to.

He opened his eyes, looking at the ceiling, faded and cracked as it was.

The first thing he became aware of was the taste in his mouth, the lingering metallic tinge clinging to the sides of his tongue. The taste of a woman's body. The room smelled of sex, heavy and thick.

Instinctively he reached out, touching an empty bed, and all at once, he was awake, aware of the sound of a heavy thumping echoing through the house.

Jacob sat up in bed, pulling his hand from the damp sheet next to him and springing from bed. What time was it? Who the hell was hammering on the door? And where was the girl?

He got halfway there when one of the questions was answered.

'Jacob Taylor!' The voice rang through the thin wood shaking in its frame. 'Devils Lake Police Department! Open up!'

He stopped dead in his tracks in the middle of the living room, stark naked, and looked down at his right hand. The one he'd touched the bed with. The one now smeared with... blood?

His heart all but stopped in his chest. Numbly, he turned, stumbling in a tight circle to look back into his bedroom, a trail of bloodied footprints leading from bed, the pale brown sheets splattered with red.

'What the—'

But he didn't get to finish the sentence before the door flew off its hinges, exploding in a shower of splinters.

Jacob glanced over his shoulder, watching three deputies burst into his home.

'Don't move! Get down on the ground!' the man at the front yelled. Jacob knew him. He'd been a freshman in high school when Jacob was a senior, but he'd still made the football team. Todd Ellis was six-three and easily two-twenty. Lean. He was leading the charge, pistol raised, a Smith & Wesson M&P 9, which looked small in his huge hands.

He charged forwards, and on reflex Jacob stepped forwards to lessen the impact, shielding his head with his arms as Todd Ellis ran him down.

Jacob felt a heavy hand on his shoulder, an elbow in his spine, driving him to the floor.

He took one staggering step and then collapsed, feeling two other sets of hands pinning him, gripping his wrists and twisting them roughly up behind his back. One of the officers pressed his cheek into the carpet, into one of his own bloodied footprints, the smell unmistakeable. But whose blood was it? The girl's?

Where was she? What the hell was going on?

'Jacob Taylor,' Ellis announced, kneeling on the small of his back. Cuffs snapped onto his wrists and tightened. 'You're under arrest for the kidnapping of Lily Graham and the murder of Brian Larson and Michael Brown—'

'What?' Jacob squeezed out beneath the weight of Ellis. 'I didn't—'

'You have the right to remain silent,' he said, cutting Jacob off with a little extra pressure from his knee. 'Anything you say can and will be held against you in a court of law...'

Jacob didn't hear anything else.

A deep thundering rumble of blood struck up in his ears and darkness began closing in around the edges of his vision.

He closed his eyes, feeling tears leak from the corners. No, no, this isn't happening. Lily Graham — that had to be the girl's name... but who the hell were the others? Brian Larson and Michael... something? Murder? Jesus. The blood on her dress, her hands, her arms... she'd been there. When they were killed? Had *she*...? And now – oh, fuck. Fuck! The bathroom. God damn it, she'd cleaned up in there, washed off their blood, which meant it was all over his fucking shower, in his drains! And her... her blood, if this was hers, was on him, his bed, his sheets. And not just her blood, her sweat, too, her hair, her... Jesus Christ.

He felt sick. She was all over him. Her DNA, everywhere. Kidnapping. Murder.

He retched, gagging at the thought of it.

Ellis finished his speech and dragged Jacob to his feet just as he emptied the contents of his stomach all over his chest and knees. Whisky and beer.

'Holy fucking shit on a biscuit,' one of the other officers grunted, hopping backwards out of the splash-zone. 'Get this sick fuck out of here!'

Ellis started hauling him backwards as the officers looked around, peeking in his bedroom. They stood at the doorway, laying eyes on the bloodied sheets, and then turned their gaze to Jacob as he was dragged through the door.

Their expression told him everything.

They had no doubts in their mind.

He'd killed those two men.

He'd taken that girl.

And then, he'd done terrible things to her.

Chapter 6

It was midday and Jacob was sitting in interrogation room 2.

His hands were cuffed, and he'd been given no phone call. No lawyer had been appointed or offered, and there was no sign of him leaving any time soon. He just thought he should feel lucky he wasn't still naked.

Ellis had frog-marched him out of his home and down the steps to the waiting squad car, his dick flapping as he was half shoved, half carried. He'd been dumped into the back seat, hands still behind his back, and a minute later, one of the cops who'd been looking in his room came and tossed a pair of sweatpants and a dress shirt onto his lap. It was possibly the most mismatched outfit that Jacob had ever been in, but he thought it better to stay quiet – this wasn't a time to open his mouth, he thought. He'd spent a lot of his teenage years and young adult life acting and speaking without thinking. And most of the time he'd not grown out of that, liable to open his mouth at the bar when he probably should have kept it shut... but now, here, today? This was a time to shut the fuck up and wait for a lawyer.

The two cops remained inside his house – looking for evidence, he guessed – while Ellis came and got in the car.

He adjusted the mirror, looking back at Jacob through the wire cage behind the front seats, a 12-gauge shotgun sitting upright right in their eye-line. As though reading Jacob's mind about the clothes, he said, 'Sweatpants can be put on you and don't need zipping up – you only need to catch a crack-head's junk in a fly once to never make that mistake again. And the shirt can be draped around your shoulders without uncuffing you. More dignified for you on the walk to the station. Safer for us.' His voice was heavy and smooth, his eyes dark and cold. There was no judgement in them. But there was no hope, either. He kept his hand on the mirror, gaze on Jacob for probably ten or fifteen seconds, waiting. Waiting to see if he talked. Waiting to see if he said 'I didn't do it, you've got it all wrong, man'. Just like every crack-head and shit-heel that'd sat in that seat.

But Jacob could hear his sister's voice loud and clear. The voice of reason. 'Don't say nothing. Don't do nothing, ya hear? I'll fix it.'

She was older than Jacob. And last time he'd been in the back seat of a cop car, those had been her exact words to him. He'd taken his girlfriend's dad's Mercury for a little joyride and by the time he got back home, the cops were there waiting for him. Steph, too. And as he'd been pushed down into the car, that's what she'd said.

And he was sticking to it.

In the car.

And in interrogation room 2.

Ellis was sitting across from him, almost splitting his dark-blue uniform, the fabric straining at the shoulders as he hunched forwards onto the table.

'Look, Jacob,' he said, talking like he was a friend, like he gave a shit, like he thought Jacob was innocent. 'Just tell me what happened, alright? We have the story, but there are holes,' he said. 'Holes you can fill in for us. Holes that'll

25

help your case. We know you picked up Lily Graham off the side of the road – we had a report of a girl walking on the side of the road alone, and we got a witness saying she climbed into an early-Eighties K10 – the kind you got, right?'

He was fishing for an answer. Hell, he was fishing for a word. For anything.

Jacob just looked at his hands, the blood still on them.

'Then you drove her home, right?'

Jacob didn't answer.

'And then when you got home, you and her...' He rolled his shoulders back and forth, downplaying the charge that Jacob would be on the hook for if this went any further south. Rape. 'But what'd you do with her, huh? That's a lot of blood in your bed, in your bathroom. Is it hers? What'd you do, Jacob? Where's Lily, huh?'

Jacob's hands curled into themselves and he lowered his chin even further, didn't even want Ellis to see his face. To see the shame he felt. He never should have stopped for her, never should have taken her home. And he definitely shouldn't have slept with her.

He screwed his eyes closed, a hot, painful pang in the back of his throat.

'What I don't get though,' Ellis went on relentlessly, 'is why you killed those two guys, huh? Hell, what I want to know is *how*.'

He waited for a response that didn't come.

'Why'd you go up there, to the farmhouse. Why'd you do it? You leave the bar and go right there, buzzed? I've had some guys checking up, I know you tied one on last night. Shouldn't have been driving, should you? Hmm? You went up there, all riled up... tell me what happened?'

By all accounts, they had enough to charge him with – circumstantial evidence, he thought they called it. The bloodied sheets, the blood they'd find in the bathroom, no doubt. Maybe Lily's bloodied dress, even. Shit. The thought turned him queasy. But it wasn't the truth. And he'd obviously been seen driving, maybe picking Lily up... Yeah, they had charged him with her kidnap, so they must have some sort of witness report, right? And there'd be people at the bar who could place him, too. Hopefully, then, Ellis could put together a timeline of when Jacob left the bar and when he picked Lily up. And that would prove he couldn't have killed those two men, right? Right? Or at least, that's what Jacob hoped. But, considering they weren't giving him a phone call or lawyer... he didn't feel so confident that they were playing by the rules.

They'd kicked his door in, tackled him to the ground, guns out. They'd come for him hard. And they needn't have. But they did. Which begged the question: why?

Why had they come at him so hard? For *kidnapping*. And *murder*. Arrested. Not detained, or brought in on suspicion. Just cuffed and locked in an interrogation room without counsel.

Jacob didn't know much about law... Hell, he didn't know much about anything that didn't plant or harvest crops – he spent his days fixing and building agricultural machinery – but something was off. Something stank to high heaven here. And this storm of shit all revolved around Lily Graham, the girl in the bloodied dress.

Fuck. Fuck! Why did he pick her up? Why did he sleep with her? How could he be so fucking stupid?

There was a knock at the door then and Ellis eased himself up from the table, eyes fixed on Jacob. He opened it, shielding the gap with his body, but Jacob caught a glimpse of the man beyond. The chief of police here in Devils Lake, Jeff Harris. He was in his late fifties, about five-nine and a little portly these days. He has a big, bristling moustache and a balding head, shiny on top but still bristly around the sides. He eyed Jacob for a moment, then murmured something to Ellis low enough that Jacob couldn't hear.

Ellis took a few seconds to take it in, then started speaking back, and this part Jacob caught a snatch of. 'But what about his right to—?'

'Just do it, alright,' Harris growled. 'That's an order.' And then he turned on his heel and disappeared.

Ellis's shoulders seemed to sink a little and then he turned with a sigh. 'On your feet, Taylor,' he said, motioning him up and towards the door.

Jacob rose slowly, desperate to ask where they were going, but knowing better. But even without asking, he knew one thing: it definitely wasn't anywhere good.

Chapter 7

Taylor was ushered into the hallway, still cuffed, and guided down the corridor by Ellis's big hand on his shoulder.

At the end of it, the door bearing the word 'Holding' gave Taylor an idea where he was headed.

Inside, two breezeblock cells were separated by a set of iron bars and occupied a sixteen-foot-wide space. On the weekend, this place would have six, maybe eight drunks and druggies stuffed in it. But now, just one bearded, near-toothless meth-head occupied the cell on the right, sitting in the corner, muttering to himself, one tattooed arm resting on the small steel toilet fixed to the back wall.

'Inside,' Ellis said, pushing Jacob towards the left-hand cell and the open door.

A small concrete bench awaited him, his seat, his bed, maybe. For who knew how long.

Jacob went in wordlessly, knowing that they'd eventually have to relent, give him his phone call. Give him a court-appointed public defender. Right? The only lawyer he knew was the guy who'd handled his dad's will, his mom's death declaration. He was pretty much the only one in town and he was easily eighty now. Which meant his phone call would be Steph. What he'd say, he didn't know – but she'd understand, she'd get it, and she'd help. She'd know what to do. She always did.

And the thought of calling her was just about all that was keeping him standing right now.

Ellis's hand left his shoulder and Jacob stepped inside, the floor cold against his bare feet, and turned slowly to find the officer staring at him.

Ellis kept his eyes fixed on Jacob as he closed the door with a thunderous clank that echoed around the room. He watched him through the bars, his expression hard to read. Jacob saw disappointment there, but in what? In him? There was something else, too – confliction. Like he knew something was up. Something was wrong.

He seemed to fade away from the cage instead of walk, watching Jacob with every step backwards, pausing at the door before he disappeared through it, taking one last, lingering look at his prisoner before he moved out of sight, leaving Jacob standing in his cell, hands tight around the steel bars.

–

Jacob wasn't that hungover, but the lack of food and water was definitely stunting his recovery. There'd been no sign of anyone since Ellis had disappeared and silence reigned in the cellblock. The meth-head seemed to have come down off whatever he was on, and had slumped over with his head against the toilet rim.

Thankfully, that gave Jacob the quiet he needed to think, although there didn't seem to be much to think about. He replayed the time he left the bar to the time he'd rolled off Lily Graham and fallen asleep over and over in his head, regretting practically every decision he'd made between those two moments. But other than the self-loathing, the questions he was asking had no answers, and wouldn't until he got out of this cell. In here, he was safe. He had rights. And whether they were dragging their heels or not, it didn't change that fact. Soon, they'd come in, and they'd give him what they had to.

And it must have been the meagre comfort of that thought that let him sleep, because when they did come back in, the frosted window in the small space outside their cells was no longer filled with white light. It was just a black square.

The door to the block creaked open, and Ellis walked in with the officer that had brought Jacob his clothes when he was in the back of the car. Jacob didn't know the officer, but he wasn't hard to remember. Guy in his forties, short-cropped dark hair and a pretty impressively thick beard. And the hairy forearms to match.

Jacob came to quickly and sat up on the concrete bench, squinting in the harsh, unshaded light raining down from above.

He shielded his eyes as Ellis and the beard opened the other cage door and went inside.

'W— whaddya want?' he stammered. 'Leggo-a-me!' he started yelling as they pulled him to his feet.

He clutched at the toilet rim, a paranoid mess of a man, grunting and howling as though they were taking him to the gallows.

'I didn't do nothing! You can't make me!' he went on.

The officer with the beard manhandled his thin arms free of the shitter and dragged him kicking and screaming from the cell.

He caught an elbow to the side of the head and swore loudly, almost dropping the prisoner. 'We're letting you go, you stupid motherfucker,' he snapped, readjusting his hold on the man as Ellis stood by and watched.

Jacob came to the bars of his own cell, watching the big man, all but ignoring the beard and the meth-head as they went into the corridor, one hurling profanity, the other nonsense.

Ellis watched the duo go, and then turned his eyes back to Jacob.

He was careful not to say anything to the officer, but the look they shared seemed to say it all: this wasn't right.

Ellis cleared his throat and looked down, walking solemnly out of the cell and then holding in front of the open hallway door. His big hand raised, shaking a little, and steadied itself on the handle as he looked out.

The sound of the addict was swallowed by a distant door closing and Jacob assumed he'd been banished from the building. He had no idea what time it was, but judging by the lack of any other sound coming from the corridor, he guessed it was late. How long had he been asleep? He wanted to ask, but he didn't think it was smart, or that it would do any good.

He kept his ears pricked instead, wondering why Ellis was standing vigil at the door, and what the bearded officer was doing beyond.

The gentle clink of crockery filtered back and then he heard the footsteps, the laboured pants of a man out of breath. A few seconds later, the beard appeared, his cheek swelling and reddening from its run-in with the elbow of the addict.

He entered the cellblock, and Ellis closed the door behind him, albeit tentatively.

Jacob kept his hands on the bars, watching.

The bearded officer had a plate in his hand. On it was what looked like dinner. Smelled like dinner, too. Just a microwave meal, Salisbury steak and mashed potatoes, greens, gravy that looked more like molasses than anything else. But Jacob didn't care. He was starving, his stomach aching it was so empty. He wanted a phone call, but dinner would do.

'Open it,' the beard commanded, nodding at Jacob's cell.

Ellis approached, reluctantly it seemed, slowly pulling a set of keys from his pocket and thumbing through them.

'You,' the beard said to Jacob, 'against the back wall, turn and face it, hands flat above your head.'

Jacob released the bars and did as he was told, backing up and then turning. As far as they were concerned, he was a double murderer, possibly triple if they had found Lily Graham, which he assumed they hadn't considering he was still in there.

Silently, he obliged, turning and planting his hands on the wall above his head, his mouth salivating at the thought of dinner.

Ellis opened the door, the clank of the lock turning and the metal hinges grinding, filling Jacob with expectation. He closed his eyes, imagining how good that food was going to taste in his mouth. The only thing he'd had in there since last night was vomit.

The smell of meat filled the cell as beard stepped in.

'Close the door,' he ordered Ellis.

Jacob's brow furrowed a little. *Close the door?*

He turned his head a little to try and see what was going on behind him.

'Eyes on the wall,' the beard snapped.

Jacob did as he was told.

The door began creaking shut at his back.

A dull slap rang out and Jacob risked looking under his arm, seeing his gravied steak lying on the floor. The mash potatoes joined it, splatting on the stained concrete.

They were throwing his dinner away, going to force him to eat it off the floor? Were they that cruel? He knew he was suspected of murder, but—

Then the plate hit the floor and smashed into big jagged pieces.

Jacob stared at it.

'Hold him,' the beard ordered.

Ellis came forwards now, reaching for Jacob's arms, folding them down behind his back, his grip like iron.

Jacob finally broke his vow, the pain in his shoulders enough to unfasten his mouth. 'What's going on?' he asked.

Ellis's eyes were fixed on his as he held his hands behind his back, but he said nothing. He couldn't read the big man's expression but he could see the pulse in his temple doing double time. And it filled him with dread.

'Get him on the bench,' the beard ordered, stooping down to sift through the debris on the floor.

Ellis did so, wheeling Jacob around. He resisted a little, but he knew if he gave Ellis a reason, he could snap his wrists like twigs, so he went. Was this intimidation? Was it some kind of interrogation tactic? Maybe they were just intent on roughing him up – is this what they did to men who they thought hurt women?

But Ellis forced him down onto the bench and stood over him, hand on the grip of his pistol, the holster unfastened, and Jacob watched as the officer with the beard selected an especially jagged slice of plate and picked it up, weighing the piece in his hand.

Jacob waited, breath held, trying not to think of the worst.

But as the officer, whose name plate said 'Adams', began running his thumb down the sharp, broken edge, checking whether it was sufficient, a grim reality struck.

'Get his arm,' Adams said, pressing his thumb into the edge until he was confident it could break skin.

Before Jacob could react, could say anything, Todd Ellis had him, one hand on his shoulder, the other around the heel of his left hand. He held his arm ramrod straight, nearly pulling it from the socket, Jacob's wrist exposed.

'Hold him still,' Adams said, approaching, coming around the side.

Jacob tried to squirm but Ellis applied pressure, threatening to dislocate his arm if that's what it took.

'Woah, woah, wait,' Jacob squeezed out, 'you don't have to do this, please, please!' he started pleading, his heart hammering against the inside of his ribs.

'Shut the fuck up,' Adams growled, positioning himself next to Ellis, rotating the piece of plate around to try and get the right angle. The angle to make it look like Jacob had done it himself. One quick rip across the wrist, enough to open the veins. Enough to kill himself.

There was no doubt in his mind, that's what they were doing: staging his suicide.

'Hold him still, God damn it,' Adams ordered.

Jacob looked down at his arm, realising that there was some movement in it, that Ellis's grip had loosened just a fraction. Not enough to get free, but enough to move.

He looked up at the big man, saw maybe just a flash of apprehension there. Ellis held his gaze for a moment, and then his eyes flicked downwards, towards his hip, before jumping back to Jacob's.

He felt Adams's hand on his arm, near his elbow, could smell his breath as he leaned in, as he readied himself for the cut.

But Jacob wasn't looking at Adams, he was looking where Ellis's eyes had gone.

To his hip.

To his gun, the safety off, the grip within reach.

It was stupid to go for it.

But Jacob'd be dead in about three seconds if he didn't.

So he did.

Chapter 8

Jacob lunged forwards, his left arm still fixed in the hulking hands of Ellis, and thrust his right hand across the midriff of the big man.

His elbow grazed Ellis's stomach as he reached awkwardly for the grip, his fingers finding it.

Jacob pulled hard, and the sleek black pistol slipped from its holster, coming free into his grasp. Adams's eyes widened seeing it and he thrust the jagged piece of crockery at Jacob's wrist. But it was Ellis who stopped him, letting go of Jacob and jumping backwards out of the path of the swinging gun. His right hand swiped through the air, nearly taking Adams off his feet completely, sending the man sprawling backwards.

His shoulders rising and falling violently, Jacob brandished the weapon at the men in front of him and Ellis backed up, raising his hands, his face like stone.

Jacob swallowed, wanting to pull the trigger in recompense, but knowing it wasn't him, knowing that it would only make whatever this was worse. Knowing it was wrong.

He pushed himself to his feet, hand shaking, gun clacking in his grip, and edged towards the door.

Adams pushed himself to a stance using the back wall, his expression more readable – furious, hate-filled, murderous – and slowly lifted his hands away from his own pistol, the safety catch thankfully fixed in place.

The sudden change in situation reassured Jacob that going for Ellis's gun was stupid, but it had saved his life, and now he needed to get out of here. And fast.

He backed towards the door of the cell and felt blindly behind him for it.

Adams smirked a little, but as Jacob found purchase and pulled it open, the smile faded. As though Adams had expected it to be locked. Maybe it was supposed to have been.

Jacob looked at them, knowing if he ran, he would be a fugitive. He'd be a wanted man, on the hook for murder and escaping police custody. Innocent people don't run, he thought to himself. He needed to be smart. Or at least *smarter*. He was never smart, not like Steph. But he had his moments, and this felt like one of them.

'Your radios,' he said, his voice quivering as he gestured to the men's shoulders. 'Throw them on the ground. Your phones, too.'

'Fuck you.' Adams sneered.

But Ellis seemed to understand there was a gun in his face and reached slowly for his shoulder, unfastening the radio from the epaulette of his shirt and holding it at arm's length. He took out his phone with the other hand, holding them together.

'Throw it out of the cell,' Jacob ordered.

Ellis obliged, tossing them through the bars and towards the other side of the room.

'Now you,' Jacob said to Adams.

Before he could answer with another 'Fuck you', Ellis turned and picked the radio from his shoulder, too, dragging the phone from his pocket, throwing them out next to his own.

'The fuck you think you're doing?' Adams hissed at him.

'I want to sleep in my bed tonight, not in the dirt,' Ellis said evenly, his deep voice ringing in the cell.

'Harris is going to hear all about this,' he threatened as Ellis turned back to face Jacob, keeping his hands aloft.

Jacob thought asking Adams to throw down his gun was asking for trouble; he was more liable to try and shoot Jacob than anything else. No, he'd gotten rid of their ability to call for help, and when he closed the cell door it would latch automatically, trapping them in here until morning if he was lucky. He still didn't know what time it was but there was no light coming in through the window, so he had a couple of hours at least. Hopefully more.

He needed to get out now, though. Get to Steph.

He made his way to the corridor slowly, pulling the cell door closed with a satisfying clang. As he edged backwards, he saw Adams lowering his hands, readying to go for his gun.

Jacob wasn't going to give him the opportunity. He turned and darted through the open door, just hearing the slither of steel on leather behind him as he did.

Adams's gun coming out of its holster.

But it was too late. Jacob was away. And though Adams's fervent cries for help immediately erupted behind him, there were no gunshots chasing him out of the room, and mercifully, as he passed the interrogation rooms on his left and emerged into the bullpen, he found it empty, the clock on the wall telling him it was a little after midnight. In bigger towns there'd be multiple officers out here, but

Devils Lake was small, and two officers on the night shift was more than enough. Enough to handle any trouble in town, and enough to murder a prisoner in their cell, seemingly.

Still, he had to keep his wits about him, and as soon as he knew he was alone, he pushed the pistol into the back of the waistband of his sweatpants and ducked out into the night, barefoot and terrified.

Chapter 9

Though Jacob lived at their folks' place out on the highway, Steph, thankfully, lived in town. She was older than Jacob, forty-six now, divorced, two kids, one off in college, the other sixteen and full of piss and vinegar. She was off at her dad's across the border over in Minnesota, living there since she and Steph had a major bust-up a few months ago.

Jacob loved Steph's girls and had loved watching them grow up, too. But he couldn't lie that he wasn't glad they weren't there. That he wasn't going to wake them up an escaped prisoner on the run and wanted for murder.

She lived in a little two-storey in a quiet part of town. Family neighbourhood. She and her husband had gotten married out of high school, bought it not too long after. He got a job working for a big grain merchant in town and did well for himself. They had no trouble buying the place on his salary alone. Steph worked at a bank out of high school and was training up to go on to be a financial advisor when she got pregnant. She always had a head for numbers, along with everything else. She took off to have her eldest, Lizzie, and her husband – *Greg* – douchebag as he was, earned enough that it made sense for her to stay off to look after her. Especially with no parents on Steph's side, and just Greg's mom, who lived a way out of town to pick up the slack. And then Kaya came along and they

41

were juggling two and Steph didn't have any chance of going back. So she never did. Just stayed at home while Greg worked.

It had been a fine setup for a while, but once the kids were in school, Steph wanted to do something more. Wanted to work. Greg did, too, and didn't like having to juggle childcare and his job. Wanted to keep things as they were. So they compromised, neither happy, and slowly, over the years, drifted apart.

It wasn't a unique story by any stretch, but it was what happened. And now Steph was in her late forties, with two mostly grown girls, no career, no husband, and just her half-drunk brother as a consolation.

And now here he was, creeping down the back alley behind her house in his best shirt, tip-toeing towards her back gate.

He stopped at it, holding on to the top to peek over. The light in the living room was still lit, the lamp in the corner with the chiffon drape over it, dimming and warming the light coming off it.

Jacob breathed a little sigh of relief. He had no desire to wake anyone up or make more noise than he had to. He was hoping he had until daybreak before Ellis and Adams got free, and he might just need that time to explain it all to Steph and for her to get done kicking the shit out of him for what he'd done.

And with that in his head, knowing he was in for a beating, he eased the back gate open and slunk through the garden and up onto the back porch, creeping up on the window, wondering how the hell he was going to start.

And if there was any way to make it sound any less terrible than it all was.

Steph was sitting on the couch, the television on in front of her, a glass of red wine in her hand. She was staring vacantly into space and when Jacob looked at the TV he saw why — her show was paused, the image not moving.

Jacob glanced back at his sister, the empty look in her eyes, the empty bottle of red on the coffee table. As much as he would have wanted to unpack what he was looking at, ask her about it, help her, talk to her... right now, he needed her. And not *this* her. He needed the old Steph, the one who'd slay dragons for her little brother.

So he shoved that sense of brotherly duty down inside and knocked lightly on the glass.

Steph started and looked over, blinking a few times before she saw him there in the dark.

'Jacob?' she mouthed, shaking her head and getting up. 'What the fuck?' She drained her wine glass and put it on the table before coming over, and Jacob once again had to force himself not to think too hard about that.

She approached and knelt in front of the low sill, flicking the latch and easing the sash up.

'Jesus, what are you doing here?' Her brow creased. 'And what the fuck are you wearing?'

He wanted to tell her everything, right then and there. But the only thing he could do was shake his head, tears forming in his eyes. He reached in and took her hands, squeezing them tightly, so glad that she was there.

'Steph,' he all but sobbed. 'I fucked up— I fucked up bad.'

She took her hands from his and clasped them gently, hushing him.

'It's okay,' she said, not knowing a goddamn thing. 'It'll be alright. Whatever it is, we'll fix it.'

And though the situation was utter shit and he knew she was wrong…

Thankfully, it still made him feel a whole lot better.

Chapter 10

When he finally finished telling her, she just stared at him.

'You're a fucking idiot,' she said after a few seconds. And not like a jokey *You're such a fucking idiot*. And she reiterated that when she followed it up with, 'No, seriously, is it all the booze or did you fall off the roof and land on your head or something? How fucking stupid can you be, Jakey?'

She reached out and smacked him on the upper arm.

'Ouch,' he said, leaning away from her. 'Seriously?'

'You're lucky I don't punch you in the fucking face!'

He was starting to regret coming here. 'So what am I supposed to do?'

'You're supposed to have not fucked a random teenager you picked up off the side of the road covered in blood!'

'She wasn't a teenager,' he reminded her. 'She was at least...' Best not to overcook it. 'Twenty... two. Ish.'

She just closed her eyes. 'That's just two years older than Lizzie. You know that, don't you? That's sick, Jacob—'

'Okay, okay!' he cut in. 'I get it. But it's done now, alright? Can we focus on the other stuff? The arrest, the cops trying to *murder* me in my cell? Isn't that just a little more pressing?' He squeezed his thumb and forefinger together for effect.

Steph sighed.

Only siblings could talk like this to each other.

'Okay,' she said then. 'Barring your extreme stupidity, this does seem to be a bit suspicious otherwise.'

'A bit?' Jacob snorted.

'Yeah, more than a bit, I guess.' She let out a long breath, thinking. 'They're obviously trying to cover something up.'

'I figured that much out myself.'

'And they're trying to pin those murders on you even though they've got no proof. But if you're dead, you can't deny it... So the question is why? And who actually killed those guys? Sounds like the only person who knows, other than the police—'

'Is the girl, yeah,' Jacob finished for her. 'But I don't know where she is, and that doesn't really help me.'

'So you got to get out of town, right? Go hide somewhere,' she said, leaning forwards on the chair. 'And then I'll find a lawyer and we can build a defence for you. Once it's solid and there's proof you couldn't have done it, we'll bring you back.'

Jacob liked the fact the curtains were closed so no one could see him but was also aware he wouldn't see anyone coming for him, too. It was one in the morning and though he'd relieved Adams and Ellis of their phones and radios, he had no idea how long they'd stay in their box before getting out.

'Where?' Jacob asked. 'Where do I go?'

Steph shrugged. 'The hell should I know? I haven't done something like this before! North, south, east, west... pick a direction. Drive 'til your gas tank is empty and the license plates are a different colour and then check into a motel in cash. Get a pre-paid phone at a gas station and call every three days. Shouldn't take long to have some

46

evidence, the drunks at that bar know you pretty well, and the cameras there'll place you, right?'

'Right,' he said, eyeing her. 'Sure you haven't done this before?'

She offered him a brief smile. 'I got some cash here, not much, but enough for a week or two somewhere shitty. You can take my car. Just make sure to park it out of sight when you get there so you don't get clocked by the police. And don't tell me where you are, either.' She pointed a finger at him, getting up.

'You mean right now?'

'Yeah, you want to wait until your friends get out of that cell and start setting up roadblocks?'

Jacob rose slowly, watching as Steph made her way to the door. 'You never asked,' he said. 'While I was telling you.'

'Asked what?' She paused and looked back at him.

'If I did it – if I killed those guys.'

She laughed. 'Jesus, Jacob, you think I don't know you? You're dumb, but you're not *that* dumb. And besides, you're a good guy. I know you wouldn't – *couldn't* – do something like that.' She gave another smile and then headed into the kitchen.

He followed her as she went to the cupboard and grabbed a cookie jar from the top shelf, pulling it down with both hands and taking the lid off.

It was stuffed with crinkled small bills and she pulled them out in wads and laid them on the counter.

'Pizza fund,' she said. 'I'd put in any smalls I had ready for family nights, you know?' She looked up at him, a sadness in her eyes. 'Wasn't many of those towards the end, and now...'

He came forwards and took her in his arms.

She resisted, and then hugged him, putting her face in his chest. Though she was older, she was smaller than him. Her brown, wavy hair, a few grey strands starting to creep in, pooled on his shoulder. 'Fucking hell, Jakey,' she muttered. 'I don't know what I'd do if I lost you.' She grabbed hold of his shirt in handfuls and squeezed the fabric.

'I'm right here,' he said, knowing how close he'd come to not being. He tried not to get choked, but he could feel his throat aching, his eyes stinging. 'It's all going to be okay, right?'

She nodded, not saying anything, and then with a snivel, pushed him away and beat gently on his chest with her fists. 'You've got to get out of here,' she said, her eyes shining. 'Before the sun comes up, before the dust settles. Here, take this.' She opened a kitchen drawer and rummaged in it for a moment, pulling out an old smartphone and offering it to him. 'It's one of Lizzie's old ones, but it still works fine.'

He nodded, taking it off her, glad to have some sort of lifeline. 'What's the passcode?'

'It's my birthday.'

He looked up at her.

She arched an eyebrow. 'Seriously? Eleven-oh-six.'

'I knew that.'

'Uh-huh.' She sighed, smiling at him like you would a dog that'd ripped up its bed. Like you were pissed, but you couldn't really blame it because it was too stupid to know the difference. 'You just keep your head down. I'll handle the rest, make some calls in the morning.'

He let out a long, shaky breath. 'I knew coming here was the right call,' he said.

She scoffed. 'I'd have been pissed if you didn't.'

He smiled at her and she scooped the cash off the counter and held it out to him.

'Maybe stop at a thrift store on the way,' she added, looking him up and down. 'You sort of stick out – and that's kind of the opposite of what we're going for.'

He chuckled softly, glad to find a glimmer of humour in this, and looked down at himself.

'Yeah, I guess I do,' he said, hugging her again, this time kissing her on the head.

'Stay safe,' she whispered, shoving him towards the door now. 'Get out of here. Let your big sis handle everything.'

He gave her a little wave and a nod and then slipped from the house, grabbing her keys from the hook next to the back door as he did.

Feeling her eyes on him, he went down the steps and then doubled back down the side of the house to her waiting car, an old Subaru Legacy with rust along the arches. It was a common enough car around here, perfect for brutal winters thanks to its four-wheel drive. The definition of not sticking out.

He slotted in behind the wheel and backed out of the driveway, glancing up at the house to see Steph inside the front door, watching through the glass, silhouetted in the darkness of the hallway against the kitchen light behind her.

She lifted a hand.

He returned the gesture.

And then he drove away, wondering which direction to head, and if it was the stupidest idea in the world to go home.

He thought it was, but then again, he'd never been the smartest guy.

Chapter 11

His own clothes, food, cash, his gun.

He was starved and needed to eat. And hitting a McDonald's drive through didn't seem very prudent. He also didn't think hitting a thrift store was a great idea, either. He'd need to go in, speak to people, choose clothes... No, that'd just increase the risk. He also had about three hundred bucks in the breast pocket of a jacket in his closet. And if this took longer than he thought, he might need it.

And as for the gun... if anyone came at him to try and finish the job, he wanted to have some way to protect himself.

In and out in five minutes, he promised himself.

If the cops hadn't been to Steph's, then they wouldn't be here. They were still in the cell. He had time.

It's all he kept repeating to himself as he turned off the highway and into the estate, rumbling through the darkness towards home, keeping his eyes peeled and roving for any hidden squad cars tucked behind the neighbours' houses.

He breathed a sigh of relief as he pulled up behind his Chevy, swinging in a circle so he was facing the exit before killing the engine.

Jacob made one last sweep of the area, dead quiet in the dead of night, and then climbed out, a thin sheen of nervous sweat coating his skin.

He'd never known the night so quiet.

The spread of homes here wasn't any kind of built-up area. Hell, there was barely a road connecting them. It was as though the person who built them in the 70s thought that this is where the centre of town would end up being and missed by about five miles. But despite there being nothing much around them, there were always noises. Road noise. Birds. The hum of electricity in the cables. Noise from someone's TV drifting in the breeze. Trees rustling.

But tonight, there was nothing.

Like the whole place was frozen in time. Like that moment of stillness between the flash of lightning and the roll of thunder.

No, no, cut that shit out, Jacob, he told himself, stealing towards the house.

He approached, readying himself to fish the spare key from above the frame. But he didn't need to. The door wasn't even shut, let alone locked.

He laid his hand on the wood, pausing for a second, wondering if, the second he opened it, Todd Ellis was going to tackle him through the rail at his hip and down into the car port. Snap his fucking spine.

He swallowed, pricking his ears, listening for any sign of anyone inside.

He heard nothing, and knew he couldn't just stand here with his dick in his hand.

Jacob pushed inwards and the door swung with a gentle creak, revealing the interior of the house. There was no muzzle flash, no click of a cocking gun. Was he safe?

His heart thudded against the inside of his ribs as he stepped inwards, being as quiet as he could.

He made it just one step before something crinkled under his bare heel. Jacob stopped and looked down at it, seeing a white envelope lying on the carpet. Like someone had opened the door and tossed it in before disappearing.

Jacob stared at the thing. 'Mail,' he muttered. 'I don't have time for mail right now.'

Without another thought he sped forwards with the list in his head, grabbing clothes, the cash, his gun... or not – okay, so the cops took the gun, not surprising, he thought – now, food. He cleared the cupboards, dumping canned spaghetti and who knew what else into a rucksack before heading back towards the door. He'd find somewhere quiet off the road to change. He couldn't risk turning the lights on or dawdling here.

As he made a run for the door he stepped on the envelope once again, this time pausing.

There was no other mail – and the mail guy always put it in the box on the side of the house.

Something niggled at him and he stooped, picking up the envelope.

He clutched it tightly as he went for the car, still bare-footed, and climbed in, tossing the rucksack and the letter into the passenger seat.

Jacob turned the key and headed for the highway, zipping quickly off the stoney verge and onto the asphalt.

The tired engine of the Subaru whined, but he was thankful that Steph's prudency was on full display and he had more than three-quarters of a tank to play with.

Though as he drove, knowing that he should leave Devils Lake far behind before stopping, he couldn't shake the desire to know what was in the envelope.

As he closed in on an old track that led down to an old fishing jetty on the shore of the lake, he slowed. 'Fuck it,' he muttered, pulling off down the track. There'd be no one down there and he'd have some privacy to get changed standing in the headlights instead of having to do it in the pitch darkness.

The car jostled along the rutted road until the trees finally broke and he emerged into a clearing, the head-lights cutting out onto the water. The distant lights of town twinkled across the lake, the biggest natural body of water in North Dakota. It was never still, never tranquil. It always sloshed and bucked like something was festering beneath the surface, Jacob thought. The level rose and fell, the water salty. In the summer when it was hot, the water would drop, the saltiness would grow and fish would often wash up dead.

They didn't call it Devils Lake for nothing.

Jacob left the engine running and put the car in park, watching as a thin mist drifted across the surface of the water.

He flipped the courtesy light on over his head and rubbed his tired eyes. It seemed like saying aloud that it had been a long day was sort of redundant at this point.

With a sigh, he turned to the passenger seat, wondering if he'd actually brought anything edible at all or if it was just cans of kidney beans and whatever else had been sitting in that cupboard for the last ten-plus years.

But even though he was going for the food, his hand landed on the envelope, pulling it towards him.

It was unmarked, and as he turned it in his hands, a faint smell, sweet and floral, seemed to emanate from it. A wave of pleasure and sickness rolled over him, his mind dancing back through what happened last night. The smell, the

53

feel, the taste of Lily Graham's body. The way she moved and the way he moved in her.

He shuddered in his seat, tearing the letter open, reading before he'd even unfurled it fully.

It simply said:

Jacob —
    I'm so sorry this happened to you. I never meant for you to get involved. If you're reading this, I can explain everything.
    You can find me where the water meets the sky.
    Lily

He lowered the letter, his lips moist, fingers tight around the paper.

Where the water meets the sky...

How could she know that?

That was his and Steph's place. It always had been. No one else knew about it except Steph's girls... Did Lily know them? Did she know Lizzie?

He swallowed hard, the paper still clutched in his hand, and shoved the car into reverse, backing in a circle before burning out of the lot in a cloud of smoke.

It blew out across the water and swirled, swallowed by the darkness as Jacob drove into the night.

Chapter 12

Nothing made sense.

He rolled the words over in his head. *I'm so sorry this happened to you. I never meant for you to get involved…* The letter made it sound like she knew him, like she knew who he was, and… No, no, she couldn't? Surely? They were strangers… He'd picked her up from the side of the road by pure chance… Hadn't he?

His head was spinning with it all.

And as though that wasn't enough, to ask him to meet her where the water meets the sky? That was enough to turn his world upside down. There were only two people on earth who knew what that meant, where that was. Him and Steph.

As kids, when their dad would drink and being there was a bad idea, they'd escape. Steph would lead him down through the woods to the water and they'd sit and she'd hold him. A little inlet in the trees calmed the water, stilled it, and in the evenings when the sun went down, it'd fall just perfectly so the light spilled in.

They'd sit there, listening to the gentle lap of the shore, watching as the setting sun merged with the water. And if you caught it just right in the summer, there'd be a moment, just a moment where the sky and the water were one. Where they merged and melded and you couldn't see where one ended and the other began.

This was the place where the water met the sky.

And not another living soul knew about it.

So how did Lily Graham?

Jacob drove quickly, heading back the way he'd come. Heading towards home once more. This time without regard or care.

The only thing that mattered was the truth, and he'd get it out of her no matter what.

He wrestled the car off the road and rallied between the houses, blasting past his own towards the treeline.

The track got rougher and he turned towards the lake, slowing and skidding to a halt beyond the furthest house.

Out here in the scrub grass at the side of the highway, several cars had just been abandoned over the years, left to rot. And though he didn't intend to disguise his parking spot, he'd done a pretty good job of it. He didn't think anyone would look twice at the rusted Subaru among the other vehicles. But still, as he grabbed his boots from the passenger footwell and pulled them onto his dirty feet, he kept his eyes sharp, looking for any flashing blue lights on the road.

There was a slight chill in the air, the darkest part of the night weighing heavily on Devils Lake, so he grabbed his jacket too and pulled it on, leaping from the car and moving quickly into the trees, down a hidden pathway he and Steph had worn in years ago when they were kids. Whatever meagre light was coming from the bug zappers and porch lamps behind quickly died away and Jacob was in darkness. If he didn't know the route so well, he would have gotten lost. But he could run this with his eyes closed – he as good as was.

As he looked down, staring into the inky blackness before him, he wondered if Lily Graham had walked this path the night before. And if so, how she'd known about it?

He could ask these questions until the sun came up, but until he found Lily, he'd not get any answers. She was smart, he'd give her that — she'd not only managed to be involved with, or responsible for, the murder of two men and then pin it on Jacob, but she'd also managed to leave him a trail that only he could follow. If any cop or anyone else found that note, there'd be no way that they'd find her from her clue. Did that mean she knew he'd escape? Or that she simply didn't know they'd try and kill him? Did she think they'd let him off for lack of evidence?

He shook his head. More questions.

His stomach was empty, his mind addled by the hunger. He felt like he was dream-walking, like his legs were moving through a swamp. Jacob's breath was ragged, echoing in his ears as he churned forwards, breaking through the brush and collapsing onto his hands and knees in the clearing.

He didn't think he'd been running, but the way he was panting, he thought he must have been.

The starlight playing off the mirror-like inlet dimly lit the clearing, enough that he could see the backs of his hands in the dirt.

'You came,' a delicate voice rang from in front of him.

He inhaled sharply, pushing himself to his knees, too weak to get to his feet.

Lily Graham, dressed in clean clothes now, a world away from the girl he'd picked up on the road the night before, stepped forwards. She was in a pair of flared jeans with a thick puffer jacket to ward off the cold. Behind her he could see a big hiking rucksack and a blanket spread out against a tree, where he expected she'd been sitting, waiting for him.

'You need some water, food?' she asked, hands firmly in her pockets, her voice even, like he hadn't just been through hell.

'What?' was all Jacob could ask. 'I don't...'

'It's okay,' she said then, unpocketing her hands and holding them up, signalling for him to stop. 'Let me explain, okay? I never meant for this to happen, it all just went a bit... nuts. Things got out of control.'

He just shook his head, his mouth flapping.

She came towards him and he recoiled a little.

Lily slowed her approach, crouching and brushing her curled, dark hair behind her ears.

He could smell the sweat coming off his own skin, his own breath. He was on the ragged edge, filthy and unwashed. Half crazy. But Lily looked fine, good, even – she looked showered and stable, the paranoid, blood-soaked girl with the frantic eyes gone. In her place a young woman with a hard look on her face.

'What happened?' was all he managed.

'I'm sorry to have left like that,' she said, not elaborating. 'But I had to. I knew they'd be coming.'

'Who?'

She didn't speak for a second, her eyes flashing in the darkness. 'Everyone.'

He shivered a little, a cool breeze washing in from the water.

'B–but—' he started before she reached out, her finger, warm and soft, touched his lips.

'Shh,' she said, withdrawing it slowly. 'You won't understand until you see. This town, Jacob... It's not what you think. There are people here who aren't who they say they are. A place that's…' She visibly shuddered. 'Just watch, please.'

He kept his eyes on her as she reached into the pocket of her big coat and pulled out her phone.

She unlocked and rotated it, a video already loaded on the screen.

Jacob squinted, blinded by the sudden brightness, and watched as she pressed play.

Chapter 13

Lily Graham was sitting in the driver's seat of her 97 Toyota Corolla when she hit record on her phone, the device sitting in a cradle hanging from the windscreen so it recorded her from the front.

She was hunched forwards a little, staring out of the windscreen.

'Oookay,' she said, elongating the word with a sigh. 'We are here. And by *here*, I mean *here here*. Not like before. It took some doing, but we finally found it,' she said with audible relief. Despite that, she was still a little anxious – visibly so, drumming her fingers on the wheel, her left knee bouncing furiously as she trundled onwards.

The old brakes squealed as she eased to a stop and put it in park, letting the engine idle.

Her eyes swept the farm in front of her. The trees had broken and given way to a fence that ringed around a property sat atop a small rise. There was a metal gate in front of her, a wooden sign stood next to it saying 'Welcome!'

She read it a few times, wondering why, if they were so friendly, that this place had been so dang hard to find. Why no one wanted to talk about it or tell her how to get there.

Lily got out, walking towards the gate, which was chained shut, and leaned on it, looking out across the fields.

A large expanse of land with tilled crop-lines rowed with stakes and small shrubs and plants ran up to a farm-yard. A big metal barn stood on the left, it's old blue paint rust-streaked. A red hay loft with open doors, a small tractor parked in its mouth stood in the middle. And on the right, a wooden-panelled farmhouse, three stories and tired, sat sentinel, weathered through the years but still there in all its original glory.

All she officially knew about this place was that it was owned by a guy called Haller. Unofficially she knew a little more… and she'd heard a *lot* more.

Hearing the sound of her engine, a head popped up between the crops.

Lily held her hand up to her forehead to shield her eyes from the sun, and lifted her other hand in greeting.

He stared back at her, surprised to see someone at the gate, she thought, and then lifted a hand in response. The man rose to his feet and dusted himself off, pushing the brim of his cowboy hat up to reveal his face.

As he walked over, Lily saw that he was in his late twenties, his skin dirty with the earth, his dark, curly hair and unkempt stubble lending itself well to that *rugged farmhand* look. His t-shirt was worn and threadbare, his jeans nearly the same, his hat worn, its wide brim shading his face. But despite that, he was handsome, and his broad smile full of white teeth would be enough to bowl any girl over.

'Hey there,' he called, sidling towards the gate with a practised walk. He extended his hands out and took hold of the top rail, showing off his well-muscled arms, his strong hands. 'Haven't seen you around here before. Something I can help with?' he asked, hamming up the farm-boy accent a little.

Lily looked down bashfully, hiding a smile. 'Yeah, hope so,' she said. 'I'm looking for someone.' She glanced up at him, closing one eye against the sun. 'I think I might be a little turned around, honestly. I don't quite know where I'm supposed to be or where I'm at.'

'Well, you found your way *here*, and that's a good thing.' He laughed disarmingly. 'They'd call that a stroke o' good fortune where I'm from. Maybe I can help. Who is it you're looking for? We don't get many visitors, but who knows, maybe your luck will double.'

'Oh, she's definitely not here,' Lily said back. 'She died a long time ago – but I'm looking for where she used to live. I'm...' she started, stumbling a little. 'I'm alone, I guess you could say. I didn't know my parents, but I've been trying to look for where they're from, where I'm from, I guess.'

'And that led you here?'

'It's led me all over,' she said sadly. She hooked a thumb over her shoulder. 'I'm living out of my car right now. Should've called it quits months ago, I think, this wild goose chase.'

'Why didn't you?' he asked, leaning on the gate now too so that their elbows were just a foot or so apart.

She shrugged. 'Dunno. Guess the idea of going home... Didn't much feel like going home.'

He nodded slowly. 'Yeah, I know the feeling. It's tough, looking for somewhere you belong.'

Lily stared up at the farm. 'You lived here your whole life?'

'Me?' he laughed. 'Gosh no. I blew in with the wind, oh, five years ago, or something.' He grinned. 'One night turned into one more, and the rest is history, I guess. There's a few of us here like that – strays, you could call us. David is good like that.'

'David?' Lily asked.

'David Hall, owns the place. Always has,' the guy said. He put out his hand to her then. 'Sorry, I didn't introduce myself – Aaron.'

She took his hand and shook. 'Lily,' she said.

'That's a pretty name. For a pretty girl.'

Lily blushed and hid another smile.

'Hey, tell you what,' Aaron said, edging closer to her. 'If it's your mom you're looking for, then David will be the one to ask. He's not here right now, but tonight we're putting on a little shin-dig. It's a bonfire, a barbeque. There's music, dancing, that kind of thing. We do it every Friday. Just a little thing to cap off another week of hard work. Everyone's welcome, whether they live here or not.' He gave her a big, sustained grin. 'You couldn't have come on a better day – your luck's doubled after all, by the looks of it.'

She stared at him for a little while, searching his face. And then she gave a short nod. 'Yeah, okay, maybe,' she said. 'No, yeah, I'll come – like you said, if there's anyone who'll know, it sounds like this David guy.'

'If your mom was here, he'll know. Hell, if your family's from around here, maybe you're related to him!' Aaron laughed.

Lily joined in, knowing he was staring at her.

'Alright then, I gotta get back to work. You want to stick around here, or—'

'No, I gotta head back to town, get some gas, some supplies for the road… or whatever,' she added.

'Right, yeah, sure. Well, fire's going by six, so come by whenever.' He put his hand on his chest. 'Aaron,' he called pushing off the gate and walking backwards. 'I'll keep an eye out for ya, Lily.'

He gave her a tip of his hat, and then all but jogged back to the crops.

Lily watched him go, casting an eye over the farm once more, her gaze sharp, her mind working furiously, before she too left the gate and got back to her car, wheeling it in a quick circle before leaving the place in her rear-view.

She watched it shrink and then disappear behind a bend, feeling the unease it'd laid on her dispel only once it was out of sight.

Lily breathed a gentle sigh of relief and tightened her grip on the wheel, closer to the truth than she'd ever been before, and determined to see this through, no matter the cost.

Chapter 14

Lily drove back to town in silence, not even thinking about the fact that the radio was off. She had one hand on the wheel, the other massaging her mouth in thought. She was doing her very best not to get worked up, to temper her excitement. It felt like her entire life had revolved around this for the last year.

And it pretty much had.

It had taken a lot of digging, a lot of research and travel. A lot of tears. But now, finally, she felt like the thing she'd been working towards for so long… it was now within reach.

She wound back to town on autopilot, pulling into the creatively named Devils Lake Inn & Suites motel, just off the highway next to town.

The place was a little tired, a two-storey U-shaped building that wrapped around a parking lot. It'd been pretty quiet when she'd checked in, with maybe a third of the rooms occupied. Devils Lake wasn't exactly a hotspot for tourism but plenty came for the fishing and the boating in the summer months.

She'd requested a room as far away from anyone else as possible as she was a 'light sleeper' and needed to get her rest. In typical motel-clerk fashion, they just sort of accepted what was clearly a lie and gave her a room in the corner. She wondered just how many people came through motels like this one pedalling fake stories, wearing fake faces, living fake lives.

She was just another one of them now, she guessed. Who was Lily Graham, huh? No one. Just someone passing through.

Lily had made as much effort as possible to blend into the background and not draw attention. But despite her discretion, she'd been unsuccessful. And that was reassured by the Devils Lake PD patrol car waiting outside her room.

She grumbled, pulling in next to it. There wasn't much point trying to dodge him. The guy was relentless, and seemed to have the nose of a bloodhound.

As Lily came to a halt, Officer Todd Ellis stepped from the car and leaned against it, the whole vehicle rocking under his weight as he did.

He straightened his belt and puffed out his big chest, looking around the forecourt with a mild amount of displeasure. Lily had been through enough motels to know that their clientele wasn't always the savoury sort, and that cops rarely had a pleasant relationship with these places.

Lily climbed out, squinting in the sunlight at Ellis, taking him in. He was much taller than her and at least double her bodyweight. She didn't much fancy shouting about her business across the roof of her car, so she walked around it so they were both standing between the two vehicles.

Ellis extended his hand. 'Hello again, miss,' he said, giving her a brief nod of the head.

She wondered if poking the bear was the right choice and decided no. She took his outstretched hand, noting how it all but enveloped hers, and the stark difference in his dark complexion from her own pale one. She had spent many long days and nights inside behind her laptop, and had grown to miss the sun on her skin. She'd all but become a shut-away, this case consuming her. The truth she'd always wanted to find but never could.

Until now.

'Hi,' Lily said flatly, pulling her hand from his grip. 'Was there something you needed? I got a lot of work I need to get on with, so—'

'I'm sorry to bother you like this.' He hooked his thumbs into his belt, hunching a little so he was less imposing, she thought. 'I just wanted to see if there was anything you needed help with? And what you were doing out there at the old Hall place?'

She all but scoffed. 'Wow, word travels fast around here, huh?' She'd only left there fifteen minutes ago.

Ellis didn't comment on that, just sort of stuck out his bottom lip and moved his head side to side like an *I guess so* sort of thing.

She stiffened a little. 'It's a free country, isn't it? And the road out there's a public one—'

'Yeah, you're right,' he said, cutting her off for a second time, standing straighter now so he dwarfed her. 'But I also know there's nothing out there for you to find. So it begs the question of what exactly you were looking for?'

'Nothing in particular,' Lily said, screening the question. 'Just asking around. It's an interesting property. That against the rules?'

His eyes narrowed. 'And what *rules* would they be?'

'You tell me, Officer Todd Ellis of the Devils Lake Police Department,' Lily said coolly, reminding him of his station and what it was supposed to stand for.

He took the hint, quietening for a second before he spoke again. 'Look, I don't want to cause you any trouble here. The opposite, in fact, I'm trying to save you some trouble, and some time, is all.'

'Oh, so you're just being a good guy, looking out for little old me?'

'Young woman, attractive, travelling alone...'

Lily smirked incredulously, looking down to hide it.

'You go poking around out there...'

'I might not like what I find?' she asked, still looking at the ground.

He hesitated, then sighed, slumping back against his car with a deep thud. 'Jesus,' he muttered, shaking his head. 'This isn't me, alright?'

'What isn't?' Lily asked, caught a little off guard by it.

He pocketed his hands and looked out across the fore-court. 'You know I was supposed to play football? College with a full ride?'

Was this a new tactic? Disarm her with some wistful story? She played along. 'What happened? Blow out your knee playing the big game at the end of the season? That's the usual spiel, right?'

'I wish... No, it was something a lot stupider than that. I played a good game, end of the season, went out with some friends, got shit-faced, got behind the wheel with my girlfriend in the passenger seat. Rolled the car off the highway, I got out without a scratch, she broke three ribs, an arm, dislocated shoulder, fractured eye socket. Her parents pressed charges.' He shrugged.

'And that's supposed to what, make me feel sorry for you? Take pity on you so I stop asking questions?' Lily asked bluntly. There was no room for weakness. Not now.

'No, I've come to live with it. With my choices. I just promised myself, from then on, to make better ones.' His eyes came to rest on her. 'I'm not here because I want to be, I'm here because I got to be. I know that the chief didn't exactly give you a warm welcome when you two, uh, *crossed paths...*'

'You could say that.' She thought back to it, to how a simple question about a simple name had her being pulled over on the way back to the motel and as good as threatened to leave it alone.

But she wasn't easily scared. Not by the chief, and not by Ellis, either. No matter how many times he came around.

'But Devils Lake is a friendly town, I swear,' Ellis went on, holding his hands up. 'I'd love to show you around – God knows this place isn't a great representation of it.' He gestured around. 'Maybe I could take you out to dinner, or—'

She was the one who cut him off now. 'I don't know whether you were told to do that, or if you seriously just lack the ability to read a situation, but either way, the answer is no, politely, but definitely.' She offered just the briefest of smiles. 'And a word of advice, if it was sincere – if you're going to ask a girl out, don't stalk her first. And don't show up in uniform and demand her time, either. People yearn for a time where they feel comforted by the presence of a police officer, not intimidated. Just something to bear in mind.'

He seemed to shrink. Something she didn't think was possible.

Todd Ellis cleared his throat awkwardly and stood, keeping his eyes to himself. 'Noted, and apologies,' he said quietly. 'That was never my intention, and I... Fuck it,' he muttered, climbing into his car and starting it. He began backing out, pausing to roll down the window and take a last look at her. 'If you're looking into the Hall place... well, hopefully I don't need to tell you to be careful. Do I?'

She stared back at him, then just shook her head, almost imperceptibly.

'You still got my card?' he added. 'Not for dinner, just for... if you need something. Alright? No strings. I promise.'

She looked at him for a few seconds, trying to gauge his angle. 'Better choices?' she asked.

His brow crumpled and he nodded slowly. 'Yeah. Better choices.' And then he backed up and turned, driving out of the motel forecourt, leaving Lily alone, wondering at where his orders ended and his good intentions began.

No time to think of that now. There was lots to do and she couldn't take her eye off her prize.

Not now.

Not yet.

Chapter 15

Todd Ellis pulled out of the Devils Lake Inn & Suites parking lot, watching Lily Graham shrink in his rear-view mirror, and hung his head a little.

He swore under his breath, knowing that he'd failed. Failed the task he was given by Jeff Harris, the chief of police here in Devils Lake. Namely: kill Lily Graham's investigation.

He didn't know who she was, or what her intentions were. But any time someone showed up in town and started poking around like she was, it meant they were some kind of journalist, investigator, or something just as bad. No hits came back on any 'Lily Graham' matching her. She said she'd been robbed, lost her wallet and ID. She was just getting by on cash right now. That's the story she'd peddled to the chief when he'd pulled her over. Which meant the name was bullshit, as was the pretence under which she was here.

The chief had elected to be hands-off with the whole thing. He couldn't get too close, didn't want to draw her attention anymore. She was an unknown entity, he'd told Ellis. Liable to do some real damage if left unchecked. You don't just show up in Devils Lake and ask about the Hall Farm without knowing your quarry, he'd said. Which made her dangerous. And he was relying on Ellis to keep her on a short leash. If she got out of hand, it was on him.

And he knew rolling back to the station as he was would only draw the chief's wrath. But what did he expect him to do? Threaten her? That's not who he was and didn't intend to be any time soon.

Ellis had heard stories about the Hall Farm, had a rough idea of the kind of place it was, and the kind man David Hall was – friendly by all accounts. But what went on out there? Hard to say. Outsiders didn't get a look in. And insiders didn't come out. People in town would nod to David, be pleasant to him when the market came to town and the Hall Farm stall popped up, selling its blackberries, its apples, its corn. And, hell, if they didn't grow good shit. People didn't like the place, but they liked the food, so they tolerated it, it seemed. Not like the people who lived there ever made trouble, either. The opposite, actually. Kept to themselves, real quiet. Real friendly. Real innocuous. Still, though. Place scared the hell out of everyone. Like if you got too close or asked too many questions, you'd just get sucked in like a black hole and *poof.* You never came out.

Ellis shivered a little as he wound down Walnut Street to the station, readying himself for his ass kicking.

He parked the cruiser and got out, looking up and down the empty road before he adjusted his belt and headed inside, spotting Harris the second he did.

The man rose from his desk in his office and waved Ellis through the bullpen towards him.

'Close the door,' he ordered before Ellis had even gotten in there.

He walked slower than he usually did, thinking about what he was going to say. There was no decent way to do it, he thought. Rip the band-aid off, his mother used to say. Get it over with.

'Well?' Harris asked, standing behind his desk with his hands on his hips.

Ellis shut the door gently, his back to his chief, and took a deep breath, turning around. He shrugged immediately, hoping no words were better than the ones he had.

Harris mimicked it emphatically, raising and dropping his shoulders in an exaggerated fashion. 'What the fuck's this? Huh?'

'I don't know what to tell you. She went out to the farm, she got turned away at the gate, far as I know.'

'She went out there?' Harris's face contorted a little and he stilled his shrugging. 'How the *fuck* did she find it?'

Ellis could only shake his head. He really didn't know. But it was a big town and he wasn't surprised *someone* talked. A lot of people didn't have much love for the place.

'God damn it,' Ellis muttered. 'But she's dropping it?' He lowered his head and looked right at Ellis. 'You talked to her, right?'

'I did,' he said. 'But I don't think she's going to leave it alone. Least I didn't get that sense.'

'Didn't get that sense?' Harris scoffed. 'Jesus Christ, it was the one fucking thing you had to do today! She's just a fucking girl, you big fucking ape.'

Ellis bristled but said nothing, not sure if that was a racial slight or just reference to his stature. Either way, he didn't like it, and he didn't like Harris. 'What did you expect me to do, exactly?'

'I gotta spell it out for you?'

'Yeah,' Ellis replied coldly. 'In big neon letters.' The badge was weighing heavily on his chest all of a sudden.

Harris read his expression, the tension in the big man, and deigned not to say the words Ellis knew he wanted to. Intimidate. Threaten. Hurt. More, if necessary.

'Get the fuck out of my office,' he growled instead. 'Ride a desk for the day. For the week,' he added. 'If I look up and don't see the back of your fucking head hunched over that desk, you and me are gonna have a problem. You understand me?'

'Loud and clear,' Ellis said, drawing a slow breath. 'That all?'

Harris waved him away and Ellis obliged, opening the door with some force, letting it bang against the wall as he strode into the bullpen, tempted to defy Harris just to see what he'd actually do. Ellis wouldn't mind taking him on, but he knew enough about Harris to know a guy like that never fights fair. And he'll do anything not to lose.

Which didn't make him fear for himself – but it did make him afraid for Lily Graham.

Chapter 16

The day slipped away. As well as his paperwork, Harris had seemingly told all the other officers they could also dump their busywork on him. And they'd jumped at the chance.

So by six that evening, when everyone else was clocking off and heading out, he could barely see over the stacks of files around him, even with his height.

But his momma had taught him well, taught him to suffer in silence when it came to it. Keep his chin up, his dignity. And that's just what he'd done. Devils Lake had always been his home, and it was a good place. A place he wanted to protect, to keep safe. To keep right.

Whether Harris had his hand in the wrong pot or not, that didn't affect Ellis's ability to act by his own accordance and do what he, and God, judged to be right. And though he definitely didn't want to sit here all night, he would if that's what it took.

And judging by the height of the files, it would.

It was a little before nine in the night when his radio crackled and his name echoed across the empty room.

Ellis was at the coffee machine, slurping down his third cup since quitting time. He walked unhurriedly back to his desk, picking up the two-way on its cradle next to his computer. Perhaps he should have read more into the urgency of Harris's tone. Or perhaps he should have been more perturbed by the fact it was Harris himself and not one of the on-duty officers working the night shift.

But either way he lumbered over and picked it up. 'This is Ellis,' he responded, holding the two-way to his mouth, and the coffee in his other hand.

'Jesus Christ,' Harris spat, 'where the fuck you been? I told you I wanted you chained to your desk!'

Ellis lowered the radio slightly, deliberating over whether to go and flush it down the toilet or not. But then he thought there might actually be something wrong, so instead he just said, 'I'm here now. What's up?'

'What's up is you need to get your ass out here right this fucking second.'

'And where is *here*, exactly?' Ellis queried, taking a long, hot sip of bitter coffee.

'Where do you goddamn think, numb nuts?'

The voice disappeared. Although Ellis wasn't a detective, he didn't need to do any sleuthing to know that Harris meant the farm. Ellis was well aware that every Friday they had a 'party' of some kind out there. What exactly that meant, he didn't know. But he knew asking about it was a good way to put yourself in their crosshairs. And that was somewhere you didn't want to be. Who *they* were was a mystery, but they seemed to be threaded through every level, every echelon of Devils Lake. So it was way more risk than it was worth for a simple question.

As Ellis made for the door, he realised this would be the first time he'd be going out there, to the Hall Farm. He'd driven the road once or twice, knew exactly where it was, but to venture beyond that gate?

He had no idea what awaited him.

But judging by Harris's call…

It was nothing good.

Chapter 17

Ellis drove the empty road out to the farm, and though he wasn't sure what to expect, silence wasn't it. Harris had sounded near frantic on the call, but as Ellis wound through the forest, his headlights cutting through the thin, lingering fog that drifted off the lake, lighting up the hushed trees, scattering needles of light into the darkness, nothing moved. Nothing sounded. So, really, what did await him?

He was in his cruiser, but didn't use his lights, or his sirens. The idea was *not* to draw attention to this place, he surmised. If he wanted everyone, blues and sirens going, then Harris would have put out a call over the radio, not rung Ellis's desk directly.

The gate came into view ahead and as Ellis approached, it opened for him, a young man in a tired red shirt with a grim look on his face pulling it open to accept the officer.

Ellis wound down the window as he approached, but the young man turned away, shielding his face. Clearly, he didn't want to talk, so Ellis just kept his mouth shut and trundled by, watching as the man closed it behind him and then all but ran out of view, slipping into the crops lining the road and disappearing.

'What the fuck…?' Ellis mouthed to himself, watching the crops fall still, swallowing the man whole with no indication of where it might spit him out.

He felt a little prickle on the back of his neck, a cool sheen of sweat forming under his collar. His heart beat slow and hard in his chest as the rear bumpers of cars came into view. There were a dozen parked in the farmyard. A few old trucks, but a mix of other vehicles, too, ones less suited to farm life. A black Mercedes, a Lexus, an Escalade… A Ford Expedition. One of the new ones, with a cream leather interior and a host of other extras. Ellis knew because it was the chief's car. Though how he afforded it on his salary, Ellis wasn't sure – but there was something about this whole place that reeked of corruption. He'd seen some of these vehicles before, around office buildings, city hall, even.

He eased to a stop and looked around.

On the left, a big metal barn lay quiet and closed. Ahead, a big red hay barn stood with its door open, a few guys standing in the mouth. There was light coming from inside, and the second they clocked Ellis's car pulling up they pulled it closed and stood sentinel outside it, arms folded.

Between the two buildings, Ellis could see a path reaching down to a clearing surrounded by trees and flowers. A big fire pit was set up with logs positioned around it. The fire was burning brightly but no one was sitting there.

Ellis had heard of these Friday-night parties, notorious as they were in Devils Lake.

The door to the farmhouse opened then and Chief Harris stepped onto the porch, eyes fixed on Ellis, a mean look on his face and his hands on his hips. He gestured heavily to Ellis, beckoning him over.

Ellis took a breath and killed the engine, stepping from the car.

The two guys standing at the mouth of the barn, one with long hair, the other with a beard, seemed to lose their nerve a little as Ellis stepped between the cars and passed them by. They quietened as he passed, staring up at him as he went by, wearing his uniform unapologetically, hoping they'd say something. He didn't much go out for violence, but he was in a shit mood, he was dog-tired, and he didn't like whatever this was already.

The old boards of the porch creaked under his weight as he stepped up onto them, hands on his belt.

'Jesus, man,' Harris said. 'You fucking walk here? What took you?'

Ellis cleared his throat, looking around. 'Why am I here, sir?'

'Come inside and you'll goddamn see why,' the chief replied gruffly.

'I mean why *me*?' They did everything they could to keep outsiders out, here. So what was the reason Ellis was being brought in? He didn't really want to step through that door if it was to be stripped naked and put on a sacrificial altar. He didn't really think that's what they did out here, but you could never be too careful when it came to this kind of thing, he thought.

'It's not just you, you oaf,' Harris spat. 'Adams and Fitzhugh are already inside.'

'Oh,' Ellis replied with. And what can I do that they can't? he felt like asking.

'Goddammit, man, get in the fucking house,' Harris said, grabbing him by the arm and doing his best to move the big man.

Ellis let him, reluctantly, and he went in.

A tall man with grey hair that fell to his shoulders and dark eyes, keen like those of a bird, was waiting in the hall.

'My goodness, Jeff,' the man said, his voice smooth and quiet. 'I do wish you wouldn't take His name in vain as you do.' A hand extended from the man and hung in the air before Ellis. 'We haven't met. My name is David Hall. Welcome to my home.'

Ellis stared at him, and then thought it best not to spit in the face of the guy, a veritable legend, or ghost story, depending on who you asked.

'Todd,' Ellis replied, shaking his hand briefly. 'Something I can help you with tonight, sir?'

Hall smiled. 'Yes, Jeff will fill you in, but I wanted to introduce myself to you personally. I've heard a lot about you, and I'd like it if we could talk some time. You can come back and—'

'Yeah, yeah,' Harris said, cutting in, 'you can give him the business later. Time is a little short here, don't you think?'

Hall's eyes flashed for just a moment at the indignity of being cut off. But like a cage snapping shut on a pouncing beast, he got it under control. So quickly that Todd wasn't even sure he'd seen it. But the gooseflesh on the nape of his neck told him he had.

He offered a brief smile, having no intention of meeting or speaking with the man. Of letting those claws, those teeth, sink into him.

'Of course, Jeff,' David said. 'What was I thinking. Take him through.' He offered the door to the living room to them and Harris went in, walking past the foot of the stairs.

Ellis followed, glancing up towards the landing, seeing a snatch of a pale face hiding behind the corner there. A girl, probably ten, maybe a little older, with long, dark hair. She ducked back behind the corner in an instant and was gone.

Ellis put his eyes on Harris's back. He didn't want to ask. Didn't want to know what went on here. Who that was. Who these people were... Well, he did. Desperately. Wanted to know it all. But he couldn't ask, couldn't take that plunge. Not here. Not in this place.

He rarely felt nervous. Could count the number of times he had done on one hand. Waiting for the cops when he crashed his car. The first time he had sex with a girl... And now, it felt like.

What was he walking into, and once he saw...

Was there any getting out?

Chapter 18

Ellis followed Harris into the room, slowing before he even saw.

He smelled it first, that harsh metallic tang. Not a lot of bad shit went down in Devils Lake despite the name. It was a safe enough town, the kind of place your kids could go and call on their friends, could go and get some ice cream, could walk home after the street lights came on without any trouble. Ellis thought that was why the smell stuck with him so much. Only a few times before had it invaded his senses like it was now. A head-on car crash between a semi and a mini-van with five people in it. A suicide in a bathtub. And a guy trimming a tree with a chainsaw when his ladder slipped and he cut off one of his hands and hacked into his thigh down to the bone.

In each of those cases, there'd been more blood than he'd ever seen before. And in each of those cases, the smell had been like this. Sharp and metallic, threatening to slice up the inside of your nose.

Harris skirted the room on a strange path, and then finally, Ellis saw why. The blood had run from the two dead men on the floor and all but filled the room. Adams and Fitzhugh were in their regular clothes, standing at the far side, talking in hushed voices, their arms folded. They stopped and looked up at Ellis, and not with any sort of warmth.

Ellis didn't feel like having a staring contest, so he turned his attention to the scene at hand.

There were two men on the floor, one on his back, the other lying on his side, his legs bent awkwardly like he'd bounced off the couch when he'd fallen.

The blood smeared on the arm told Ellis he probably had. The other guy just seemed to have keeled over backwards, his arms at his sides, palms up, covered in blood, too. Ellis looked over their injuries. The one on his back, a stocky guy with a balding head — Ellis didn't recognise him, or at least didn't know his name. But he'd seen him around somewhere at some point. His chequered shirt was all torn up around the belly and Ellis could see at least four — make that five — separate stab wounds. Someone'd gone after him with some serious malice. The second guy was taller, greying hair, and a long, curved nose that was pressed into the gore around him. Ellis could see that he too had a gaping wound in his stomach, but this one lower and off to the side, just above his hip bone. There was also a slash across the palm of one of his hands, and a cut across his upper arm, too. Ellis tilted his head a little. But the one that'd killed him was the single stab wound to the middle of the chest, likely severing the aorta.

He wasn't a detective, and he didn't know all that much about murder or human anatomy, but he knew enough, and attributed what he did know about biology to his mother's love to hospital shows. Grey's Anatomy, House, Scrubs, even.

But despite the two dead men here, he didn't think the killer had been all that skilful. Just intentional. Just... angry.

'You getting a picture here?' Harris asked sourly.

Ellis looked up. He was, but he didn't think the chief wanted to hear it. Not by his tone or his expression.

Still, the scene played in his head for him. The stocky guy went down first. The killer had been in close quarters, within arm's reach. And by the way he'd gone down, he didn't even know what was happening until probably the third or fourth thrust of the knife. Just *stab, stab, stab, stab, stab, stab* into the gut in quick succession. It felt hasty, rushed almost. No real desire to hit any one thing, just a desire to hit anything. Just to get that blade in there again and again, do as much damage as possible.

The second guy, the tall one, saw what was going on, tried to intercede. The killer stepped back, slashed at the incoming hand, sliced the palm. The man pulled back, taking hold of it, and the killer moved forwards, the desire to kill enough to keep them there, stop them from turning and running away. The first kill could have been one of passion, something decided in the moment. The second? That was intent. Murder in the first.

The killer had gotten them once in the hand, chased them and caught them in the arm. The hands came up to defend themselves, and then the killer had put that knife right into their torso. Didn't matter where. Just stuck them, driven them back.

The guy stumbled, hit the couch and fell onto it, the killer on top of them. And though the wound looked deep and egregious enough to do the work. To kill the guy. He'd have bled out from that alone. But no, the killer had wanted to make sure. Had ripped the knife free, and then plunged it into the man's heart. No doubt they'd seen the light go out behind his eyes. And then they'd climbed off, leaving the man slither down onto the floor in a dead heap.

Ellis's mind did the maths. Why was he here? What for? The answer seemed obvious, and yet it made no sense. Especially not by looking at these two fully grown men. Men who would have dwarfed her. Men who would have easily overpowered her.

Was it really possible to consider the fact that Lily Graham was involved, or possibly even responsible for this act? For a double murder? She'd been asking about the farm, had been here.

Was she the killer?

Ellis looked up at Harris.

'Well?' Harris asked. 'Are you?'

Getting the picture? Yes, pretty clearly. But what could he say?

'Two dead,' Harris went on. 'Because of you. Because of your goddamn inability to do your fucking job.' He tutted, shaking his head.

'You want me to arrest Lily Graham,' he said. Not even a question. His hands curled at his sides, the guilt, the anger setting in on him now, too. Was this on him? Had this been coming all along? Had his desire to see her as a young woman, innocent and harmless – and, hell, and he was cursing himself now... attractive – had all that blinded him from what she really was? A calculating, vicious murderer.

'Arrest her?' Harris breathed. 'No,' he said, swallowing the bile that seemed to be rising in his throat. 'I want you to bring her to me. Quickly. Quietly.'

'And then what happens to her?' Ellis hazarded to ask, casting around the room once more. At the two dead men. At his two colleagues with the hard expressions on their faces. To his boss, the man tasked with protecting and serving Devils Lake and everyone in it.

But no answer came.

There was just silence in the room.

And blood.

Chapter 19

It was early when Todd got the call.

He roused, shoulder sore and complaining at him from his awkward sleeping position. He was slumped in the corner of his driver's seat, arms folded, the cabin of the car barely containing him. He had one leg across the centre console, the other in the driver's footwell, and it was, possibly, the most uncomfortable sleep he'd ever had.

He'd not stopped searching until after two, driving up and down every road, looking for her. He'd gone to the motel multiple times, camped out on the highways, even just sat and watched her car, which he'd stumbled across at around eleven that evening, tucked into a pull-off in the woods at the side of the road about a mile from the farm as the crow flew through the woods. That'd taken a good two hours of his night, and by the time he decided she wasn't coming back for it, the hour was late, and his eyes were heavy, his body exhausted.

So he'd found his own spot on the side of the highway and pulled up, tucked in behind a mini-billboard for the gas station two miles down the road, where he tried to keep his eyes open for as long as he could.

What time he finally dropped off, he didn't know, but it felt like he'd had no sleep at all now that he was awake.

'Ellis,' came the gruff voice of the chief. 'You out there, you big fuck?'

His radio crackled in the centre console and he jerked awake, reaching for it. 'Here,' he said groggily. 'I'm here.'

'Asleep,' the chief replied sharply. 'You find Graham?'

Ellis's thumb hovered over the talk button.

'Course you didn't. Know how I know? Cause I did.' The sigh was cut off halfway through as the chief let off the button his end. His voice swam back a second later. 'I'm sending you an address, think you can get there?'

Ellis wanted nothing more than to go home, shower, and fall into bed, pretending like last night never happened. He'd not been able to shake the stench of blood from his nose, and didn't know if he ever would again. The vision of that room had been haunting him since last night. Appearing in strobe of each passing streetlight, the shadows behind each tree. He couldn't wrap his head around it, couldn't imagine it. Couldn't imagine her doing it. There had to be some explanation beyond the obvious. But he knew there wasn't. He knew Lily Graham was responsible, and that it was on his shoulders. He should have stopped her, should have done his job. The weight of those men's lives weighed heavily on him. So much so that he barely hesitated in his answer.

'Yeah, send it across,' he said coldly. 'I'm on my way.'

Before it had even arrived, the radio was back in the cradle and he was pulling onto the road, stiff and strung out, but determined to make this right. Though, as he drove, he wondered what that entailed. Whether there'd be any justice to be had, and if so, what that looked like? The chief had brought him to the farm to see those two men, to see what they were up against… to light a fire in him. To make him see the terror that was Lily Graham. To convince him she needed to be stopped. Whatever the cost.

Ellis drove to the address at speed, keeping his sirens and lights off, the hour early and the roads quiet.

He pulled off the highway outside of town and trundled into a housing estate filled with 70s ranchers, their gardens bleeding into one, a dirt road cutting between them. Low-priced when they were built and worth nothing now. Originally, this part of what was still technically in town was supposed to blossom, Devils Lake expanding around the shore to link up with the newly rezoned areas. Fifty years ago, the town had been on the up. But it turned out no one really wanted to come here. So the idea withered on the vine, all but stranding those who bought all the way out here. Most of the people who lived in these houses had done so since they were built, and would do until they died.

So what was Lily Graham doing out here?

Ellis trundled forwards until he saw the back of another squad car ahead, along with the chief's SUV. There were no lights or sirens from them, either. And the way that the chief was waving him to slow down, he figured out quickly that they were doing this quietly.

Todd eased off the gas and came to a stop and climbed out. Adams and Fitzhugh were standing next to their car, wearing their uniforms now, and checking their equipment. Adams was ensuring the magazine on his service pistol was full, and Fitz was securing the straps of his ballistic vest.

Ellis watched them, wondering if that was overkill for one girl.

Chief Harris snapped his fingers in front of Ellis to get his attention. 'Eyes on me, big boy,' he said.

The nicknames were getting old. Fast. 'Whose house is this?'

'Does it matter?' the chief replied hastily, keen to tell Ellis what he was supposed to do. Ellis's stern look elicited an eye roll. 'Some prick named Jacob Taylor. He was seen picking up a girl from the side of the road late last night. She climbed into that truck right there' – the chief pointed at a black Chevy pick-up under the car port next to the house – 'and came here. And now we're here.'

'Someone just called that in?' Ellis asked dubiously. The name was familiar to him, but he couldn't place a face to go with it.

The chief sighed, frustrated by Ellis's questions. 'Yeah. The guy said that the driver was weaving in his lane, drunk, maybe. And the girl he picked up looked small – wasn't sure if it was a kid or not. So the guy figured he best call it in. You satisfied with that answer, Officer Ellis, or do you need more encouragement to do your fucking job?'

Ellis pursed his lips and looked up at the house, nervous at the look in Adams's and Fitz's eyes. 'And we're sure she's in there?'

He seemed to labour over the answer for a few seconds, sucking on his cheek. 'No,' the chief said, the word slow.

'So then what the hell are we doing here?'

'We're here to get the prick that picked her up – correction, the prick that *kidnapped* her. Snatched an innocent girl off the roadside, and we're doing our duty.'

'I don't understand…' Ellis began. 'You said she *climbed* into the truck—'

The chief hung his head. 'This is simple,' he interjected. 'The girl's not here, but the guy that picked her up is. And he's gonna tell us where she is, or we're gonna put him away for kidnapping and murder. You understand that?'

90

Ellis didn't know how to answer. He thought a 'no' would get him into more trouble, so he just slowly nodded. The charges wouldn't stick, and this would shake out right in the end, wouldn't it? Even in his head it didn't sound convincing.

'Now let's get on with this, it's already getting hot and it's not even seven in the goddamn morning yet.' He turned, wiping the forming sweat from his brow, and started towards the house, motioning his two cronies to fall in.

He was right, it was getting hot, but he didn't think that was why the chief was sweating.

And as Ellis started forwards, slowly unfastening the clip on his pistol, he realised it wasn't the reason he was sweating either.

Chapter 20

They filed onto the porch slowly, the chief beckoning Ellis to the front of the group. 'You're in first,' he whispered.

Ellis stared back at him. Not sure about any of this, doubting all of it. Was he being walked into an ambush? Was Lily Graham actually in there, sitting in the hallway with a shotgun? Was this the chief trying to take him out without getting his hands dirty?

Or was this something different...? Who was Jacob Taylor and how was he wrapped up in this? Just an innocent bystander sucked in by the storm surging through Devils Lake? Or was there more to him? And did the chief really want to get him for kidnapping and murder, try and put crimes on him that'd never stick? It made no sense. It would just drag him through the system and spit him out. Lots of time, lots of paperwork... And the chief had done all he could to keep this whole thing hush, free of any red tape so far. So why decide to do it this way now? It made no sense.

The only thing that made any sense was that this was some concocted excuse to just wipe Jacob Taylor out. Kill him here in his home. And all because he'd come into contact with Lily Graham? She might have told him things, Ellis thought. Things about the farm, about Devils Lake that the chief would do anything, everything to keep hidden.

So was all this just a ruse to commit a plausibly sanctioned killing?

Ellis's skin prickled at the thought. He couldn't let that happen, could he?

Either way, Ellis figured he didn't have a choice at that moment. There was no turning away, no disrupting this. It was happening and there was nothing he could do to stop it. And at least if he was in first, he'd have a chance of taking Graham alive. The way that Adams and Fitz were bristling, and the cold look in the chief's eye... it confirmed his suspicions.

Ellis nodded, reaching for the door knob, but the chief took his wrist out of the air, holding it a few inches from the handle.

'Hold on,' he muttered, pulling Ellis a little closer to him. 'The two men that Graham murdered last night? They were friends of mine. Brothers. Michael Brown and Brian Larson. Two good men, alright?' His eyes flashed a little. 'You with us?'

Ellis stared at his chief, reading what he was putting out. Was he good with what was about to go down? He felt like he was being inducted, that this was some sort of test.

He nodded, afraid of what would happen if he didn't.

The chief slowly released his hand, motioned for him to draw his weapon.

Ellis obliged, heart beating hard, and slipped his Smith & Wesson from its holster, flexing his great hand around the grip. The thing had always felt small to him, but it didn't detract from how dangerous it was. A 9mm bullet was just that in width, less than three centimetres in length, and weighed less than ten grams. An average-sized man was probably eighty to ninety kilos, and around one-point-seven-five metres tall. Which meant that a person weighed around eight thousand, five hundred times more than a single bullet. And was just one fifty-eighth of a man's size. And yet, despite all that, if you put one of them pretty much anywhere in a human body, if left unattended, they'd likely die of blood loss. And if you hit any sort of organ or artery, well, death came much quicker and was much harder to stave off.

And that always amazed Ellis — the fragility of humans. How close to death we all were at all times. And how few people actually managed to get themselves killed. Though, three officers busting into your house ready to execute you in your sleep was a very likely way to meet your maker sooner than intended.

One bullet would be enough to finish Jacob Taylor off. Their pistols held seventeen rounds each. Fifty-one between the three of them. Enough to kill him fifty-one times over. And that was what was going to happen if Ellis didn't do something about it.

'On you,' Adams said, at Ellis's shoulder, all but leaning against him to get him inside faster.

In first, fire first. That was what was expected of him.

His hand closed around the knob and he turned it, finding it locked. There was a momentary sigh of relief, but he quickly realised that they wouldn't be dissuaded of their quarry that easily.

'Jacob Taylor!' the chief called, leaning against the jamb. 'Devils Lake Police Department! Open up!'

Ellis glanced at the chief, who nodded Ellis forwards.
Break it down.

There was no escaping it now. Ellis inspected the fifty-year-old door, took a breath, and then threw his shoulder into it. The old wood splintered, the single bolt lock no match for his bulk.

The door swung inwards, bouncing off the wall, sending splinters into the corridor. Fitz and Adams shoved him from behind, desperate to get inside, the wildness coming off them in waves, killers in that moment, two men further from the badge than any Ellis had known.

He surged forwards, arms wide, blocking their line of sight, their firing line into the house.

And there he was, suddenly. Right there in the living room, just a pasty white guy who looked on the wrong side of forty with a pudgy belly and the beginnings of some serious alcohol-induced man breasts. He was side on, his dick hanging out, the smell of sex permeating through the stale air in the small house.

Jacob Taylor. Ellis barely recognised him. He had been in high school with him, if he remembered right, a senior when he was a freshman.

Ellis catalogued what he saw, what he smelled, what he felt. He wondered what had happened here, had this guy...? And Lily...? A pang of anger, of jealousy rose in him, but his sanity mercifully returned. Adams's pistol was rising at his elbow, ready to execute this man. Ready to fill him with bullets. Ready to kill him where he stood.

Taylor went wide-eyed, clocking Ellis before he turned away, taking one step towards the bedroom.

Ellis stepped sideways to block Adams's shot and surged forwards. What would become of Lily Graham after all this? He didn't know. If they found her, they'd kill her. But right now, he didn't know where she was, and it didn't matter. The man standing in front of him didn't deserve to be put down like a dog.

Protect and serve.

Due process.

Justice. Real justice. Not this outlaw bullshit.

Ellis tackled the man to the ground, a mewling, wheezing cough escaping him as Ellis knelt on his back and hastily folded his arms up, starting the process before Jacob could catch a bullet, hoping the words would be enough to stop his colleagues from doing anything rash.

But even as he began: 'Jacob Taylor – you're under arrest for the kidnapping of Lily Graham and the murder of Brian Larson and Michael Brown—'

'What?' the man beneath his knee squeezed out. 'I didn't—'

'You have the right to remain silent,' he said, leaning on him a little more to cut him off. 'Anything you say can and will be held against you in a court of law. You have the right to an attorney, if you cannot afford one, one will be provided to you. Do you understand?'

The man beneath him had fallen silent, eyes fixed on the doorway ahead.

Ellis looked up, seeing what he was looking at – Adams and Fitzhugh standing in the empty bedroom, standing over a bloodied bedsheet.

Ellis's blood ran cold.

What had happened here?

And where was Lily Graham?

Chapter 21

Ellis was at his desk at the station, knee bouncing furiously beneath the top as he rolled the situation over and over in his head.

They'd hauled Taylor in and thrown him into one of the interrogation rooms. But despite the rights that Ellis had read him and that the constitution gave him, he'd been given no counsel, and no phone call, either.

The chief had disappeared from the station moments after they'd arrived, saying to hold tight, don't do anything. Don't talk to Taylor until he got back.

But what then? What would happen when the chief did arrive?

Ellis didn't want to think about it. But if he could get in there first, get Taylor to talk, get him on record providing a statement that he didn't, *couldn't* have committed this crime, then it would be entered into the system, and whatever the chief was planning couldn't come to pass. Right?

He swallowed, standing and drawing a slow breath, Adams and Fitz watching him as he made his way to the corridor leading to the interrogation rooms and cellblock.

He'd burn for this, he knew that. Harris wasn't one to be crossed. But he didn't care. Jacob Taylor was more than likely innocent of a crime against Lily Graham, and definitely innocent of any crimes against the Hall Farm.

He was on the hook for the murder of Brian Larson and Michael Brown – two killings he did not commit. And all he needed was for Taylor to say that.

He paused outside interrogation room 2 and pulled out his phone, setting a voice note to record before slipping it back in his pocket and ducking inside.

Taylor was there at the table, hands still cuffed, his right bloodied – but Ellis wasn't jumping to conclusions. He needed Taylor's version of things. He just hoped that Taylor had enough sense to talk.

But as he sat down, the look in his eye said he wouldn't. Ellis sized him up in silence for a minute or so, and then decided there was no point waiting any longer.

'Look, Jacob,' he said, his voice soft, placid, friendly, he hoped. 'Just tell me what happened, alright? We have the story, but there are holes.' The story the chief was pedalling was double murder, kidnap. Rape, even, if he could use it as a club to get at Taylor. 'Holes you can fill in for us. Holes that'll help your case. We know you picked up Lily Graham off the side of the road – we had a report of a girl walking on the side of the road alone, and we got a witness saying she climbed into an early-Eighties K10 – the kind you got, right?' He hoped the question was simple enough to elicit an answer. Or even a word. He'd settle for a nod. 'Then you drove her home, right?'

The man across from him didn't answer.

'And then when you got home, you and her…' He stumbled over the words a little, the thought of it more than unpleasant. Like Lily was something to him other than just a young woman he'd found attractive. Found intriguing. He did his best to make it a playful question, like they were two boys at the bar recounting war stories, but struggled with it. 'But what'd you do with her, huh?

That's a lot of blood in your bed, in your bathroom. Is it hers? What'd you do, Jacob? Where's Lily, huh?' If he could get the answers, then there'd be no reason to keep him. They could release him before anything else happened.

But Jacob wasn't talking. He went inwards, hunching over, staring at the table. The man closed his eyes, afraid of what was to come. Of what was happening.

Ellis was running out of time. The chief could be back any second. He had to keep going. It was all he could do. 'What I don't get though is why you killed those two guys, huh? Hell, what I want to know is *how*.' Come on, Jacob, tell me you couldn't have done it. That you were at the bar. That's all I need! Say it!

But he was waiting for a response that wasn't coming.

'Why'd you go up there, to the farmhouse. Why'd you do it? You leave the bar and go right there, buzzed? I've had some guys checking up, I know you tied one on last night,' he bluffed. 'Shouldn't have been driving, should you? Hmm? You went up there, all riled up... tell me what happened?'

Come on, Jacob. Just give me something. Anything.

But before either of them could say a word, there was a knock at the door.

Ellis's stomach dropped and he pushed back from the table, heading to answer it.

He pulled it open a foot, seeing Chief Harris standing there in the gap, eyes like fire, hands on hips, moustache bristling.

'What the *fuck* do you think you're doing?' he muttered, the acid in his voice burning Ellis's skin.

Ellis swallowed the lump in his throat. 'I was—'

'Shut it. I don't give a shit,' he breathed. 'I told you to fucking wait. Not to go in there. And not to fucking speak to him. Or are you deaf as well as stupid, huh?'

Ellis blinked slowly, tempering his anger. He had to stand firm. Had to keep standing up for the law. But what could he say to that? No, I'm not deaf, I just decided to disobey an order?

Harris shook his head. 'Get him the fuck out of there. Throw him in a cell. And don't fucking go near him again, alright?' Harris's finger was in Ellis's chest now.

'But what about his right to—'

'Just do it, alright,' Harris snapped. 'That's an order.' He turned and stormed back down the corridor towards Fitz and Adams who were leaned against the wall at the far end, eyeing Ellis viciously.

He sighed and pulled the door wide, turning to the man in cuffs at the table. 'On your feet, Taylor,' he said, beckoning him towards the door.

Fear flushed in his eyes, but he got to his feet slowly.

Ellis wanted to tell him.

That this wasn't right.

That he'd do his best to make it so.

But as the man walked out of the room, he felt the overwhelming urge to say nothing.

To not make promises that he wasn't sure he could keep.

Chapter 22

Ellis locked Jacob Taylor in his box and stepped back into the corridor.

The chief was standing a little way down, waiting for Ellis to approach.

He walked over to the chief, slowly. 'What are we doing here?' he asked. The waiting was interminable. He was ready to be out of the dark. If the chief had ill intentions, then Ellis wanted to hear the words. Loud and clear.

'We're doing our jobs. Keeping this town safe,' he replied.

What a line.

'You know Taylor didn't do this. Didn't kill those two men.'

He moved his lips around beneath his moustache. 'That what he told you?'

'He didn't say anything.'

'Then we don't really know, do we?'

Ellis narrowed his eyes. 'What about Graham? What are you going to do with her when you find her?'

The chief stared back. Dead-eyed. 'You're walking a dangerous line here, Ellis. You should know that.'

He puffed a little, raising to his full height, throwing a shadow over the chief. 'And how's that?'

'You need to understand how things work around here. And the sooner you do, the easier your life will become. Now why don't you head on home, huh? It's been a long night for you.' He clapped Ellis on the arm, hard enough that most men would have moved. Ellis didn't budge an inch. 'Get some sleep,' the chief said. 'And then, come on back tonight, around midnight. Got a special job for you. Adams will be here to walk you through it.'

'What for?' Ellis asked as the chief turned and walked away.

The only response was the one he didn't want to hear. 'That's an order.'

The chief disappeared out of sight at the far end of the corridor, leaving Ellis standing there, still as a statue, going over what he'd just heard in his mind.

Come back tonight when no one else was here. To do a special job.

He glanced back over his shoulder at the door to the cells.

A special job involving Jacob Taylor.

Ellis just hoped that come midnight, he was going to be asked to kill the man. And not just bury the body.

He clenched his fists at his sides and let out a long breath. He'd be here at nine, just in case.

Jacob Taylor, you don't even know, he thought to himself, *the only thing standing between you and the end of a rope right now is me.*

He shook his head and surged forwards, towards the door. He was remiss to leave Taylor's side at all, but Harris was right about one thing. It had been a long night, and he was practically dead on his feet.

He needed sleep, needed to eat. Needed to think. Because even if Taylor made it past tonight alive, they wouldn't stop hunting him. Or Lily Graham.

And as Ellis stepped out into the early afternoon sunlight, he wondered at what point the chief would stop asking for his help...

And start hunting him, too.

Chapter 23

Ellis was parked down the street in his own car, an early two-thousands Tacoma, one of about a hundred in Devils Lake. He'd never appreciated the invisibility of it until now.

He was parked just at the corner of 3rd Avenue and Walnut Street, with a clear line of sight to the station. No one really rolled down this road on the way there, so he knew that if the chief, or Adams, or Fitz were headed to the station to take care of Taylor, they wouldn't drive by him.

He'd managed a few hours of restless sleep, mercifully, but now, he was wide awake, his heart beating steadily beneath his uniform. The chief hadn't mentioned whether he should or shouldn't be wearing it, but he thought anything he could do to remind those around him of what they stood for might be a good choice.

It was now 11:30 p.m., and though he'd been sitting there since before ten, nothing had moved. No one had gone in or out.

Ellis knew from the schedule that there were two officers on duty, sitting inside the building, and another two on patrol around town, with four more standing by on call. That was the normal setup for a normal evening. And it all seemed to look normal to him so far.

So why were his hands sweating so much?

This was why.

As though on cue, Adams's black RAM 1500 came haring around the corner and mounted the curb in front of the station, parking itself right outside the door.

Ellis's hand was already around the door handle.

Adams exited the vehicle and jogged up the steps into the station wearing his uniform.

'Shit,' Ellis muttered to himself, cursing the several hundred yards of space between him and the front door.

He was halfway there, verging on a run, when the two officers on duty exited through the front door and made a beeline for their cruiser.

Ellis slowed to a halt in the middle of the street as they wheeled backwards onto the asphalt and then sped off down the road, blowing through the red light at the intersection and hauling ass up College Drive.

He watched them go, realising that Adams was now alone in the station with Taylor. He repeated the curse word and then sped forwards, hurdling up the steps and inside, praying that a gunshot wouldn't echo through the halls before he got there.

But when he threw the door open and went inside, the only thing he was greeted with was silence and an empty room.

'Adams?' he called out tentatively.

A moment later, a bearded face appeared in the doorway to the kitchen, the first door in the corridor that led to the cells.

Ellis hid his relief as Adams arched an eyebrow. 'You're early,' he said, a little surprised, a little suspicious.

Ellis tempered his ragged breath. 'Yeah, I was just hanging around, so...' A poor excuse, but Adams either swallowed it or didn't care.

He moved back into the kitchen and Ellis approached, seeing him emptying some leftovers from the fridge onto one of the plates from the cupboard.

'Midnight snack?' Ellis queried.

'Something like that.'

'If you're hungry we could head down the street, get a bite, talk a little?' Ellis offered. Adams had the same cold aura he'd carried when they were outside Taylor's house. If he could get him away from here, maybe he could talk some sense into him, calm him down.

'It's not for me,' he answered steadily.

Ellis swallowed. 'Prisoners aren't supposed to have plates.'

Adams set about putting the food in the microwave, hitting the timer for two minutes and setting it on low.

'Come on,' he said, turning back towards Ellis. 'I need your help with something.'

'What is it?' Ellis asked as Adams stepped past him and into the corridor, heading for the cells.

He was met with silence, but followed anyway. He had to, didn't he?

As the microwave hummed away behind them, Adams walked the length of the corridor and let himself into the cellblock, pulling keys from his pocket.

Jacob Taylor was lying on the concrete bench on his back with his knees up when they went in, but Adams veered right, going for the other cell, where a known drug addict was being held until he dried out. The guy was in and out of here so much the toilet seat had moulded to the shape of his ass. He had a real problem with anything he could snort, smoke, or stick in his veins, and he was never pleasant to deal with. So what Adams was doing, Ellis wasn't quite sure.

He beckoned Ellis to come with him, and out of the corner of his vision he caught Taylor holding his hand up to shield his eyes from the overhead lights.

Ellis's attention snapped back to the addict as he started talking. 'W— whaddya want?' he stammered, holding his hands up. 'Leggo-a-me!' he wailed as Adams grabbed him by the arms and pulled him up.

He swiped at Adams, getting free and diving for the toilet bowl, hooking his nail-bitten fingers around the steel rim and locking in.

Adams grabbed him by the shirt and tried to pull him, readjusting until he got him by the waist, trying to drag him free, grunting as he did.

'I didn't do nothing! You can't make me!' the addict screamed, his voice echoing around the bare concrete room.

Taylor watched from his bunk and Ellis stared back at him.

With another heavy grunt, Adams wrestled the guy free and dragged him, screaming like a child, from the cell.

Halfway out of the door the addict managed to manoeuvre himself to a stance and throw an elbow into Adams's skull.

He hissed and swore, almost losing his grip. 'We're letting you go, you stupid motherfucker,' he growled, pulling and then pushing the prisoner into the corridor where he ejected him from his grasp and pointed towards the exit.

In the way they usually did, he reeled off nonsensical accusations about police brutality and suing the department.

When Ellis turned back, Taylor was on his feet, standing at the bars of his cell, staring right at him.

They kept their eyes locked as Adams threw the prisoner out and locked the front doors behind him. On his return journey he ducked into the kitchen, the microwave's hum stopping as he pulled the plate out. And then he was walking back towards Ellis.

With each step, Ellis's heart ratcheted up a gear. You're not supposed to give prisoners plates because they can smash them and use the shards as weapons. On each other. On officers. Or, as the report would likely read in the morning, on themselves.

Adams appeared a moment later, plate in hand, the food steaming. Ellis wasn't quite sure of the point of heating it at all if Adams was going to do what he thought, but it seemed like a question of little consequence now.

'Open it,' Adams said, nodding at Taylor's cell, eyes fixed on the man inside.

The tone said it wasn't worth arguing. Not over this. But Ellis needed to figure a way out, and fast. But how to do it without incurring Adams's wrath, and the chief's?

He racked his mind as he approached the door, dragging his keys from his pocket as slowly as he could. He thumbed through them, inserting the correct one into Taylor's lock.

'You, against the back wall, turn and face it, hands flat above your head,' Adams ordered Taylor with that same flat, inarguable tone.

Ellis watched, brow beading with sweat as the condemned prisoner went to the back of the cell.

Adams stepped closer to Ellis, ushering him inside.

Ellis opened the door and stepped through, Adams moving past him. 'Close the door,' the man said.

Ellis swallowed. Lock us in, was what he was saying. We're not leaving until we're done. He stared down at his hand around the key and withdrew it from the lock, swinging the door slowly to the jamb, easing it up against the metal so it was shut but not locked.

Thankfully, Adams's eyes were fixed on Taylor, like a farmyard cat watching a rat, readying itself to pounce.

Ellis took in a long breath, turning back to the cell. He reached slowly to his weapon and slipped the safety catch off the holster, just in case, as he watched Adams's steady, unshaking hand around the plate. The man was not only okay with killing Taylor, he wanted to. There wasn't a shred of doubt in him.

Which meant that if Ellis was going to do something…

He needed to do it now.

Chapter 24

Taylor turned his head a little, hands still on the concrete, and Adams quickly corrected him. 'Eyes on the wall,' he snapped.

Slowly, Adams loosened his grip on the plate and the whole thing tumbled from his fingers, turning slowly in the air before landing face down on the ground.

The food, meat, gravy, mashed potatoes, splattered on the polished concrete, the plate shattering under its own weight.

Adams, voice dripping with venom, turned to Ellis. 'Hold him,' he ordered, his right hand hanging at his hip, perilously close to the grip of his pistol.

Ellis didn't have any other ideas. Not yet. So he went forwards, taking Taylor's arms from above his head, ignoring the confused look on his face as he stared at his dinner on the ground.

'What's going on?' he asked, allowing his arms to be folded down, a thin hope audible in his voice.

'Get him on the bench,' Adams said as he bent down teasing the broken shards of plate apart with his index finger, searching for the best, the sharpest, one.

Ellis began moving Taylor and the man seemed to glean an understanding of what was happening, resisting a little. But if Ellis let him go here, he'd run across the room and

Adams would stick him with a shard, or just draw and fire, putting five rounds in him before Ellis could do anything.

So he held firm, putting the man on the bench as instructed.

He could see Adams testing the sharpness of his desired shard as he pushed Taylor down.

'Get his arm,' Adams said, approaching.

Fuck. This was it.

Could he just release Jacob, swing for Adams, knock him out? And then what? He'd have to kill him if he wanted to keep the truth of what happened secret. But then what? Hide the body, pin it on Taylor? Neither were good options. No, there was a way out of this. For him. For Adams. And for Taylor. He just didn't know what it was yet.

'Hold him still,' Adams ordered as Ellis took Taylor's left arm in both his hands, bringing it to his side, exposing it to Adams.

He looked up at Taylor, hoping to God he had more fight in him than he was currently displaying.

He pleaded, 'Woah, woah, wait, you don't have to do this, please, please!'

Then fight, Ellis thought. *Fight for your life, for Christ's sake!*

'Shut the fuck up,' Adams snarled. 'Hold him still, God damn it!' He moved up next to Ellis, squeezing next to him and reaching over his arms to get to Taylor's wrist, trying to assess the angle, the right way to do it so it looked like Taylor could have done it himself.

Ellis's stomach began to churn. Come on, Taylor, do something!

He looked down at the man in his grasp, the man that'd be bleeding out all over this cell in about three seconds if he didn't try something right now.

Taylor looked back.

He wasn't going to do it. Not on his own at least. Not without help.

Dammit! If this got Ellis killed... But there was no other way. He looked down. Just a second. A flit of the eyes. To his hip. To his holster. To the unbuttoned safety catch. To the Smith & Wesson that could be pulled free.

Just don't shoot me, Ellis thought, as Taylor lunged for the weapon.

He lifted his elbow just a little so Taylor could pull it cleanly, and thankfully, he managed.

Ellis released his arm and stood straight fast enough that he almost bowled Adams over, his arms already raising next to his head, his own pistol suddenly levelled right at him.

He willed Taylor not to shoot, but in that moment, he wasn't sure if he'd made a grave mistake. Had he just given his life for Taylor's? And in the end, would it even make a difference?

Behind Ellis, Adams got to his feet, using the wall for support, and ran the back of his hand across his spittle-flecked lips before he slowly lifted his hands, too.

Taylor backed slowly towards the door, groping behind himself for it. Ellis hid a sigh of relief, glad he'd left it open now. This could all go sideways very fast if they were all locked in here.

The door creaked open and Taylor stepped through it, gun still raised and pointed at them, shaking in his hand.

'Your radios,' he as good as stammered from beyond the bars. 'Throw them on the ground. Your phones, too.'

Not as dumb as he looks, Ellis thought – thank God – as he reached for his radio, pulling it off his shoulder. He took his phone out, too.

From behind him, Adams spat a, 'Fuck you.'

'Throw it out of the cell,' Taylor commanded them.

Ellis did so, hurling his through the bars and into the cell of the recently moved-on addict. Well out of reach.

'Now you,' Taylor said to Adams.

Before he could try anything stupid, Ellis took the liberty of doing it for him, turning and pulling his radio free, unclipping it from his shoulder with the kind of slow precision he hoped wouldn't get him shot. As he reached into Adams's pocket, he asked, 'The fuck you think you're doing?'

Ellis lifted his head, meeting his colleague's eye, and matching his hard look. 'I want to sleep in my bed tonight, not in the dirt.'

'Harris is going to hear all about this.'

I'm sure he will, Ellis thought, as he turned and threw out the other radio and phone, right next to his own. Now run, he thought, willing Taylor to turn and haul ass out of there.

And thankfully, he did.

He'd barely turned his back before Adams was tearing his gun free. But the only thing he found in front of him was Ellis, his huge hand resting on the top of the barrel, pushing it back down.

'Hard to make that look self-inflicted,' he said as Taylor's footsteps receded down the corridor.

Adams swore under his breath and jostled past Ellis, grabbing the bars, letting forth with a stream of cries for help, for release, his voice echoing through the cellblock, ringing loudly, but reaching no one.

Ellis rubbed his tired eyes and went to the concrete bench where Taylor's life had nearly ended just a moment ago.

He eased himself down with a little groan and leaned back against the wall, closing his eyes while Adams shouted himself raw.

It would be a long night. But with what he'd just done…

Ellis wasn't sure if he even wanted to see the morning.

Chapter 25

It wasn't until eight the following morning that someone arrived at the station. Whatever Adams had told the officers on duty had cleared them out for the night. Ellis had been curious, but he'd not said a word to Adams after Taylor escaped. Decided it was for the best.

After about thirty minutes of straight screaming, he collapsed against the bars and put his head between his knees, muttered to himself under his breath. Whatever fate awaited Ellis, he figured it probably wasn't great for Adams. This was a big ball fumble, surely. Whatever the chief was trying to protect, or prevent Taylor from saying or doing… it was enough to order Adams to kill him. So what punishment would await the man?

When the door sounded, Adams leapt back to his feet and started yelling again.

Fitz came running in, wide-eyed. 'What the fuck happened?' He looked left and right at the two of them, then seemed to notice the distinct lack of Jacob Taylor, or his blood spread across the floor.

He quickly unlocked the door and Adams rushed out of the cell, slowing in the hallway, not really sure what to do next.

Ellis got up and went calmly to the door, rubbing his stiff neck.

'What happened?' Fitz asked, sizing him up, an unmistakeable suspicion in his eye.

'Taylor got loose,' he replied coldly. 'Took my weapon, held us at gunpoint.'

'How'd he manage to get your weapon?' Fitz asked accusatively.

Ellis shrugged. 'I must have been pre-occupied trying to stage his suicide. If I'd have known what was expected of me before going in there, I might have been more cautious.'

Fitz eyed him and then looked down. *Yeah, that's what I thought*, Ellis thought. *Grow a spine and make your accusation or get the fuck out of my face.*

Ellis trudged tiredly towards the door, grabbing his phone and radio from the floor as he went.

He was halfway down the corridor when Adams stopped him. 'Where the hell do you think you're going?'

'Home,' Ellis replied, removing Adams's hand from his chest with ease. 'To sleep. Whatever the fuck you guys are doing… I want no part of it.'

Before he could move off, Adams took him by the wrist. 'You're already a part of it. You started this. And we're gonna finish it.' There was that same wild look in his eyes.

The wild look that told Ellis that when they found Taylor, they were going to kill him.

Which told Ellis that as much as he wanted to end this night and go home to bed… his day hadn't even begun yet.

–

He successfully avoided the chief's wrath by agreeing to Adams's suggestion that they not tell him what happened until they'd found Taylor and *taken care of him*.

Ellis suggested they split up to cover more ground, that Adams should go back to his house to see if he was there, or had been there, hoping he wouldn't be that stupid.

Since his arrest, Ellis had looked into Taylor, and knew he had a sister in town. Stephanie Taylor. Smart lady, by all accounts. And with no parents in the picture, a boy in trouble will always run to his big sister for help, Ellis surmised. So if he wasn't there, he was sure she'd heard from him. Jacob had no one else in the world. So even if his plan was just skip town, Ellis figured he'd go there first.

As such, if Ellis didn't catch him, he figured Steph would know where he was, or headed. And at the very least, he'd get a little peace of mind that Jacob wasn't liable to be scooped up by Adams, Fitz, or anyone else that wanted his head on a pike.

He walked unhurriedly down the street to his truck and climbed in, taking a second behind the wheel to centre himself. What exactly was he wrapped up in, and what was his endgame here? Once he pulled Taylor's head from the noose, then what? If the chief wanted blood, it was likely that his would have to stand in for Taylor's.

Another thought came to him, then... What was so important about Taylor? About what he knew? What was so crucial to keep hidden about Lily Graham and the Hall Farm?

'One thing at a time, Todd,' he said to himself, cranking the key in the ignition. 'When you find Taylor, you can ask him what's so important. But first, you gotta find him.'

And with that, he pulled slowly into the street and headed for Stephanie Taylor's house. And he hoped, the truth.

Chapter 26

Ellis pulled up outside Stephanie Taylor's house at a little after 8:15 a.m.

He eased his truck to a stop across the street and stared up at the place. It was a little tired, like a lot of the houses in Devils Lake. It was a wooden-clad two-storey detached house, sitting snug with its neighbours, a little wooden porch out front, a fenced yard.

Stephanie Taylor was divorced, two kids basically grown. Lives alone. Other than that, Ellis didn't have much on her.

He surveyed the house. Lawn unkempt, overgrown. No one was keeping up with the maintenance. Car in the driveway, old Subaru dusty with the North Dakota summer.

Ellis massaged his chin for a few seconds, thinking. Would Taylor come here? No cars had rolled by in the last minute or so. The street was quiet, and he'd know the area, could slip in without anyone knowing. And it was walking distance from the station.

Honestly, Ellis wasn't sure if he wanted Jacob Taylor to be there or not. If he did find him… what then? Maybe they could run together. Ellis sort of felt like it was getting to that point. He just couldn't believe he'd been so blind for so long as to what kind of men he'd been working alongside. Had he really just been that oblivious, or had he been wilfully ignoring signs all along?

He wrestled with it as he climbed from the truck and headed across the asphalt towards Steph Taylor's house.

The old wood bowed under his weight as he climbed up onto the porch, the structure creaking as he stood before the door, looking at the windows to his flanks. Blinds drawn. Early, sure, but still...

The front door had a glass pane but it was covered, too.

Trying to hide something?

He lifted his hand, listening to see if he could hear voices – multiple, he hoped. But there was no sound at all.

Ellis knocked.

Knuckles first, politely.

No reason to bang the door down, not yet.

When no answer came, he repeated, louder this time. Loud enough for it to be heard all through the house. There was a shuffling noise beyond the door.

He leaned into the wood. 'Stephanie Taylor – it's Officer Todd Ellis with the Devils Lake Police Department. Would you mind opening up for a minute?'

He closed his eyes, listening more closely. The hurried patter of feet. How many sets?

Impossible to tell.

The door opened a few seconds later, a slightly flustered looking woman standing before him. Her hair was greying around the temples, her eyes bagged. She looked tired, but Ellis was struck by her resemblance to Jacob Taylor.

Unmistakably his sister.

'Hi,' she said, hovering in the gap, keeping the door closed enough that Ellis didn't have a look down the hallway. 'What can I do for you?' she asked quickly.

'Everything alright in there, ma'am?' Ellis replied carefully.

'Yeah, why?'

'You look a little out of breath.'

'No, not at all,' she said. 'What do you want?'

Asking to go inside was probably a little premature. So how to handle this?

What about the truth, Todd? He thought. You're already up to your neck in this shit. 'Your brother, Jacob, is he here?'

'No. Is that all?'

'You're not even going to ask why I'm asking about him?'

'I'm guessing he drove away from a traffic stop? Got into a bar fight? Man's an idiot,' she answered quickly. Without missing a beat. 'But he's not here.'

Ellis nodded slowly. Big sister trying to protect her little brother. If he handled this wrong, she'd never let him in. *Truth, Ellis. Be that man.*

'Look, some bad shit has gone down, alright?' he began, dropping all pretence. If he had a hat, he'd be kneading it in his hands. But he didn't, so he kept them at his sides, as unthreateningly as possible. He guessed that Jacob would have told her everything, and if not, Ellis doing so might soften her up to help. 'The police are after Jacob. And...' He looked down at his chest, at the badge there. Where Steph had also looked when he'd said *the police* like he wasn't including himself in that cabal. 'Last night, they tried to kill him. He's... God, he's mixed up in something, and I don't know what it is, alright? Not the full extent of it, at least. But there's a girl in town, and Jacob is in the firing line now. Look, I know I'm not really making sense right now, but… if it wasn't for me, Jacob would be dead, okay? And I'm trying to keep it that way. Trying to keep him alive. So if he's not here, I need you to tell me where he is, or at least that he's somewhere far away. And if he is…' Ellis swallowed, balling his hands into loose fists. This was it, the choice. 'Then we need to get him out of town. Right now. Before they find him.'

Steph stood there for a few seconds, eyes narrowing almost imperceptibly. 'Why?' she asked, after what seemed like an age.

'Why what?'

'Why do you want to save him when everyone else wants him dead?'

The question was simple. The answer was, too. 'Because he's innocent. Innocent of what they've accused him of. And I can't stand by and let them do that.' He stood a little straighter. 'It's just not right.'

Stephanie Taylor surveyed him for a few more seconds, and then shook her head. 'Well, I believe you. But Jacob's not here. He took off this morning – I don't know where. And I have no way of reaching him. I told him to run as far as he could. And I hope he has the sense to follow my advice. Now, if there's nothing else—'

She made to shut the door, but Ellis put his hand out, stopping it.

'I'm sorry, he said, but… If I could take a look around inside, that'd make my life a lot easier. I just got to make sure.'

She kept pressure on the door. 'You got a warrant?'

'No,' Ellis said. 'But if I don't make sure he's not in there… it won't be me that comes back next time. It's not a threat, I'm just telling you what's likely to happen.' He took his hand off the door. 'It's your choice.'

Steph Taylor appraised him, seemingly trying to assess whether he was full of shit or just trying to be decent.

Eventually, she decided it was the latter and with a sigh, pulled the door wide.

'Fine,' she said. 'Come in, then. But you aren't going to find what you're looking for.'

He gave her a nod and stepped in.

I hope not, he thought. *I really hope not.*

Chapter 27

Ellis stepped inside, not realising quite how warm the summer morning was until he entered. Though he didn't think the heat was the reason that he was sweating. He ran his sleeve across his forehead, wanting nothing more than to unbutton his shirt, tear off his tie, and throw his badge in the fucking lake.

But he couldn't quit, not yet.

Even if Taylor was long gone, he needed to know why. Why him? Why had the chief chosen him? Why had Lily?

The girl. He couldn't get her out of his head. Couldn't imagine her killing two men. Couldn't imagine her *not* doing it. She was an enigma to him. She made him want to run a hundred miles and do everything he could to find her at the same time.

They'd had three or four exchanges – who was he kidding, he knew it was three – and each time it had been electric. There was something about her. He felt it. And Taylor had, too. But how'd he done it? How had he gotten her to…

'You thirsty or something?'

Ellis turned to see Stephanie Taylor standing in the hallway, hands in her back pockets.

'I got some coffee on,' she said, nodding towards the kitchen.

'Coffee would be great,' Ellis replied. *Offering coffee? Can't be too hurried to hustle me out of here, then.* Either Taylor wasn't there, or she was really confident Ellis wasn't going to find him. Either way, he could do with the caffeine. To think. To function. 'Black, one sugar,' Ellis added as she gave him a nod and headed into the kitchen.

He paused in the living room and looked around. Two couches pointed at a TV, necessary for a family of four. But they were at least twenty years old – bought when they *had* been a family of four. Pictures on the shelves of kids when they were young. None of the dad. None of the kids grown up. Two daughters, not far apart in age. Ellis surveyed the place. It was a time capsule. An echo of a happier time.

Any pictures of Jacob?

He made a slow lap, found what he was looking for on the hallway wall. Pictures of Stephanie and Jacob together. As kids. At her high school graduation. Pictures of Mom and Dad from way back when, aged and yellow.

'What kind of man is your brother?' Ellis called softly, the smell of coffee filling the air.

'What?' came the reply.

'Your brother,' Ellis said, coming to the doorway and leaning on the frame. 'What's he like?'

'You talked to him, didn't you?' Steph replied, looking up from behind the drip filter machine.

'He wasn't exactly chatty.' Ellis folded his arms. 'I'm just trying to figure out how he got so wrapped up in this.' He eyed her, tried to read her expression, her body language, and had to admire how she carried herself. How guarded she was with it all. 'You saw him last night, right? Around one, probably? How much did he tell you?'

She shrugged.

'He tell you about the girl?'

She looked up, just a flicker of fear in her eyes.

'Yeah, she's at the heart of it all,' Jacob replied.

'Who is she?'

The million-dollar question. 'She goes by Lily Graham, but I don't know if that's who she really is.'

She drew a slow breath, raised her chin. 'Jacob's not like that, you know. He wouldn't – I mean, he wouldn't *usually…*'

Ellis closed his eyes and looked down. Jacob was barely older than him. He couldn't judge the man for doing what he wanted to do himself. But if he'd forced himself on her, that was a different story.

'But he did? They had sex?' The word had to be said.

She nodded, the shame clear in her face.

'What'd he tell you?'

'That she, uh, crawled into his bed, that he was, uh, drunk…' She stumbled over the words. 'He'd never… what you're accusing him of, I mean.'

Rape. That was clearly the word she wanted to say. 'You sure about that?'

'More than anything. Jacob's a good man.'

Ellis couldn't figure out what he was wrestling with the most; whether he wanted to find Jacob or not. *Not*, he thought. If Jacob was gone, like she said, things would be a lot easier. For him. For everyone.

'Did he give any indication of where she might be? The girl? She wasn't there when we arrived at his place this morning. Thanks,' he said, accepting the cup of coffee being offered to him.

She shrugged, then shook her head for good measure. 'No, I don't know. I mean, he took off, so… who knows where she is, right? Hopefully gone, too?'

Ellis watched her speak. Whether she was lying about Jacob or not, she wasn't lying about Lily. She hoped she was gone.

But somehow, Ellis didn't think so. What had happened at the farm maybe hadn't been the plan, but it wasn't the end of this. Not by a long stretch.

He tested Steph. 'She killed two men. Or at least, that's what I believe. I don't know how. Or why. But I think she did it. And then afterwards, she went home with Jacob. It's the only thing that makes sense. Why exactly that makes him deserving of death, I can't say. But one thing's for sure – standing in your kitchen isn't going to answer the question. She's the only one that could do that. And Jacob's the last one to see her. So if you know where he is, I really need to speak to him. If I can find Lily Graham, I can—'

But he didn't get to finish. A dull thud echoed from the hallway and cut Ellis off mid-sentence. Something solid thudding against a wall.

He looked at Steph, saw her eyes widen.

Ellis put his cup down on the counter and she began to shake her head.

He turned from her, stepping back into the corridor, looking down its length. Towards the front door.

Towards the closet under the stairs.

'Wait,' came Steph's crestfallen voice from behind Ellis. 'Please.'

But he couldn't. If Taylor was here, he had to get him. Talk to him, at least. Try to figure this out. He couldn't go back to the chief and say he wasn't here. It'd be his head on the block instead of Taylor's then.

Ellis stood before the closet, hand reaching for his empty holster. He looked down at it, suddenly aware that the man behind the door had his gun. Was probably pointing it right at him through the thin layer of wood.

'Jacob Taylor,' he said, heart beating out of his chest. 'This is Officer Todd Ellis.' God, he could hear his own voice shaking. 'Last night, I saved your life. You know that to be the truth. Now, come out, please. I just want to talk to you.'

He waited.

There was silence.

He could feel sweat beading under his jaw, his heart thumping in his ears.

A few more seconds, he thought. Then I'm going to open it.

But before he could, there was a creak behind him. Todd Ellis turned around, seeing Steph Taylor standing there, a glass bowl raised high over her head.

His mouth opened to speak, but he didn't manage to get a word out before it came down.

And then there was darkness.

Chapter 28

There was a crash like breaking glass and then a huge bang like someone had dropped an anvil on the floor, so heavy the whole house shook under his feet.

'Jacob...' came the tinny voice of his sister. 'You can come out now.'

Jacob Taylor let out a quivering breath and lowered the pistol he'd been holding up in front of him, ready to fire if the door opened.

'Fuck,' he muttered, his mouth dry and his bladder aching. He really thought he was going to piss himself, he was so scared.

He groped for the handle in the darkness and swung the door open, squinting in the sudden onslaught of light.

The baseball bat that'd been against the wall, that he'd knocked into the door when he'd shifted position, that had made the noise that had drawn Ellis, fell into the hallway with a loud clack, rolling sideways into the leg of the man on the ground.

Jacob stared down at him, lying flat on his stomach, arms at his sides, a small pool of blood forming around his head, a hall of broken glass spread around it.

'Jesus,' he mumbled, the gun hanging loosely in his grip. 'What did you do?'

Steph was standing there, lifting the toes of her bare feet to avoid the spreading liquid. 'I... I...' she stuttered. 'I just saved your life.'

Jacob looked back at Ellis. Was that the truth? Had Ellis just been trying to lure him out so he could take him back to his cell and finish the job? Or had he been telling the truth. His words rang in the air. *I saved your life. You know that to be the truth.* Did he? Ellis had held his arm while that bearded maniac had tried to slash his wrist. He'd glanced at his gun, sure, but otherwise... Jacob shook his head. No, Steph was right to do this. Was right to act like she had.

'He's not dead,' she announced after a second. 'He's breathing, look.' She pointed at his slowly rising and falling back. 'He's just unconscious.'

'So what happens when he wakes up?'

Steph pursed her lips. 'Come on,' she said. 'Help me with him.'

'Help you with him?' The question was one of shock more than anything. 'Help you how?'

'We can take him down to the basement, tie him up. So when he wakes up—'

'You're serious? Look at the fucking size of him! How the hell are we supposed to do that?'

'Quickly,' she said, already bending down. 'Because if he comes to before we get there, we've got a pretty big fucking problem, don't we?'

Jacob cursed, knowing she was right, and crouched, taking his shoulder.

'Roll him over, and then we'll sit him up, drag him by the arms if we have to.'

'Fucking hell,' Jacob grumbled, following her lead. 'This is fucked.'

'Yeah,' she panted, 'it is. But it's better than the alternative, right?'

Better than every alternative, he thought.

'And once he's all trussed up, you're going to finish telling me what the fuck happened with that girl in the woods.'

There was no messing with Steph, and Jacob couldn't lie to her. Not ever. Not even if he wanted to. But he didn't want to. What Lily had shown him, what she'd found out, what she'd seen... Jacob had lived in Devils Lake his whole life, and he never could have imagined what was going on right under his nose.

She'd killed those two men. But he couldn't say they didn't deserve it, and worse.

Ellis left a smeared trail of blood as they guided him towards the basement door, the rubber heels of his boots squeaking on the kitchen tile as they hauled him awkwardly to the stairs. They clapped on each step on the way down, and by the time they reached the bottom, they were both slick with sweat and practically gasping for air.

The basement was stuffy and poorly ventilated, an old washer dryer and laundry sink against one wall, a workbench against the other. There was random stuff lying around, camping gear and fishing gear, old sports equipment from the girls, an ancient set of golf clubs that Greg had left behind and she'd never touched.

'Hold him,' she said, letting go and stepping towards a couple of spare dining room chairs stacked in the corner. She dragged one over to the wooden pillar in the centre of the basement and put the back against it, grabbing a long, red extension cord that was hanging on the wall on the way past.

'Get him up,' she said.

Jacob stared at her. 'Seriously?'

'Right,' she said, realising Ellis probably had thirty pounds on him.

Together, they managed to pull him up onto the chair and fold his arms behind his back. Steph looped the wire around his wrists, clove-hitching the cable around each before securing the ends behind the pillar.

Their dad had taught them when they were kids. To fish. To sail. Steph had always picked things up faster. And retained them. Jacob remembered basically nothing, and just watched in awe of his sister as she *trussed* him up, as she'd said she would.

'Now what?' he asked, stepping back and staring at Todd Ellis, his head hanging over his chest, the cut skin on his hairline from the glass bowl leaking blood down his face. It dripped slowly from his nose.

'Now?' Steph said, stepping next to her brother. 'Now you tell me what that crazy bitch told you — about the farm, about the people there...' She swallowed, taking Jacob's hand and squeezing it tightly. 'About everything.'

Chapter 29

Steph stood there, blinking at him. 'A cult?'

'That's what she said. That they take young women, and they poison their minds.'

'Poison their minds?' Steph repeated back to him. 'What the hell is that supposed to mean?'

Jacob didn't quite know, either. They were Lily's words, not his.

She shook her head then, the pair of them standing in the kitchen, shooting glances at the basement door in turn. 'I'm sorry, tell me again who this person is supposed to be?'

Jacob sighed. He hated when his sister took this tone with him, the one that made him feel ten years old. 'Lily Graham. She's an independent journalist, alright? She's doing this huge piece on modern cults in America, and she's investigating one that's supposed to be here in Devils Lake.'

She put her hands on her hips. 'At the Hall Farm? The stall that sells blackberries and strawberries on Sunday mornings at the farmer's market?' She arched an eyebrow, muttering something under her breath as she sat at her kitchen island and pulled a tablet on the counter towards her.

'What are you doing?' Jacob asked, coming forwards a little.

'Checking.' She tapped on the screen.

'Checking what?'

'To see if *any* of that is true.' Her brow crumpled as she scanned the results on screen. 'There's no hits for any Lily Graham as an independent journalist. Nothing online, at least.'

Maybe it's her first article. Maybe that's not her real name. They were the first two things that came to mind. But neither of them seemed like a good hill to mount a defence on. 'I'm only saying what she told me.'

'And I'm only saying that she's completely full of shit.' Steph basically snorted. 'You picked up a shoeless girl off the side of the road, fucked her, and got lied to. Hell, if there was anything in the house worth stealing, she probably would have grabbed it on the way out!' Steph shook her head at him. 'You got taken for a ride, Jakey. It's okay. A young woman who needs help, attractive, you're drunk—'

'No,' Jacob said suddenly, louder than he'd intended. 'It wasn't like that. It's *not* like that. She wasn't lying, okay? She showed me the video of her going to the farm, she showed me her notes, her research, articles about missing women from around the state. It's real, Steph. The Hall Farm… Fucking blackberries? No, there's something going on up there.'

'And you're going to figure out what it is, huh? Save the girl? Save *all* the imprisoned girls up there?' She tutted and closed the tablet. She'd heard enough. 'Do you hear yourself? Who are you right now?'

He set his jaw. Proof. He'd need proof to convince her. He'd come here to tell her the truth of what happened, the truth of what Lily had told him. But she needed more. She needed to see it. To hear it from Lily. To see the videos, the clippings. Which meant he'd have to get Lily and bring her here. Or bring Steph to her.

'Let's go,' he said. 'We'll meet her. And then you can decide for yourself.'

'And leave the jolly green giant tied up in my basement? I don't think so.' She huffed.

'Fine, you want to stay here? Do it. Ask him when he wakes up. He'll tell you. About the farm, about Lily. He's the one that hauled me in yesterday. The one that interrogated me. The one that...' He cleared his throat. 'The point is that he'll know. Okay?'

Steph stared back at him. 'Okay. I'll ask him.'

He breathed a little sigh of relief.

'I still think you need to get out of town,' Steph said then.

'And what about when they come looking for him?' He nodded towards the basement door. 'You want to be here when they do?'

Steph pursed her lips. 'I can't just leave him down there tied up.'

'Do you really have another option?' Jacob came forwards, leaning on the kitchen island, staring at his sister.

She stared back at him. 'How does this end, Jake?'

He held her gaze as long as he could, then broke, looking down. 'I don't know. But if I run now, I'll never be able to stop. I'll be a murderer. And now, with this...' He stole another look at the basement door. 'You're in this now, too. So...' He let out a long, rattling breath. 'Whatever it looks like, we have to see it through to the end.'

She was still for a while, and then nodded. 'I think you're right.'

'I'm sorry, can you repeat that?' Jacob asked with a smirk. 'I need to hear it again.'

She sneered at him. 'Yeah, yeah, first time for everything, right?'

He came around the counter and hugged her, resting his head on her shoulder, arms wrapped around his sister. 'I love you,' he whispered.

She reached up and held on to his wrists, squeezing tightly. 'I love you too, Jakey.'

He meant to let go, but found it hard to do so. And the way she was clutching him, it seemed like she felt the same way.

So they just stayed there in her kitchen, holding each other.

Wishing for this to all be over.

But knowing there was a long way to go before it was.

Chapter 30

Jacob peeked through the curtain on the door, checking the street in both directions before he opened the door and slipped down the driveway towards the Subaru. He'd driven straight back there that morning after leaving Lily at the lake, so filled by her story, by what he'd seen. So ready to tell Steph that it wasn't as bad as it looked, that he *was* innocent, and what the truth of the whole thing was. The Hall Farm, the cult, the way the cops were in on it. Everything.

He didn't know if it was his intention to help Lily, or what that help would look like. But giving that information to Steph was paramount, even Lily agreed. So that if Jacob did need to go into hiding, if he did need to run, that Steph knew the whole story. But he hadn't quite considered how preposterous the entire thing was until he'd repeated it back to her, the most cynical, pragmatic person he knew.

But Lily would convince her. Once she heard it come from her mouth, saw the video, the proof she had. Jacob knew it.

He slid in behind the wheel and cranked the key, aware suddenly of how quiet the street was. How nothing was moving. The skin on the back of his neck prickled and he hunched forwards over the wheel, scanning the space before him once more, acutely aware of the sharpness of

Ellis's gun in the small of his back, tucked in the waistband of his jeans.

He drew three, short breaths, the air struggling to expand his chest, and then he drove, slipping the car into gear and pulling quickly into the street, struck by the urgency of his task now. The noose was closing in, and if they didn't come here looking for him, they'd come looking for Ellis. And by the time they did, he wanted to be long gone. Him and Steph. Somewhere far away, with good lawyers.

Lily was staying at the Devils Lake Inn & Suites, room 24. She'd told Jacob to come find her when he was ready, after he'd spoken to Steph.

He thought of her as he drove, replaying their meeting at the lake's edge, at the place where the water meets the sky, over and over in his head. He still didn't know how she knew about that place, how she knew what it was called. But he trusted her. Trusted she wouldn't lie to him. He couldn't explain it, but there was a connection between them that felt strong and sudden.

He could practically still feel the warmth of her hand on his face as she cradled it, staring down at him in the splintered light of the dawn. Her smile filling him. Her voice soothing him. And the videos she had of the Hall place, he knew she wasn't lying. She'd gone back there that night, had gotten footage of them welcoming her in, of them taking her to the fire. Of them sat around, singing, passing food, laughing, clapping along. Of the man she'd spoken to at the gate earlier that day. Aaron. Of the way he'd sat by her, spoken to her with a softness and tenderness so disarming that it was easy to see how this place took girls in. The glint of his eyes in the firelight, the electric caress of her thigh with his hand, all caught on video from the ultra-wide camera hidden in the lapel of her jacket.

It'd been minutes before he'd whispered in her ear that he wanted to talk, and she'd let him lead her by the hand towards the house. Even then, watching that, knowing she was just working, that it wasn't real, Jacob'd felt this intense, insane pang of jealousy.

She and Aaron had gone up together and gone inside, sat on the sofa and talked, and he'd revealed things so intimate and personal, you couldn't help but fall for him then and there. But that was the point, Lily had said. That he was what was called a *honey pot*, that his job was to bring girls in for them, to make them feel like that.

And it wasn't long before he'd asked her to wait there, that he wanted her to meet someone she'd love. That he wanted her to meet the owner of the house, David.

She'd agreed, and then the video had gone dark, the sound muffled. She'd taken off her jacket, or the camera had stopped transmitting, maybe. Jacob didn't know.

But he hadn't had time to ask before Lily spoke again, before she told him what happened – how David came in, how he thanked her for coming, how he explained that they took in people who were lost, how they gave them a home, how they gave them purpose.

And the next thing she knew, she was being given a tour of the house. Aaron encouraged it, led her to a beautiful bedroom, told her that it could all be hers. There was a dress on the bed. She was told to change. That he'd be just outside.

She did so, wanting to know what came next. Needing to know. She tried to record it, she said, but the camera must have failed or lost signal. She took a knife with her, a small, folding thing, just in case. Held it in her hand, hidden. But when she came outside, Aaron was gone. She went downstairs, slowly, and in the living room, she found two men waiting for her.

She asked them what was going on, where was Aaron? They told her he'd be back soon, to come inside and wait. They gave their names. Brian. Michael. They said they were good friends with Aaron and David, that they looked after the place. They smiled broadly. But their eyes betrayed them.

Lily went inside, her heart beating fast, her mouth dry.

And when they came towards her, she knew…

So she…

Jacob hadn't needed to hear more. He could piece the rest together. From the blood on her dress. From the shake in her voice. From the tears in her eyes.

'We have to save them,' she said, clasping his face once more. 'We have to end this, Jacob. There's so many girls. I can't do it alone.'

He'd not told Steph any of this. Not yet.

And he'd not told her that he'd nodded when Lily had said that.

That he'd agreed to help.

Whatever she needed. Whatever it took. Whatever it cost.

And that when he had, she'd closed her eyes and kissed him.

Tenderly.

And that there'd been no hesitation in him when he kissed her back.

Chapter 31

Jacob rounded the corner and jostled up into the parking lot of the Devils Lake Inn & Suites, slowing the Subaru to a crawl, but not stopping as he looked around.

He had no doubt the cops knew where Lily was staying, too. And just stopping and getting out felt like the stupidest thing he could do. Especially when they were likely to open fire the moment they saw him. So with one foot lightly pressed on the gas and ready to floor it, he trundled towards room 24, not seeing any cars, or any signs of life.

His fingers grew sweaty on the wheel as he got close, eyeing the exit back onto the street.

Maybe the cops hadn't come here? Maybe they'd been and gone? He wouldn't know unless he tried.

'Screw it,' he muttered, easing on the brake and pulling into the space outside 24. He'd barely stopped when he noticed that the door wasn't even closed, and his mind instantly leapt from wondering if she was there to if he was already too late.

Without another thought he leapt from the car and charged towards the door, not bothering to slow or pause for any noise inside before he burst in, throwing the door wide.

It swung across the carpet and stopped, catching up on an overturned chair, banging into it and swinging back towards him.

He let it knock against his foot numbly as he stared inwards at the stripped bed, the clothes strewn across the room, the ransacked desk, drawers ripped out and tossed. Hell, they'd even torn the shower curtain out of the bathroom. It was lying on the floor across the threshold.

Jacob swallowed the lump in his throat and risked a step forwards, his boot crunching on what seemed to be shards of broken glass crushed into the carpet. He looked around, saw remnants of what looked like the bottom of a drinking glass. Just broken in the melee or thrown against the wall in frustration?

He wasn't a detective by any stretch but it wasn't hard to tell that they were looking for something. Lily, probably, but then likely anything she had on the cult. She'd told him that they'll do anything to stay hidden. That's why they'd gone after him. It's why they'd try to kill him. Wipe out all traces of Lily and her investigation.

He felt a pang of anger, felt his fists close at his sides as he pressed forwards, pulling Ellis's gun from his waistband like he was going to do something stupid with it.

Jacob moved forwards, eyes flashing around the room, searching for something, anything that'd tell him what had happened here. Had Lily been here when they arrived? Was this purely a search or was there evidence of a struggle? Of violence?

Jacob paused in the middle of the room and looked around. Bed stripped. Pillows on the floor. But no blood, nothing to suggest they'd hurt her.

He felt a little relief, but still the deep gnawing sense of dread in the pit of his stomach wouldn't let up.

His eyes moved downwards, to the floor, and among the glass he could see dirt. And dirtied footprints.

He lifted his own feet to see if they were his, but they weren't. His boots were heavy, treaded work boots. These ones had smooth bottoms, like the cowboy boots his father used to wear. All at once his mind flashed to the video that Lily had shown him of her first approach to the farm. Of the young farmhand that had come over and introduced himself. Jacob hadn't noticed his boots, but he'd been wearing a cowboy hat. And where you found the hat, you usually found the boots.

His blood ran a little colder as he envisaged that piece of shit, Aaron, coming here, busting in, threatening Lily, taking her, dragging her towards his truck. Maybe hurting her.

Jacob screwed his eyes closed, turning and heading back towards the door, breathing hard, shoulder pumping as his mind rolled over the possibilities of what could be happening to her right now.

Then he was back in the sunshine and practically running towards his car, thinking of the next move, and the gun in his hand.

The last place he wanted to go was to the Hall Farm, but if Lily was there… If there was even a chance, he needed to try. To try and get to her. To rescue here. He couldn't abandon her to that fate.

He climbed into the Subaru and backed quickly into the parking lot, swinging around and driving hard onto the road, the whole car rocking, bouncing viciously as he headed out of town.

He knew where the farm was, everyone did, and gave it a wide berth. But he wasn't headed straight there. Not to the front gate. No, he'd have to be smarter, quieter.

What awaited him, he didn't know. But he feared he'd be using Ellis's gun far sooner than he hoped.

Jacob had never shot anyone. Had never been a violent man. But these people, these... animals... they didn't deserve his concern, his pity. No, if he had to use force, if he had to shoot, if he had to... kill. Then he would.

He'd do it for her.

He'd do it for Lily.

Chapter 32

Jacob hit the highway and drove fast, almost completely disregarding his status as a wanted man. If the goal was to not draw attention to himself, driving twenty over the limit probably wasn't the best way to do it.

A sheen of sweat had developed on his forehead and he ran the back of his hand across it, realising only then that he still had Ellis's pistol firmly in his grasp. A sickening twinge developed in his guts and he lowered it, grimacing at the thought of what was to come, knowing he couldn't turn away from it, but wondering where he'd find the strength to do what he needed to.

His head turned as he passed the spot that he'd picked Lily up from two nights prior. Just an unassuming stretch of empty highway. But one that'd be seared in his mind forever.

He slowed just a little, then stomped on the gas once more, accelerating hard, nearing his destination.

The Hall Farm was on the next road over, about five miles if he drove. But less than a mile as the crow flew, he figured, if he took the direct route through the forest. The same route he figured that Lily had taken when she'd made her escape.

Jacob watched the trees build at the roadside as he drove, looking for a good opening, somewhere he could pull off the road and leave the car so it wouldn't be spotted right away by anyone driving past.

It was still early and the roads were quiet, the ground dry, so he didn't have to worry about tire tracks.

The line that divided the road from the shoulder rumbled under the tires as he crossed it, stepping down off the asphalt onto the grass and then down into the ditch, the old springs and shocks squeaking as he rolled into the trees, guiding the Subaru between what he thought was an elm and a silver maple, their stout trunks and thick canopies offer ample shadow and coverage.

He pushed forwards until the undergrowth rattled along the bottom of the car, and shrubs scraped the doors. Then he killed the engine, allowing the forest to cocoon him for a moment. He could scarcely see the road from his position, and for the first time in almost two days he felt safe, tucked away, hidden. He would have stayed there forever if he could, just let the trees swallow him whole. But it wasn't to be. The best he could hope for was that they'd stand guard over the car and keep it hidden until he got back.

There was a sour taste in his mouth and his hands felt stiff from clutching the wheel and the gun so hard. Steph had fed him coffee and a little breakfast, but his stomach still felt raw and empty, full of bile and little else.

This wasn't a time to wallow, though, to lament over better times, easier times. Now was a time to be a man, to do what was right.

With a heave of the door against the saplings littering the forest floor, he climbed free and got his bearings, heading deeper into the woods before he lost his nerve.

It was a slow walk, meandering through the trees, following game trails and trying to avoid hidden holes and ditches. After a hundred steps, the car was already gone, the noise of the road completely silenced. He was alone, and losing his nerve by the moment. He did all he could to keep Lily in his mind, the last words of her story, the look on her face burning behind his eyes as he ploughed onwards.

The woods deepened, the sound of birdsong echoing around him as he pushed onwards. The wind rustled through the foliage, the trees swaying gently, creaking and sighing as he moved through them.

And then, seemingly, it faded away all at once.

The birds stopped.

The wind died.

And when Jacob looked up, he could see a fence ahead, the tops of ears of corn staying stock still, and in the distance, between the thinning trunks in front of him, a metal barn, a hay loft, and the Hall Farm.

The whole place was bathed in sunlight – a perfect picture of rural life, he thought. It looked warm, inviting. The kind of place you'd see and think that it was safe. That it was an oasis. That you'd found home.

Even now the light was splintering through the thinned canopy, bathing him in the warm touch of the sun. But he couldn't be lulled into a false sense of security. Not here.

He slowed, holding his breath instinctively, and lowered himself closer to the ground, all but hidden by the long grass.

The approach was tentative and he took each step carefully, conscious that his boots crunched in the dry brush, conscious that his heart was louder still. *Thud. Thud. Thud.* Against the inside of his ribs.

He did his best to steady his breathing, creeping forwards, eyes fixed on the fence ahead.

Something glinted in front of him, hidden in the grass, and he paused, looking down at it.

Slowly, he reached out, parting the long strands of grass, peeling them away gently until the thing, just a few inches from his right shin, revealed itself.

A stretch of razor wire, laid eight inches off the ground, strung between the trees.

His blood ran a little colder, the thought of the steel barbs hacking into his flesh enough to make his skin break out in gooseflesh.

He stared at it, wondering why it was so important to keep people out, why they'd go to this length...

And then an even worse thought seized him.

It's not to *keep* people out.

It's to stop people *getting* out.

Chapter 33

Jacob guided his foot over the wire slowly, setting it gently down on the other side before he even dared breathe. His other foot followed and then he was over, turning, moving slowly towards the fence, wondering how many had made it this far just to get sliced up and fall.

But what happened to them after? Were they hauled back, treated, then thrown in some sort of dungeon? Or were they just left to bleed out as a stark reminder of what happened when you crossed these people?

Or were they simply shot? Put down like a dog?

The last thought only occurred to him as he reached the fence and watched two men in their forties make their way along the perimeter, hunting rifles slung over their shoulders.

They made a slow loop of the fields, patrolling, eyes turned inwards at the crops and the people working among them.

People… No, women. As Jacob turned his eyes across the fields, all he could see were women. He counted half a dozen, busying themselves collecting the blackberries and strawberries that the Hall Farm stall sold at the farmer's market. The ones everyone in town gobbled up. Utterly unaware of what went into growing them.

He'd never touch another berry again.

And if he got out of this, he was liable to burn that fucking stall to the ground. God. God! How could he be so naïve? How could this be going on under everyone's noses all along? For years, decades! Razor wire? Armed guards? This was more of an internment camp than anything else.

He had that sour taste of sick in his mouth again.

Wait and watch, he told himself, eyeing the guards, their backs to him. He couldn't see anyone else that was armed, but a few men were standing around in the yard in front of the metal barn. They might have been armed, it was too far to tell.

God, what was he doing? He couldn't see Lily, but she'd be imprisoned somewhere if she was here. Three buildings. He'd have to check them all, wouldn't he? Fuck. Fuck! How was he supposed to even get up there, though? How was he supposed to reach…

He became distinctly aware of someone watching him then, and turned to see the head of a woman poking above the corn right in front of him.

She'd been kneeling, and had now stood up, no more than twenty feet from him.

The woman was probably thirty, maybe a little less, the gauntness in her cheeks, the thinness of her hair betraying her age.

She slowly reached up with a gloved hand, dried husks in her fist, and wiped her brow, just staring at him. Almost in disbelief.

Jacob's heart all but stopped as he stared back, praying that she wouldn't scream or call out. He raised a shaking finger to his lips and hushed her, begging with his eyes for her to keep quiet.

Hers were bright and dark, shining in the sunlight. She lowered her hand, a deep crease forming in her forehead, her lips beginning to tremble. But she didn't make a sound, just mouthed the word 'Help'. Silently. But louder than any word Jacob had ever heard.

Before he could communicate back, or even process it, a voice rang across the open space.

'Hey!'

The sharp call of a man.

Jacob lowered himself instinctively, all but pressing himself to the ground, just a thin layer of grass between him and the wooden fence before him.

There were heavy footsteps, and a moment later Jacob saw one of the armed men rushing through the corn. He was taller than the woman, his shoulders poking above the juvenile crop.

'What the fuck d'you think you're doing?' he barked at her.

She recoiled, turning and lowering her head. 'N-nothing, sir,' she stuttered, her voice thin and tired.

Without hesitation, he lowered his right hand and then sent it flying upwards, a sharp and fierce backhand striking her cheek.

She cried out, so suddenly Jacob flinched, and clutched her face.

'Eyes on your work,' the guard snapped, taking her by the back of the head, his big fist clenched around the nape of her neck. 'There ain't no room for idle hands here.' And before he gave her a chance to answer, he shoved her onto her knees and out of sight.

A few snivelling sobs echoed through the plants and the guard stood over her to make sure her focus was back on her task at hand before he slowly turned and moved away through the corn once more.

Jacob waited for the man to rejoin his comrade and return to his sweep of the perimeter, and slowly lifted his head. There was no sign of the woman now, just the small echo of her cries hanging in the still air.

Every fibre of him wanted to help her, to call her to him, to whisk her away through the forest and to his waiting car. But he knew he couldn't help her. Not now, not yet. Not like this. No, he needed Lily, he needed Lily to bring the whole thing down. To burn it down if they had to.

He thumbed tears from his eyes and began moving left, skirting the fence towards the blackberries. High crops growing on frames. It was mid-summer and they were in full swing, the bushes thick enough to hide his approach to the back of the hay loft. The rows ran up the hill and he hoped he could skulk the length of one unnoticed, the beginning of the crop just ten feet from the fence.

He reached it, the voices of the two patrolling guards just filtering back to him. They were walking away, and he hoped would have no reason to look back while he was in the open.

Still, he waited, hesitated, Ellis's gun almost slipping from his grip his hands were sweating so much.

He wanted nothing more in the world than to turn around and go home, forget this ever happened. But how many lives would be lost if he did? How many women would end up here, never to be seen again?

Jacob wasn't a hero. He knew that much. He didn't even know if he was a good man. But he knew if he walked away now, he'd never live it down. He'd carry it always, and he'd never forgive himself.

For the first time in his life, he felt like he was staring death in the face. Felt like this could be the day that he died. The day he was going to see his father, his mother again.

Was this how his father had felt during the war? Crouching in some foreign place, weapon in hand, knowing that death was just a trigger pull away? That a bullet could come from any direction at any time? That you could be dead before you even heard the shot?

He promised he'd ask him one day.

But right now, there wasn't time for those kinds of thoughts.

He needed to move. And he needed to move now.

Chapter 34

Jacob levered himself over the fence, flopping to the ground, doing his best to stay low. With a little plume of dirt and dust he scrambled forwards into cover, barely able to fill his lungs his chest was so tight.

When he reached the cover of the blackberry bushes, he froze on his hands and knees, straining his ears to listen for any hint of the guards running towards him. A small part wished for it. So he could turn, hurdle the fence and flee back to his car. So he could say he tried everything he could. But there were no footsteps, just the distant rattle of cicadas somewhere in the distance.

He raked in a few breaths, trying to gather himself, then pressed on – getting up to a shaky stance and heading forwards.

The rows of bushes stretched out ahead, and were thick enough that Jacob thought he could press himself into one for further cover if it came to it. Though the thought brought him little solace.

The distance was less than a hundred metres, but it felt endless as he wound his way up, stepping cautiously, pausing every few feet to listen, to wait. He sort of hoped it would never end, but before he knew it, he was at the top, the bushes ending just in front of him.

A small grassy bank led up onto the flat farmyard, the back of the hay loft, a big red building with a sloped roof.

The kind they used to keep hay in above, and livestock below.

Jacob had worked in agriculture all his adult life, had spent his years repairing farm machinery. And had been to countless farms. But there was none of the stamping or chuffing of horses coming through the wood like usual. The barn was eerily silent.

As he thought that, he realised that he'd missed work yesterday. That his phone had been taken, his life taken from him. It all felt like such a distant memory now, clocking out on Thursday afternoon and heading straight to the bar.

Another life.

Another Jacob.

He peeked from the blackberries and looked along the length of the back of the barn. A rolling door was ajar, unlocked. He needed to get in there, check to see if it's where Lily was being held.

Jacob was so intently focused on the door that when it opened and a man stepped out, he didn't react at first. His brain stuttered and on reflex he threw himself to the ground, rolling into the bush with a loud rattle of stems and thorns.

A few blackberries shook loose and rained down on the dry earth.

He heard the crunch of boots turning to look, holding his breath, not daring to move, clutching the pistol so tight his hands ached.

The man muttered something to himself about birds, hawked and then spat on the ground, and sidled off towards the other crops.

Jacob meant to let out a sigh, but it was more like a sob. What was he doing here?

No, no, you can't think like that. You have to do this.

He peeled himself from the ground, the thorns of the bush tugging at his clothes and skin, and scrambled up the little bank in front of him on his hands and knees, all but scuttling towards the open door before he slipped inside.

The interior was cool and dark, and with the sun no longer on his back, he felt better. He wiped the sweat from his eyes with a dusty sleeve and took stock of the interior.

Ahead, the big front double doors were half-closed, letting in a long shaft of light that split the room in two. There were six stalls on each side, a mezzanine running above them, stretching around three sides of the barn. But there was no hay up there. No animals here, Jacob thought, then recanted that statement. There are animals, just not the kind you think of first.

He moved right, into the shadow, pausing at the first stall to look inside. He'd seen it before the iron rings on the stall walls to tether horses. And at first, that's what he thought he was looking at. But then he saw the chains. He went inside, the thin layer of straw and sawdust on the concrete floor congealed and thick, the smell of old urine pungent in his nostrils. A bucket sat in the corner, empty but uncleaned, a few tenacious flies circling it.

His hand stretched out, pulling the chain affixed to the back wall, searching for the end buried somewhere in the muck at his feet, hoping to God when it came free that he wasn't going to see what he was expecting.

But as it came free, all of his dread was realised.

Jacob lifted the chain, thin for holding a horse, but plenty to hold a human. Especially a woman.

At the bottom of the chain, swinging freely, the iron splattered with some unknown dark liquid, were a pair of shackles. They looked downright medieval, small enough to lock tightly around the delicate wrists of a female.

Jacob grimaced and closed his eyes, lowering the chain back to the ground with a gentle plink.

He turned back to the room, surveying it, looking around at the stalls before him. Twelve of them. For twelve girls. His mind reeled with it. They were really just locking women up here? Chaining them to the walls, making them defecate in buckets? But for what purpose, to what end was this barbarity going on?

Before he had chance to think of an answer, he got a chance to hear it firsthand.

He hadn't noticed among the roar of his own blood and thoughts in his head. But now it was clear, ringing in the cool silence of the barn.

Just a gentle whimper rising from one of the stalls to his right.

Chapter 35

Jacob moved quickly, checking each stall, his brain just screaming Lily's name over and over at him.

First stall, empty.

Second, empty.

Third, empty— No. Jesus, he barely saw her, curled up in the corner.

'Lily!' The word came from his mouth before he could stop it and he threw himself forwards onto his knees, reaching out for her without hesitating.

His hands touched her shoulder and she convulsed, one huge jerk that threw him backwards.

Jacob tumbled into the damp, sawdust under his heels, and looked at the girl. She picked her head up, staring at him wide-eyed. It wasn't Lily, but… she was in a white dress? The same as the one Lily had been wearing two nights ago. His brain struggled to comprehend it all. She was thin, probably in her early to mid-twenties, with dark hair that looked greasy in the gloom. There were rings beneath her eyes that looked like they'd been drawn with charcoal, and her lips were so pale they were almost the colour of her skin.

He felt a pang of fear, then sadness as he looked at her. She pushed herself onto her hip, hands fastened together, the chain snaking beneath her and then up the wall. There was a putrid smell coming from the bucket next to her, and the dirt and grime on her skin, combined with the sallow look of her cheeks, told Jacob she'd been there for days, at least. Probably longer.

'W-what...' Jacob started, unable to find the words.

The girl looked at him, her lips moving in a silent chant.

He shook his head, a heat building in his throat, making it ache as tears formed in the corners of his eyes. 'I'm... I'm going to get you out of here' was all he managed. Though he didn't know how the hell he was going to make that happen.

Her eyes flashed to his, a sudden focus there so unnerving he recoiled a little more. 'No,' she said, not making any effort to hush her voice.

'Shh, please,' he urged her, holding up his hands to try and calm her, a frantic aura radiating off her as she moved onto her knees, curling them under her like a cobra rearing up on its tail.

'I'm not going anywhere,' she said plainly. 'I'm staying right here. Right here until I'm better.'

'Until you're better?' He could only numbly parrot the words back to her, like they were a foreign language. 'Why... why are you here? Are you sick? Are you—'

'I'm being punished,' she said, blinking as though it were common knowledge. She pulled her hands towards her stomach and laid them there, crossing them gently. 'But I'll do better. I'll get better. And when I am, I can go back. And we can try again. He promised.'

Jacob was the one who blinked now, in astonishment. In shock. In disgust. The way she was clutching her stomach... Did he even want to know? Want to consider the truth of what was happening here, at this place?

He couldn't help this girl, not here, not now. The only way he'd be able to was with Lily. To get her out, and then take this place down together. They had enough evidence between them to go to the state police, right? To the FBI? To someone who could fucking do *something*! Anything!

'Have you seen another girl?' Jacob tried then, steeling himself as best he could.

She shook her head quickly. 'I've been here, repenting. I'm not allowed to be with the others.'

The tears began to form at the corners of his eyes again. He thought, then slowly turned his head towards the door, the farmhouse visible through the gap, drowned in bright sunlight in the farmyard.

'Where are the others? How many?' When he looked back at the girl, she was staring back at him with an unnerving calmness.

'Inside, of course,' she smiled, as though it were a silly question.

'How many?'

'Not enough,' she replied with a small, closed-lipped chuckle. 'Never enough.'

A coldness spread through Jacob and he pushed himself to a shaky stance, the girl watching him the whole way.

He backed up slowly, eyes fixed on her as she lowered herself back to the floor, stacking her hands beneath her ear, curling her knees to her chest like a child, her mouth moving once more in that silent chant, that silent prayer.

But to which God, Jacob wondered as he turned towards the farmhouse.

And to what end?

Chapter 36

Jacob came to the door and paused, desperate to get away from the girl and everything she reminded him that this place was.

He needed to be single-minded. Focused. He needed to be strong.

The pistol shook in his grip, but he was gaining strength with each passing moment, a deep-seated, cold rage burning in him, burning away the fear and the apprehension.

From his position inside the barn Jacob could see clear across the farmyard, but was hidden from anyone looking in by the shadow the door afforded him.

The area was clear. He could see nobody around, could hear no voices. And the farmhouse was just forty feet away. He looked down at himself. Dusty and tired. A plaid shirt, jeans, boots. Would he stick out that much if he just walked across the space?

He swallowed, wondering what would really happen if someone saw him.

Jacob crept forwards a little more, standing at the corner of the door, making sure the coast was clear.

The girl in the stall made a small noise and he jolted, looking back. She fell quiet almost immediately and he lamented leaving her there. But he had to. As he turned his attention back to the door, however, he noticed a chair parked at the side of the room, a cowboy hat sitting on it, a water flask at its side.

His jaw tensioned, teeth clamping together. Aaron. The one who'd taken Lily. Who'd met her at the gate. Had he been the one who stepped out of the barn a few minutes ago? Jacob continued staring at the hat, a stark realisation coming over him: when was he coming back?

He'd left his hat, his water. He wouldn't be gone long, surely. Already on his way, maybe.

Fuck. Jacob's heart kicked up another gear and he stole another glace at the farmyard before sailing across the doorway and back into shadow on the other side.

Without missing a beat he picked up the hat and pushed it onto his head, pulling the brim low.

Even if Aaron didn't catch him, the girl had seen him, and she might talk. *Would* talk. Hell, she was so twisted up by this place she'd likely want nothing more than to report someone poking around.

That thought spurred him on and without hesitation he walked into the sunshine like he was supposed to be there. Or at least that's how he hoped it looked from the outside. He had the pistol in his hand, hanging at his side, trembling viciously.

Jacob didn't breathe until he was on the porch and opening the door, didn't dare look around or do anything else until the door latched behind him and he sank back against it with a little whimper of his own.

When the rushing of blood in his ears subsided, the noise of the house replaced it. The tick of a clock in the living room, the drip of a tap in the kitchen. The muted voices of women upstairs somewhere.

Jacob looked left and right, trying to ascertain if he was alone down here. He was, it seemed, but as he peered into the living room, he couldn't help but notice the huge red stains on the threadbare carpet, covering it almost entirely.

Two men's worth of blood, he thought morbidly. Is this where Lily had killed them?

Or was it from something else?

He wasn't sure which thought frightened him more.

Lily wasn't down here, though, and with the women's voices growing clearer the longer he listened, he figured that the only way was up. And if nothing else, he could knock the house off his list and proceed to check the final building.

Careful of the creaking stairs, he slowly made his way up, stepping on the outer edges of each step to minimise the noise. It was something he'd learned as a kid and it was the first time it'd ever actually come in handy.

He never thought it'd be life-saving, though.

As he got to the landing, the women's voices got clearer, emanating from the door at the end of the hallway to his right.

He walked towards them, the door ajar. He detected two, no, three voices.

Jacob paused a few feet short and moved to the wall, looking through the sliver of space between the door and the frame, able to just make out the dim room beyond.

The windows were covered, the room lit only by candles. They flickered, casting a warm glow against the back wall, cutting through the curling incense smoke. Jacob's nose wasn't capable of teasing apart the scents, but it was heavy and intoxicating, enough to make his head swim, even from here.

Jacob could see the brass footer of a bed, a patterned quilt, an ornate headboard. And the three women, young, slim, beautiful, naked, lying atop it, their arms draped across one another.

They spoke quietly to each other, their words hushed, intermingled. And then they stopped, looking up towards the door.

Jacob froze. Had they seen him? Heard him?

The woman on the right sat up, her long, auburn hair spilling down over her slender shoulders and over her small, round breasts. She was in her late twenties, healthy, nubile. A world away from the half-starved woman in the barn. She stared into the gloom with a strange look on her face, one of enamour, of worship, even.

'My blood is your blood,' she said then, her words ringing in the still, thick air.

The other women repeated it, sitting up now too so that they were all shoulder to shoulder. 'My blood is your blood.'

Jacob lifted a hand to rub his eyes, not even sure what he was looking at, whether they were speaking to him or themselves, or something else entirely. God, these fumes. What the hell was this? His chest was tight, his vision pulsing. It was all he could do not to cough and splutter.

He couldn't take his eyes off the women, though. The curve of their stomachs, their long legs, entwined and smooth. The gentle ridges of their ribs beneath their breasts, their long hair, their big eyes, glinting and reflecting the flickering of the flames around the room.

He watched, almost through someone else's eyes as his left hand began to reach out for the handle, his desire running rampant, willing him, compelling him to go inside, to—

A man's voice cut the smoke. 'Show me,' it said.

Jacob's hand retracted, his eyes leaping to the dark shape that swam across the sliver of bedroom he could see. A man. Someone else in the room.

He looked on, watched as the redhead, eyes fixed on the man, pulled in a few deep breaths, her shoulders rising, ribcage expanding as she inhaled more of the incense, a wicked, salacious grin spreading across her face, revealing a slit of yellowed, almost brown teeth.

Jacob shuddered, revulsion and yearning riling against one another inside him. And yet, he couldn't look away.

He watched as she turned from the man at the foot of the bed and reached to the bedside table, to the cup there, what looked like a stemmed glass made of some opaque material.

She turned back, holding the cup up to show the man, then raised it.

The other two women watched the cup rise, and then slowly tip towards them.

They lifted their heads, closing their eyes as the liquid poured out, shimmering, almost black in the half-light.

It splashed over them, their faces, their bodies, covering them in what looked like oil – but Jacob knew it wasn't. Even among the smoke he could smell the coppery, metallic tinge of blood.

And though he wanted nothing more than to collapse and empty the contents of his stomach all over his boots, he could not tear his eyes away.

The women breathed deeply, their chests heaving as the blood spilled over them, looks of ecstasy seizing their faces as they reached up, their fingers splayed and stiff, rubbing the liquid over their skin, spreading it around their throats, up their cheeks, down their bodies, their midriffs, their thighs, their hands pushing them apart, low moans escaping the bed as they did.

The man stepped forwards then and climbed onto the bed, wiry, nude too. Jacob made him out to be older, in his sixties, his lithe frame betraying a life of farm work.

His course, bony hands reached out, tracing the lines of the women's legs, over their shins and upwards as they luxuriated in their bath of crimson.

It was then that Jacob realised he wasn't alone in the corridor.

There was someone standing behind him.

Chapter 37

'Aaron?' the person behind him said, the word hushed like he was conscious of the people in the room not hearing. 'What are you doing here?'

Jacob stayed still, the scene in front of him escalating quickly, the man now on his back on the bed, the women slithering all over him like bloodied pythons, low moans radiating from the bedroom.

And this person behind Jacob thought he was Aaron. Of course – he was still wearing the hat.

But the second he turned around, the guy would realise, and then what?

Jacob's mind worked furiously, clouded by the smoke. But the fear was still real, still palpable, the gun in his hand still solid, still deadly.

Was he going to have to turn and shoot this guy? Did he have any other choice?

The stranger stepped forwards, as though to reach out for Jacob's shoulder.

Out of time.

If he fired the gun, he'd alert the entire farm.

But the stairs were there. One hard push. If he turned, kept his head down, would he be able to take a run at the guy before he realised he wasn't Aaron?

He didn't have much choice.

Jacob pulled in a sharp breath and turned, lunging forwards with as much strength as he could muster, lifting his head at the last moment.

A man in his fifties was standing there in faded jeans and a denim shirt, his eyes widening as the realisation struck.

Jacob's hands found his chest before he could make a sound and shoved him backwards. The man was caught off guard, the impact enough to wind him, prevent him from calling out as he staggered backwards, heels tipping over the edge of the stairs.

His hands flailed in circles, worn-to-the-steel toe caps of his boots rising in the air as he fell, carrying halfway down the stairs until he landed hard on his back with a nasty crack, bounced and tumbled backwards, landing upside down on his neck, it looked like, coming to rest at the bottom without a sound.

He didn't move, just lay there in an awkward heap on his front, head at an odd angle, arms pinned strangely beneath him.

Jacob looked at his hands. They were shaking violently. Had he just…? Was the guy…?

His stomach twisted up, his legs threatening to buckle as he stared down at the man at the foot of the stairs.

He would have stayed rooted to the spot if the door to the bedroom hadn't opened. Without thinking he turned his head, seeing the man, slick with blood, standing there, one hand on the door handle, the other at his side, blood dripping slowly from his fingers.

He was lithe, tall, with bright, sharp eyes. His body was muscled and lean, his penis still erect.

The man stared at Jacob and Jacob stared back, neither of them moving, or recognising the other. They remained there in silence for a few seconds, and it was only broken when one of the women climbed off the bed and stood next to the naked man. Whether it was the gun in his hand or the fact that she didn't recognise Jacob, he couldn't have said. But without warning, she let out the loudest scream Jacob had ever heard, the sound enough to bowl him backwards.

Run. Run. Run! That was all his mind could tell him. *You're discovered. You're found out. You have to run.*

He was halfway down the stairs before he even decided to do it. A quick glance over his shoulder told him the man in the bedroom wasn't chasing him. But it didn't matter, he still needed to get out, and he needed to get out now.

He hurdled the guy with the broken neck in the hallway and ripped the front door open, leaping down off the porch and landing hard in the dust. He stumbled, his hands hitting the ground, pushing him forwards, his breath already ragged in his throat, the sudden onslaught of sunlight blinding him as he made a hard left turn and sprinted along the side of the house.

God, what the fuck was in that room? The incense was making his head swim, like being drunk and stoned at the same time. Felt like he was running through water.

Where was he? Where was his car? The cornfield?

Jacob stopped and blinked, looking around, unsure whether the screams in his ears were still coming from the woman inside or if they were just echoing around his head.

He didn't have time to consider how warped his reality was in that moment, though. He needed to get out of there. Already he could see commotion building around him, people begin to move in the fields, shouts coming from all around. The guards. Where were the guards with the rifles?

Run! Run, you idiot!

He took off again, circling the back of the house and aiming for the blackberries. He skidded in the loose earth as he approached the bank, sinking onto his hip and sliding down.

The first shot rang out, a strand of blackberries exploding above him, showering him in leaves and little splatters of juice.

God, if he hadn't lost his footing, that might have taken his head off!

He twisted and rolled onto his front, diving into the rows, hearing more shouts rising in the fields. No more shots followed, the bushes hiding his route to the fence. But the guards were closing in, calls of 'Where is he?' and 'Find him!' chasing Jacob down the line.

They were close now, too close.

The pistol came up instinctively and he blinked hard, sweat running into his eyes as he moved. They stung and ached as he loped forwards, weapon raised and at arm's length, trained on the end of the row, the opening there. The ten feet of space to the fence.

It was just twenty yards away, not far. He wasn't even running, why was he panting? Focus, Jacob, focus! His head was pounding, the remnants of the incense haze pulsing at the corners of his vision.

A body appeared at the end of the row, just a vague shape, out of focus through his sweat-stung eyes.

He didn't think, just pulled the trigger, not even knowing what he was really aiming at.

Muzzle fire leapt from the gun, the thing kicking back in his hand, slowing him momentarily.

The bullet unzipped the air, a plume of green dancing in the sunlight as it cut a path through the crop.

The man dove forwards out of view, swearing.

Jacob advanced, pulling the trigger again, again. Two more bullets. A geyser of dust this time from the first, just short of the fence. The next one went high, taking a chunk out of the top rail, sending splinters flying.

Swearing reached his ears and he searched for the source, saw the glint of a gun barrel in the light and moved sideways, pressing himself to the bush, not even feeling the prick of the thorns.

The bellow of a rifle sang in the morning air and arms of blackberries fell to the ground around him.

Jacob returned fire, advancing still.

Two, three shots.

There was a groan, then more cursing. He didn't know if he'd hit the person, but he couldn't stop to check.

He charged onwards, firing again and again into the foliage, towards where he thought the shooter might be.

And then he was free, clear of the row and in the open. He caught a snatch of a man on his back, kicking himself along the ground, blood streaming from his leg, the rifle in the dirt.

The fence was there then and Jacob was vaulting over it, his joints and bones aching. He hadn't run in years. Hadn't put his body through anything like this ever.

He landed hard, heart slamming in his throat, and moved forwards, not stopping, not until he was at the car.

At the last second, he remembered the razor wire and jumped, throwing himself into the air with as much clearance as he could. He didn't know where it was exactly, a snake in the long grass waiting to nip at his shins and put him down.

He landed on his shoulder and rolled, clear of the flesh-hungry barbs, and stole a look back at the farmhouse, at the panic erupting around it.

Jacob hadn't checked every building, every room. God, he hoped Lily wasn't still up there, that he wasn't abandoning her to a fate worse than death.

To the man in that bedroom.

As Jacob turned and ran, he could still see his eyes, burning in the half-light. Burning Jacob's skin.

And those words... Those words just went around and around in his head as he charged through the forest towards the car, chilling him to the bone, even in the choking heat of a summer morning.

My blood is your blood.

My blood is your blood.

My blood is your blood.

Chapter 38

By the time Jacob emerged from the trees he was covered in sweat, his clothes painted to his body. He was dirtied and exhausted, sick to his stomach.

He all but collapsed into the Subaru, clutching the wing mirror to stay upright as his legs quaked.

Jacob groaned, fumbling at the handle, and crawled inside, wanting nothing more than to stop but knowing he couldn't. It took three tries to get the key in the ignition and start the engine, and as he wheeled backwards the front fender scraped against a tree.

He launched backwards then into the drainage ditch and bounced up onto the roadway, a car on the other side of the road slamming on its brakes and laying on the horn as it swerved to get around him.

But Jacob barely noticed. The engine flared as he stamped on the accelerator and the car pulled forwards tiredly, straining to pick up speed.

He drove for fifteen minutes before he couldn't any longer and pulled off the side of the road once more. The car juddered to a halt on the verge and Jacob collapsed forwards onto the wheel, sobbing, blowing snot and tears over the worn-out leather-effect plastic.

He mewled, crying into the backs of his hands, visions of what he'd seen, what he'd done playing on repeat behind his closed eyes. God, he'd killed someone! Shot someone else. The woman in the field mouthed a plea for help and he left her. The girl tied up in the barn… He'd just abandoned her, too. The women in that bedroom, pouring blood on themselves. The man with the burning eyes. Jacob shuddered, retching on whatever was flowing in his bloodstream. That wicked smoke.

He wasn't sure how long he stayed there, but when he finally managed to gather himself, he knew it was too long. If he stayed here either the farm would catch up to him, or the cops would. Either way, he needed to get somewhere they couldn't find him. He still had no idea where Lily was or of any way to find her, so the only thing he could do was try Steph.

His head was still throbbing and it was tough to keep his thoughts straight. But he managed to get his phone out and Steph's number on the screen. He hit call and waited, the line ringing and ringing until it went to the answering machine.

He swore, tried again.

Same thing.

Fuck. Come on, Steph.

Third time, no answer.

This wasn't like her. Especially not now, not today. Was something wrong? Had the cops come looking for Ellis?

Suddenly, Jacob's head was clear as a bell. Even among everything else, Steph was the most important thing in the world to him. So before he'd even put his phone in the centre console, he was already spinning the Subaru around in a circle of dust and racing back down the highway towards town.

He pulled his forearm across his face roughly, dragging the tears with it, and willed the car to go faster, racing past the place he'd emerged from in the forest a few minutes before without even a look.

Jacob reached town in a blur and headed for Steph's house, pulling into the driveway quickly, the brakes squealing as he stood on them.

He left the car door open, jumping onto the porch, his hand closing around the handle and twisting. But the door didn't budge and he knocked up against it. 'What the...' he muttered, jiggling the handle again. Locked.

Inside was dark, all the blinds still drawn.

He cupped his hands to the glass anyway and tried to see in.

Nothing moved inside.

'Steph?' he called, risking as much volume as he dared. 'It's me. Steph? Open up.'

Basement? The window was frosted, but maybe—

As he turned to go and check he stopped in his tracks on the porch, seeing Lily standing on the lawn ten feet from him. She had a wild look on her face, her hair tangled and frizzy, her brow wet with sweat.

'Jacob,' she said, sighing audibly. 'I'm so glad you're here.'

He didn't know what to ask first. 'Where were you, I went to the motel, and—'

'Yeah, they showed up there, looking for me. I barely got away, had to go out the back window.' Her expression changed, breaking, crumbling as she came forwards. 'I'm so glad you're okay.'

He shook his head. 'I went to the farm, and—'

'You went there?' Fear streaked across her face. 'What happened? What did you see?'

He came forwards a step and looked back at the house. 'How long have you been here, did you see...'

'Your sister?' She shook her head. 'I've been here a while, an hour or something. I was hiding in the bushes…' She turned and gestured to a patch of shrubbery across the road. 'I was hoping you'd come here, or—'

'Where's Steph?' Jacob's question was more direct than he'd intended, but he made no effort to hide the tension in himself.

'I don't know. When I got here there was no car in the driveway, the lights off, everything. I waited in case, watched… But, God. I thought you'd left, the two of you. I thought you'd left Devils Lake, thought you'd left…'

Me, Jacob thought. 'I wouldn't,' he said firmly. 'But I need to find Steph, I need to—'

'And we will! But please, first, we can't just stand around out here.' She held out her hands, beckoning Jacob towards her.

He clenched his jaw to stop it from shaking, needing to feel something warm, something good. Needing someone to tell him there was a way out of this. That they were going to be okay.

Jacob stepped down off the porch and walked into her arms, feeling her squeeze him tightly, her little breaths, the slight shake in her body. She was as scared as he was.

'We have to go,' she whispered into his chest. 'We have to go right now. It's not safe here.' She pried herself from him and went to Steph's car, climbing into the passenger seat. 'Come on,' she called through the open driver's door.

Jacob turned, taking one last look at Steph's house, and then began walking backwards towards the car.

Where are you, Steph?

But there was no answer from the house before him.

All he could hope was that she was okay, and that Todd Ellis was still tied up in the basement.

But as he backed out of the driveway and slid the car into drive, Lily's hand settling over his knuckles on the shifter and holding tightly, he didn't know if either of those things were true.

And he had little faith that they both were.

Chapter 39

They broke free of Devils Lake and headed north. There was a long, straight road ahead of them that ran all the way to the border. But Jacob had no intention of going that far or anything close to it. He wasn't leaving Steph. End of story.

After ten minutes, with barely a car in sight going in either direction, Jacob pulled off the side of the road onto the wide grass verge just short of the Sweetwater turn-off. Wheat crop waved gently to the west, and to the east, the pools stretched out towards the lake.

Lily had been silent the entire way, watching the countryside rolling by. But now, just as Jacob was about to speak, she did instead.

'It's so quiet out here,' she said, her voice quiet and easy. 'Peaceful.'

Jacob swallowed, curling his shaking hands into fists on his thighs.

'You ever just think about driving? Just keeping on going, leaving Devils Lake behind?' She turned to him suddenly and he jolted a little in the chair.

Her eyes were filled with tears, shining in the light coming in through the windscreen. 'I haven't been completely honest with you, Jacob,' she said.

His stomach dropped.

'Not about why I'm here, not about who I am…' She let out a shaking breath, looking down at her hands in her lap.

Jacob just waited, unable to speak.

'I came here because of my mother,' she said slowly. 'She was… She lived at the Hall Farm.' She looked up at him again. 'We both did. I was…' She cleared her throat, her voice dropping to a whisper practically. 'I was nine when she ran away, and, um…'

Jacob pictured the place, the razor wire and the armed guards, the chains in the barn, whatever the fuck was going on in that bedroom.

'She took me in the night, and we, uh, we escaped. At the time, I didn't want to, I wanted to stay — it was my home,' she said, smiling weakly. 'It was all I knew, but… But, well… you went there. You saw. Right?' She searched his face for some kind of understanding.

He just nodded weakly, trying to keep the contents of his stomach locked in there. Trying not to think about what it would be like for a young girl to grow up there. What they'd go through.

'Growing up there is… My mom knew what was waiting for me, what was coming. So we left. But we didn't get very far before…' It was clearly difficult for her to say, and Jacob didn't know whether to respond, how to respond. So he just listened. Just waited.

Lily steadied herself, taking a few deep breaths. 'One night, when some men from town came to the farm, my mom was with one of them, and she… She took his keys. She got me from the barn, and she pushed me into the car. We left everything behind. I tried to get out, to run back, to call for help, but instead of coming to help me, they just… They just shot at us. Shot at me. They hit Mom as she was pulling me back to the car.' She held a hand to her stomach and Jacob pictured it. 'We drove then, fast. As far as she could. I didn't know what was happening, or what to do. We drove all night and I... I fell asleep at some point...' She was choking on her own words, snivelling now, tears running down her cheeks. 'When I woke up, we were outside a police station in Minnesota. I looked around, at Mom, and she was asleep, but when I tried to wake her...'

Jacob didn't need her to finish the sentence.

'There was so much blood. She was...'

'It's okay,' he said, reaching across and pulling her against him, his arms around her shoulders.

'She was dead,' Lily said, needing to say it for herself. 'They killed her, Jacob.' She pulled away now, looking right at him. 'They killed her because she wanted to leave. Do you understand that?'

'I do,' he said.

'That's why I came back. So I could finally do something about it. So I could stop them. For good.'

There was something cold, something venomous in her voice that made him shiver despite the stifling heat in the car.

'But it's not just me they took something from.'

Jacob stared at her.

'They took something from you, too.'

'From me...?' A nervous perspiration beaded under his jaw, the intensity of her stare unnerving.

'I only have one picture of her,' Lily said, levering up out of the seat and pulling a folded photograph from the back pocket of her jeans.

She held it out to him.

He just looked at it, a scratch of dread at the back of his skull telling him not to take it. Not to look.

Slowly, he reached out, tugging it from her grasp.

'Open it,' Lily said. 'You need to see. You need to know.'

He didn't want to.

But he knew he had to.

He held his breath, digging his thumb into the crease and flattening it.

His whole world rocked, twisted, and then just shattered.

It had been twenty-four years since he'd laid eyes on his mother. And although she was older in this photograph, he'd never forget her face. He couldn't.

'Jacob,' Lily said.

He looked up at her, seeing in her face that she knew. That she'd always known. That... That they were...

Oh God.

Before he could actively formulate the thought the vomit came.

He scrabbled madly at the door handle, barely shoving the door open before he ejected the contents of his stomach into the air and flopped onto the grass, crawling away from the car with what little strength he could muster.

An endless expanse of ground stretched out before him.

But Jacob knew, no matter how far he went, no matter how far he ran from Devils Lake, he'd never escape the truth.

That Lily Graham wasn't Lily Graham.

She was his sister.

Chapter 40

'Jacob?'

Even the sound of her saying his own name made him feel sick.

She was at his side then, kneeling next to him, resting a hand on his back.

He recoiled from her touch, falling onto his side, holding his hands up. 'No, no,' he begged. 'Don't— Don't fucking—' The word was cut off, another huge involuntary retch taking it from him. He dragged his phone from his pocket, dialling Steph again.

Lily crouched him, elbows on knees, watching. Was she not revolted? How long had she known? Jesus Christ. Before they slept together?

He stifled another retch and waited for Steph to answer her phone.

It rang out.

He tried again. *Come on, pick up! I need you, Steph!*

'Fuck!' he hissed, throwing his phone down. 'Fuck!'

'Jacob.' Lily's voice was harder now. Stern, even. 'It's okay.'

'It's not, it's not,' he muttered hunching up into a ball, forehead on the ground. 'We're... And we...'

'Shh, shh,' she hushed him, standing and walking over. She knelt next to him now and put her arm across his shoulders.

He didn't pull away this time, just kept his face in the dirt. Where the hell was Steph? 'Did you know?'

'That we share a mother?' Lily asked.

What the fuck else would he mean?

'I did. Not always, but before I came to Devils Lake, yes. But I didn't expect to meet you, at least not like we did. That night at the farm... God, when I heard them talking like they were, when they tried to... when they tried to *fuck* me...' She *tsked* with disgust. 'I just fucking lost it. I killed them, and it felt good, but it wasn't enough. I knew that I'd have to go back, that I'd have to burn the whole place to ash before it felt like it was enough. They took her from me. And from you, too.' She looked at him for a few seconds. 'You know, when I walked into that police station, all those years ago, covered in her blood, and told them what happened? They put me in a holding room, got child services to come and take me away. No passport or birth certificate, no last name, even. I didn't know where the farm was, what state it was even in. I had nothing, no idea where I came from or who I was. Just that I was alone. I don't know how our mother found her way to David Hall—'

The man with the burning eyes flashed in Jacob's mind.

'—but she did, and she never left. Not until the night she died.' Lily tightened her grip on Jacob's shoulder. 'They took me into foster care and I took the last name of my first foster family. I grew up there, bounced from home to home until I aged out. The last home I was in, I was there the longest. But they weren't the good kind of people – hell, I don't know if there is a good kind. I don't think so. This world... the people in it. God, fuck. It's just... I never met anyone that didn't want something from me. Since I was twelve years old it seemed like everyone

183

who was nice to me wanted... well... you can guess... But at eighteen, when you're facing the streets, you don't have a lot of choices. You kind of have to do whatever you can to survive.'

Jacob kept his eyes closed, just listening.

'And that's the thing, Jacob. I'm a survivor. But not just a survivor. A fighter. I had everything taken from me. My childhood. My mother. My family. I had nothing. Nothing but this deep, aching pit of hate that never left me. I came back to Devils Lake with one goal in mind: to find that place, and to end it.

'It took a long time. A lot of searching, a lot of questions, a lot of doors slammed in my face. But eventually, I found my way here. All I had was a picture of my mother to go on – it was all she had in her pocket the night we left. The only personal effect she had. On the back she wrote *I love you. And I always will.* I don't think she ever thought she'd get out. Not alive, at least.' She stared off into the distance, across the open fields that stretched all the way to the horizon. 'I showed it around town, asked everyone I met if they knew her. It was just a random person on the street that did.' Lily laughed a little at that. At the simplicity of it. 'From there, with a name – Anna Taylor – it was easy to find the obituary in the newspaper archive, her death certificate at town hall, her surviving kids...'

Jacob opened his eyes and sat back a little.

'And then, suddenly, I had two siblings. A brother. A sister. Jacob. Stephanie. My world suddenly got so much bigger. But I couldn't come to you, couldn't involve you in any of it. Not with what I had to do, not with what lay ahead. And then, that night at the farm, things got out of hand, and I ran. And I thought that was it, that

I'd be hunted down, killed. Like her. But then, there you were.' She afforded a small smile, her fingers digging into his shirt. 'I couldn't believe it. You were just there, in your truck, asking me if I was okay. It was meant to be. Fate. It brought us together.'

His throat hurt, but he managed a few thin words. 'But when you came home with me, why did you…?'

She seemed to consider that for a time before speaking. 'You were the first person who'd been nice to me. Really, genuinely nice to me in I don't know how long. And I think, being there with you, I just felt… I don't know. Safe, I guess. There was something about you that I just felt, like magnetism. Something between us? Our mother may have been the same person, but we're not like you and Stephanie are. We never have been. And I don't know, I just felt… *It* just felt right. You know?'

'Why didn't you tell me?' Jacob asked, pulling himself to his knees, finally looking at her.

'Would you have believed me?'

'You had the photograph all along.'

'It wouldn't have been enough. I was covered in blood. You'd have called the police.'

He didn't deny that.

Before he could speak again, she reached out, cupping his face with her hands. 'I'm doing what I'm doing for her… For Mom, Jacob.'

He tried to pull away but she held him firm, her icy-blue eyes alight in the sun, piercing him. Penetrating his soul. He could hide nothing from her.

'It's you and me now. Just us,' she said. 'We're the only ones who can do this. Who can make it right. For Mom. For all the other girls. You saw, didn't you?'

He tried to look away.

'Look at me!' She dug her nails into his skin and he looked back at her. 'Didn't you? Saw what they're doing there? To them? To the girls?'

'I... I did.'

'Then you have to decide. Right now. Are you going to help? Are you going to help me make this right, save them? Save them all? For Mom?'

'I—'

But before he could answer, she kissed him.

He tried to resist, but her fingers were dug into his neck, her lips, her tongue moving over his, kindling something in him he wanted nothing more than to extinguish. But he couldn't. Couldn't resist it in that moment. Whatever it was, it was stronger than him, and he was powerless to it.

He let her do it, let this strange, beautiful girl kiss him, despite everything he now knew.

Because he couldn't deny it – there was something between them that just felt *right*.

So when she let go and met his eyes once more, her question hanging in the air, all he could do was nod.

She smiled and it filled him.

'Good,' she said. 'That's good, Jacob.'

He smiled back.

'I love you,' she said then. Without warning or ceremony.

And before he even had time to process it, she kissed him again.

Chapter 41

As they climbed back into Steph's car, Jacob didn't look at Lily.

He put it into drive and pulled back onto the road, spinning around to face Devils Lake. Which he trundled towards slowly, afraid suddenly of what awaited them there.

Lily wasted no time in laying her hand over his, holding onto his knuckles, gently rubbing her thumb across his skin.

He shot a quick glance at it, trying not to alert her to what he was feeling. It was nausea, predominantly. Fear, too, in spades. He was a mess, he knew that. His mind felt addled, twisted. And until about sixty seconds ago, he was hers, wrapped around her little finger. But then those words... *I love you?* It was like a knife to his gut, twisting.

He'd not really considered it up until that moment, but now there was something he couldn't get out of his mind: Lily Graham was a fucking lunatic.

He stole another quick glance at her and she smiled back at him. 'I managed to get out of the motel with my bag — it has everything in, all my notes, my camera too. I need it, okay?'

'Okay,' Jacob replied, forcing a smile.

Jesus Christ. Certifiable, he thought. He'd been so fixated on the police, the farm, the danger they posed to him, his family, he'd completely overlooked the fact that it seemed like the most dangerous person of all was sitting right next to him.

He told her he'd do it. Help her. Help her bring the farm down, and hell, he wanted nothing more than to do just that after what he'd seen. But what did he know about this woman other than the fact she'd murdered two people and seduced him despite *knowing* they were related. Shit – and that was assuming that she was telling the truth! Was she? Was it just to manipulate him?

She had a photo of his mother, but how could he know, really?

He cleared his throat awkwardly. 'You, uh, you never told me how you knew about that place we met – where the water meets the sky?'

She looked at him like he was dumb. Because he was dumb. 'Mom told me all about it, silly.'

'But she didn't tell you about... me? Us? Me and Steph?'

She just shook her head. 'No. I don't know why.' She looked out the window, almost mournfully. 'I guess it was too hard – for her to think about her life outside. Before.'

It was one thing he'd been thinking about since she'd said it. Why didn't his mother tell her about her life before? About her two kids, her husband, everything? Had Lily known what life outside even looked like? God, it was enough to make his head spin. Maybe she didn't want to deprive Lily of the life he and Steph had. What was that old adage? Ignorance is bliss?

How had his mother even found her way to the Hall Farm in the first place? The man with the burning eyes, he knew. David Hall. That's what Lily had said. That's who she wanted to see... who she wanted to kill. The man behind it all. The one who'd taken his mother in. Used her. Twisted her. Jacob shuddered, thinking of the women in that room. Had his mother been in that room? In that bed? Dousing herself in blood, giving herself to that creep, that evil fuck? And was Lily the result of a night like that?

She looked over at him. 'What's wrong? You shivered.'

He kept his eyes on the road. 'Yeah. Someone must have walked over my grave.' It was the first thing that came to him. He blinked, thinking of it, of what he'd just said.

Lily looked at him strangely. 'I've never heard that before,' she said.

'Something my dad used to say,' Jacob thought aloud. 'After he came back from the war, my mom said he was never the same.'

'Our mom,' she corrected him.

He suppressed another one. 'He used to shudder like that, and he'd always say it. Oh, someone must have walked over my grave.'

A small smile cracked Lily's delicate face. 'That's nice. The idea, right? Of another life, another you. A different time, a different place.'

'Not if you're dead,' Jacob said, a little coldly.

She shrugged, squeezing his hand tighter. 'There are worse fates than death, Jacob.'

He swallowed.

'You know that. And soon, they will, too.' She looked over at him again. 'Right?'

'Right,' he said, looking back at her. 'What is your plan, exactly? What do you intend to do?'

'We, you mean.'

'Right. What are *we* going to do?'

Her smile broadened. 'And ruin the surprise? I don't think so. But you'll like it, I promise. There's nothing we could do that would be enough. Nothing they don't deserve. That *he* doesn't deserve. Don't you think?'

'Yeah…' He answered slowly.

'I'm glad we found each other,' she said then, staring right at him.

'Me too,' he said, accelerating a little. Willing them to be back faster, to be in town and doing something else, anything else.

She let out a slow, soft sigh and let go of his hand, moving hers to the top of his thigh, her slim, pale fingers spidering their way up towards his crotch.

A road sign flashed by and he considered swerving into it.

Instead he just pulled his leg up, trying to shrug her off. Before she got what she wanted – which despite everything, he didn't think he could stop. 'I can't,' he said.

'Why?' She reached for him again.

'It's Steph – I don't know where she is, if she's alright or not. I can't think of anything else right now, you understand, don't you?' He risked looking at her.

A quiet rage descended over her face, her features cold.

'She's my sister,' he reminded her.

'*I'm* your sister,' she reminded him.

Jacob turned his head to look forwards, remiss that there wasn't another sign for half a mile.

Chapter 42

Jacob's knee bounced furiously as his phone was ringing and ringing in his ear.

He chewed his thumbnail as it cut to Steph's answering machine for the tenth time in a row. Jacob's mind was on her, but his eyes were fixed on the abandoned house in front of him. On the pried-open front door that Lily had disappeared through a few minutes ago. This is where she'd stashed her belongings.

Jacob looked up at the place. A veritable shit-hole on the outskirts of town that was falling down. Five hundred yards from the nearest neighbour, it was quite literally a forgotten place that was being reclaimed by the earth. A tree was growing through the porch, the windows were all missing, the outside of the building covered in climbing plants.

He took his eyes from it, staring at his phone. 'Come on, Steph,' he said, still bouncing his knee. He could leave, he thought. Drive back there. Abandon Lily, just get the hell out of town, him and Steph, like they'd planned. That was still on the table.

He looked back at the house. But then what would happen to Lily? She could die. Or she could kill someone else. Not that the men at the farm were innocent. But what of the other women there? He could call the state police, but would they believe him? There were a lot of questions up in the air. But by the time they even got out there, how much damage would Lily have done?

As much as he wanted to turn tail and run, he couldn't. Even if she was bat-shit insane, he couldn't abandon her. They were... fuck... *family*, after all. He gagged on the thought alone. If she was his sister – and he was finding it hard to deny the signs – and she wasn't right, then he had to help her, didn't he? His main fear was that if he tried to stop her from following through with this, she might well push him to the other side of the board. She hadn't said it, but he sensed a *you're either with me or against me* undertone to the ultimatum she'd posed him by the roadside.

He would stick with her, prevent her from dying, or killing. He'd find Steph. And then they'd figure out what the fuck to do together. Take her to a facility that could help her. Then call the state police. That simple, right? Right?

Even he didn't want to answer his own question.

His phone buzzed on his thigh then and he looked down at it so quickly his neck clicked. Steph.

All ok. Meet me here.

His phone buzzed again, a link to the maps app. He clicked it, saw a pin dropped on the shore of the lake. Twelve minutes' drive.

Thank God. She was okay. He almost collapsed in on himself with relief right then and there. If he lost Steph, he didn't know what he'd do. She must have fled from the house. Maybe Ellis never came around and she had to deal with a dead cop. Maybe the other guy who'd tried to off him in his cell had shown up looking. Either way, she was texting him, and that was good.

He was so transfixed he didn't even notice Lily walking out of the house and climbing in the car.

Jacob jumped as she opened the door.

'Who are you texting?' she asked, her tone accusatory. It wasn't even veiled.

He pushed it between his legs instinctively. 'No one. Uh, Steph,' he corrected himself, intentionally loosening his posture. He tried not to let on how terrified he was in that moment.

He looked at the side of the seat then, to the spot where he'd pushed Ellis's pistol. It'd been in his waistband but that was uncomfortable, so he'd shoved it down the side of the seat next to the centre console when they'd driven out to Sweetwater.

And now it wasn't there anymore.

And there was only one other person in the car.

He cleared his throat. 'Get what you need?' Change the subject.

She ignored it completely. 'Is she okay?' Lily asked him.

'Yeah. She asked me to meet her. We'll go there now—'

'We don't have time,' Lily said.

'I need to know if she's okay—'

'If she's texting you, she's okay.'

'I just really need to—'

'Jacob.' She cut him off again. 'You know what's at stake here. We can't afford any detours. We have to go. We have to do this. You said you were with me.'

He set his jaw, his heart hammering in his throat so hard the corners of his vision were pulsing black. Could she hear it? He wouldn't be surprised.

'I know,' he said slowly, the breath caught in his chest. 'But she's family. Mine, and yours.' He let that sink in for a moment. 'You want to know she's safe, don't you?'

Lily just looked back blankly.

'If you need the car, I can walk. It's not far. We'll meet you after—'

'Fine, fine,' she said, smiling again. 'Of course, I'm just being...' She sighed heavily. 'Of course we can go meet her. She's my sister, too.' She clasped the backpack on her lap tightly, staring forwards at the road ahead. 'Go on, then. Let's go.'

Jacob kept looking at her, his eyes falling to the bag. Asking about the gun was a stupid move. The one he'd gotten from his own house was in his duffle bag at Steph's. He could go get it. But not now. Not yet. Right now, he needed to see Steph, and he needed to keep Lily calm. She was smiling, but Jacob bet she was also smiling when she'd gutted those two men at the farm.

He tried to quell that thought, and his heart as he slipped the car into drive and headed down the road.

Twelve minutes. That's all it is. *And then you'll see Steph and all this will be alright.*

But despite him telling himself to act normal, to drive normal, he couldn't help himself.

He floored it.

Chapter 43

Though the phone said it was twelve minutes, he was there in eight. It was wearing into late afternoon now, the sun sinking lower in the sky.

Summer evenings were sleepy in Devils Lake, and Jacob had no trouble navigating to the spot where Steph was waiting without any trouble. Most people who hit the water in the warmer months headed to the state park or one of the resort beaches. Where Jacob was headed was neither.

The location that Steph had sent was off Highway 19, to the west of town. Despite living here his whole life, he didn't think he'd ever been to this specific spot. And he was wondering, as he drove, how Steph knew about it.

He pulled off the highway and headed down a long dirt road, following a few hand-made signs for fishing spots. A lot of anglers had their favourite spots and way-marked them like this. Small signs that led to secluded beaches.

And it seemed like that's where they were headed now. To one such secluded spot.

Lily watched in silence as they drove, and it only added to Jacob's growing sense of trepidation. There was something jarring about Steph's message. The lack of feeling, the lack of her *voice* in it. His heart beat a little harder. Could he really glean that much from so few words?

That was the other thing. What was stopping her from picking up the phone?

As he made the last turn, cutting through the sparse trees that littered the side of the lake, heading for the beach, he was barely breathing.

They broke through the foliage into the open, seeing just one vehicle parked there. An old Tacoma.

Was it Steph? How else would she have gotten out there?

Jacob eased up next to it, checking the cab. It was empty, the truck dark.

He put the Subaru into park and cut the engine. Nothing moved around them except for the lake, lapping gently at the sandy shore.

A few small boats were moored just offshore, a couple of skiffs pulled up onto the sand to keep them out of the gentle current.

Lily remained quiet, her eyes scanning the beach without any sort of nerves or hesitation. She was cool, and Jacob was sweating.

He reached for the handle, hoping she might warn him against it, and opened the door, stepping out. A little breeze was coming in off the water, washing away a good amount of the oppressive summer heat, but that still didn't make it any easier to fill his chest with breath.

Jacob held his phone up, seeing if she'd text, if she'd call. But there was nothing.

He took a few steps forwards, into the space behind the cars and called out. 'Steph?'

His words died in the rustle of the trees and the push and pull of the water.

'Steph?' he tried again.

Nothing.

Lily was out of the car now, too. She moved up next to him, reached for his hand.

He stepped forwards, as though he hadn't realised she was doing it – better than pulling it off her. God, if Steph saw him holding her hand? She'd backhand him there and then.

That thought brought him some solace, and when a crunching of stone sounded behind him, he turned so fast he almost lost his balance.

'Steph!' he said, before even seeing who it was.

And that person wasn't her.

Todd Ellis was next to his truck, hands raised and held out in front of him. He had a strange look on his face – sadness, fear. Remorse.

'Where's Steph?' Jacob asked, his voice strange and alien to him.

'Let me explain, okay?' Ellis pleaded.

'Where's my sister?' Jacob said, demanding his answer. If Ellis was loose, then that meant… No, no, Ellis would tell him where she was. That she was okay. That she was safe.

'I'm so sorry, Jacob,' he said, keeping his hands out. They shook visibly. 'I didn't mean to… Okay? I didn't mean to.'

'Didn't mean to *what*?' Jacob asked, his voice more a growl than anything else. 'Where is Steph? Where is my sister?'

Ellis laboured over the answer, taking a deep breath before he spoke. 'She's…' He looked at the ground. 'She's dead.'

The words rung hollow in the air. They cut through the din like a knife right into Jacob's heart. He wanted to ask if he was lying, if that was the truth coming from his

197

mouth. But he knew from the look on Ellis's face that it was. That his sister... that Steph was gone.

He couldn't comprehend it, couldn't wrap his mind around a world where she wasn't alive, wasn't with him, wasn't telling him how to live his life – where she wasn't there to look after him.

'Please,' Ellis said, on the verge of tears. 'Say something...'

Jacob's mouth opened, but nothing came out. No sound, no breath. He wasn't even sure if he was conscious.

But he felt Lily's hand on his shoulder then. 'Jacob,' she whispered.

He blinked.

'It's okay, Jacob,' she said softly.

He felt something being pushed into his hand then and looked down, seeing Ellis's own gun in his fingers.

'Take it,' Lily whispered. 'Take it.'

His hand closed around it numbly and he felt her guide it upwards until it was pointed right at Ellis.

The man's eyes widened, his hands moving from their position in front of him to the sides of his head.

Lily's grip steadied Jacob's arm, her lips hovering next to his ear, her body pressed against him. 'He killed her,' she said, her voice cold now. 'He killed Steph.'

'I...' Ellis began, but his words were drowned out by Lily.

'It doesn't matter how. He did it. He killed her.'

Jacob's world was spinning. He closed his eyes.

'Look at him!' Lily hissed.

His eyes snapped open.

'Do it.'

He tried to speak, but found he couldn't.

'Do it. He deserves it. Pull the trigger, Jacob. Kill him.'

Jacob croaked, no words coming.

'Do it!' Her fingers dug into his skin, her nails biting at his wrist. 'Do it!'

He jolted at the sudden volume, the intensity of her order.

His finger moved.

The gun kicked back.

Fire lanced from the muzzle, a report echoing across the surface of the lake.

Ellis staggered backwards, clutching at his sternum, a tiny, dark hole cut through his shirt between the zips of his jacket.

Jacob saw the whites of Ellis's widened eyes for a split second before the other man keeled backwards and landed heavily.

Everything was still for a moment and then a single, explosive sob escaped Jacob's lips. He collapsed forwards, too, dropping the gun and falling to his hands and knees.

Lily scooped it up and pushed it into her bag before kneeling at his side, hand on his back. She rubbed it gently, hushing him once more.

'It's okay, it's okay,' she said. 'It's over. He's dead. You killed him.'

'No… No…' Jacob mewled.

'He killed Steph.'

'No… No…'

'You did the right thing. I'm proud of you.'

He hunched over further.

'You were strong. We're going to need that. For what comes next.'

Jacob looked at her.

'We need to go. Steph is gone, but we still have so much work to do.'

He shook his head.

'It's time to get up, Jacob. You have to get up. We have to go.' She tried taking him by the shoulder and pulling him, but he shoved her away.

Lily stood straight, managing to stay on her feet.

She looked down at him, a mixture of hurt and disgust painted on her face.

'Get up, Jacob.'

He stared at her. Saw her, finally. Truly.

'Get up out of the dirt,' she ordered him. 'And get in the car.'

'No,' he said slowly, the word dripping from his mouth like venom.

'What did you say?'

'I said NO!' he roared suddenly, pushing himself up to his knees.

Lily jumped, taking a step backwards, the pistol suddenly in her hand and levelled at him.

He stared into the barrel, then lifted his eyes to hers. 'You're going to shoot me?'

After a few seconds, she lowered it. 'No,' she said, letting the weapon hang at her side.

And then she turned away, as though he were nothing to her, and strode back towards Steph's car, heading for the driver's door.

He patted the pockets of his jeans, not feeling her keys there. Lily must have taken them when she'd been in his ear.

But before he could call out, she'd already climbed in and started the engine.

She backed out quickly, swung in a circle, and then drove away from the lake in a cloud of dust, leaving Jacob there alone, the sound of the engine swallowed by the

North Dakota summer, and the man he'd just killed lying no more than ten feet from him.

Chapter 44

As waves of pain radiated from his chest, his breath strangled in his throat, his life draining from him, Todd Ellis stared into the canopy above his head, replaying the last few hours over and over in his head.

He wondered how he could have done things differently. Not just today, but his whole life. A single tear trickled from his eye and ran over his cheek and he closed his eyes.

When he opened them again, he was tied to a wooden post in Stephanie Taylor's basement.

He was staring at his knees, leaned forwards, strained against his bonds. He wriggled his hands first, feeling the tug of rope or cord around his wrists, digging into his skin.

Ellis detected the smell of cigarette smoke and lifted his head to find the source, the pain in his head all at once overwhelming. He hissed and winced, screwing his eyes closed once more.

'Yeah,' came a woman's voice from the ether, 'that's on me.'

Ellis opened one eye to see Steph Taylor sitting on the basement steps. She had her elbows on her knees, dark circles under her eyes. There was an empty coffee cup between her feet, and in one hand she had a cigarette. In the other she had a chef's knife.

Ellis stiffened a little at the sight of it, hoping there was no intention of using it.

'You remember your name?' Steph asked.

'Todd Ellis,' he said. 'Officer Todd Ellis, Devils Lake—'

'Yeah, yeah, I know you're a cop,' Steph said. 'Doesn't mean you're getting out of here. I asked your name to check if you've got brain damage, not because I wanted to know.'

Ellis sighed a little, straightening and trying to ease the ache in his shoulders. It didn't work. 'How long have I been out?'

'About thirty minutes, maybe a little more.' She shrugged. 'I did hit you pretty hard.'

'With what? A hammer?' Ellis groaned.

'I think it was a vase.' She eyed the man in the chair. 'A big one.'

He couldn't help but smile a little at that. 'Are the restraints really necessary?'

'You came into my house, pulled a gun, were going to shoot my brother. *After* you already tried to murder him once.' She sucked on the cigarette. 'So I'd say yeah – pretty necessary.'

Ellis swallowed, his mouth dry, and gathered his thoughts, noticing how foggy they seemed. This was a concussion if he'd ever had one. 'I didn't try to murder him – I saved his life.'

She harrumphed, waving the knife gently in her grip. 'Sure you did. Same as you were trying to save him by holding him at gunpoint through that door, earlier. Right?'

He picked up his head now and looked right at her. 'I don't want your brother dead. I just wanted to make sure he was safe.'

'From your colleagues, the other *cops*?'

'Yes,' he said, trying to temper his frustration. 'What he's involved with… they don't want him to see another sunrise. I do.'

'Why?' She narrowed her eyes.

'Because he's done nothing wrong, and I don't participate in the willing murder of innocent men. It's not who I am.'

'Ah,' she said, pointing the knife at him almost playfully. 'So you're the one moral cop in town full of corrupt ones. Convenient.'

'Not really,' he growled. 'Pretty much fucked myself out of a job, and maybe my own life, too.' He hung his head again. 'Once the chief finds out I let Jacob walk… Well, I'd say him and me are in the same boat.'

'You think they'll come looking for you?'

'Here?' He shrugged as best he could. 'Probably, sooner or later.'

'Then we'll see if you're lying, I suppose.'

'You're going to ask them?' He looked at her, surprised at her short-sightedness if that was her intention.

'No, I'm not a fucking idiot.' She scoffed. 'When they come in, I'll let them look around, and if you call out for help, then I know you're full of shit. If you stay quiet, it does your case a lot of good.'

'And what if they want to look in the basement?' he asked, clenching his fists and testing the give in his restraints.

'Don't worry, I got a lot more vases upstairs I'm not attached to.' She rose slowly to her feet and stubbed the cigarette out on the bare concrete wall. 'You hungry? I'm going to make some breakfast.'

'You going to feed it to me?' Ellis asked, leaning forwards against his bonds to illustrate his position.

'Depends,' Steph said, curling another smile. 'You going to bite?'

She returned almost fifteen minutes later with a tuna-mayo sandwich – not breakfast food, but he was hungry and needed to eat something. Thankfully, his mind had cleared a little in the last few minutes, and not dimmed. So he hoped that the concussion wasn't all that bad. He'd had some knocks to the head playing football, so he wasn't a stranger to the feelings.

When Steph approached slowly, doing a quick lap of his chair to make sure he was still tied – which he was – before she knelt in front of him and scooped a sandwich off the plate, offering it for his mouth.

He leaned forwards, taking a bite. It wasn't exactly dignified, especially as he had to sort of gnaw and tug at the bread to get a good mouthful. But he hoped he could show her that he meant her no harm at least.

'So,' Steph said as she continued feeding him. 'This Lily Graham...'

Even by her tone he could tell Steph wasn't a fan.

'You met her? You know her?'

He chewed and swallowed, deliberating over his words. 'Yeah, I've met her.'

'You know what she's doing here in town?'

'Looking into the Hall Farm,' Ellis replied, opening his mouth for another bite.

'You know much about that place?'

'No more than anyone else, I guess,' he said, taking another chomp of sandwich.

'She says they're a cult.' She didn't give him another bite. Wanted him to be able to speak. 'She's got Jacob all twisted up. You buy any of it?'

'I didn't,' Ellis answered truthfully. 'Not until a few days ago, at least. The chief, the other officers, they didn't just want her to stop looking. They wanted her *gone*. And then they wanted Jacob dead just for getting mixed up with her. So yeah, I'd say I buy at least half of it.'

She gave him his prize.

'Where's Jacob now?' Ellis asked.

'Gone to look for her,' Steph said, and then sighed. 'But I hope he doesn't find her.'

Ellis nodded a little. 'Yeah, that might be for the best. She's a lightning rod for trouble right now – they know who she is, and they won't stop until they find her.'

Steph fell quiet. 'What would you do?' she asked then. 'If you found her first?'

He didn't have an answer to that question. Not one that'd please her to hear, at least. 'I don't know what I could do… other than just staying out of her way.'

Chapter 45

He finished the sandwich gladly, wondering how this was going to play out. He couldn't sit here all day, and though Steph seemed reasonable, and somewhat accepting of the truth he'd given her, there was no hint of her letting him free any time soon.

'What is your plan here?' He moved a little to illustrate he meant with keeping him tied up.

'I'm waiting for Jacob to get back. And then we're leaving town.'

It wasn't a bad plan. It was practically the same as his. 'When's that?'

'I don't know. Soon, I hope.'

'And what about me?'

'We'll call the police and tell them where you are when we're clear of Devils Lake.'

He looked right at her. 'They'll likely kill me,' he said, coming to terms with the gravity of what was happening. 'I know too much... and I failed.'

'Failed to do what?'

'Kill Jacob. Kill you.' He shook his head. 'I was so oblivious for so long to who they were, what they were.' He let out a long, sobering breath. 'I don't know what to do.' There was no point hiding it now, and Stephanie Taylor was possibly the only person he could be truly honest with in that moment.

'Do you know what they're doing out there, at the farm? The truth?' She wasn't asking to check; it seemed like a genuine question. 'Jacob says it's some weird cult. But who knows for sure? All I know is that—'

But before she could finish, there was a loud knock at the door upstairs.

They both froze, looking at the ceiling.

Feet moved past the window to their right, the frosted glass stopping them from seeing who it was, but there was definitely someone out there.

Another knock, harder this time. A thunderous pounding at the door.

Adams and Fitzhugh? The two cops that had been with the chief at the farm?

Steph looked at Ellis, fear in her eyes. Her look was pleading, willing him not to call out.

She didn't have to worry about that.

The sound of breaking glass filtered down to them, a dim creaking.

'Back door,' Steph all but mouthed to him.

He balled his fists, meeting her eye. 'You need to untie me. Right now.'

'I can't,' she said.

'If you don't, we both die,' Ellis said, his voice hushed but hard. 'Please.'

She thought for a second, chewing her bottom lip. And then she came forwards, swearing under her breath as she did.

A flood of relief washed over Ellis as he felt his bonds loosen. A moment later a red extension cord hit the ground behind him, just as footsteps moved above them.

'Is there another way out of here?' Ellis asked, standing up and rubbing his wrists. He turned to see Steph keeping her distance, far enough away that he couldn't make a grab for her, the chef's knife in her hand once more, held up between them.

Smart woman, Ellis thought to himself. He had no intention of touching her, but he appreciated the common sense.

She shook her head. 'No,' she whispered. 'Just the door to the kitchen.'

Ellis turned back to it, letting out a long, shaking breath.

Two men, armed. Intent on killing. They'd have weapons drawn, ready to fire the second they saw anyone.

Two choices: hide, hope they leave, and when they don't, meet them down here. Or, take the fight to them.

Neither were good options.

'What do we do?' Steph asked then, stepping closer to Ellis.

'The only thing we can do,' he said, hopefully without too much defeat in his voice. 'We fight.'

Steph just blinked at him. 'What do you mean, *we fight*? Fight who? The police?'

He nodded solemnly, not expounding on that. Not telling her that what he really meant by fight was *kill*. That there was no other way out of this basement than right through them, and that they wouldn't walk out of here until Adams and Fitzhugh's blood was spread all over the floor.

Their footsteps circled towards the kitchen and Steph automatically brought her kitchen knife to attention. It was a standard size – twenty centimetres. Hard to wield effectively, but fine for slicing or stabbing. But did she have the skills or the stomach to do that? Ellis's father had taken him fishing a lot as a kid, and he knew his way around a knife, had gutted enough fish to know what putting a blade into a living thing felt like. But what about Steph? Could she be relied upon? The way she was clutching on to the knife for dear life, he didn't think it was a safe bet.

Ellis looked around frantically. Open staircase. 'There,' he said, pointing to it. 'Get under there, quickly,' he ordered her.

She looked at it, then at him. He was her prisoner just minutes ago, and now her life was in his hands. She knew it. So did he.

After a second, she went, nodding to herself, steadying herself for what was to come.

Ellis followed her. 'Do you have any weapons down here? Guns? Anything like that?'

'No,' she said, huddling under the stairs so the open rungs were above her and she was completely shadowed. She leaned back against the wall, clutching the knife to her chest. 'There's nothing like that. Just some old fishing stuff and some golf clubs over there,' she said, pointing to the corner of the room. 'Some tools, too.'

Ellis kept pricking his ears to check for any hint of their would-be attackers coming through the door. They were being thorough, thankfully, making sure that they checked every nook and hiding spot upstairs before they came down.

Still, Ellis wasted no time in going to the workbench and looking through what was there. An old set of screw-drivers, a few wrenches, a hammer. Nothing that could cause any real damage. Not when they were up against guns. *Fuck.* What was he going to do?

He moved on from the tools, scanning the golf equipment. A five-iron was a decent enough weapon if he could get a good swing off. He pulled out a club and held it at his side. Last resort, he hoped, carrying on the search.

Fishing stuff next. Rods, nets stacked against the wall. Tackle box. He opened it, not hoping for much, maybe a knife if he was lucky. And he was. There on the top was an old folding survival knife. Three-inch blade, rusty by the looks of it. Jesus, when was the last time this was opened?

He dragged the blade free and set it on the workbench, lifting the flat tackle box insert, revealing the deeper section, where there'd be a big pile of lures and other effects used to make them. Not that any of that shit would be of any use here, but when he did pick the insert up, he was glad he did.

It wasn't a firearm, but it was a gun of sorts. A flare gun. An old, orange, plastic one.

He picked it up and held it, the outside sticky with grime from the years it'd been there.

Ellis pressed the release and broke the pistol, the single tubular barrel folding down to reveal a flare cartridge inside. These old ones were usually sulphur-based, and sulphur burned at over a thousand degrees. So long as this thing still fired, it was liable to do some serious damage if it hit someone. Shooting it in an enclosed space was the last thing that he wanted to do, but if it came to it…

Just then, voices sounded in the kitchen and Ellis rushed back to Steph, motioning her to be quiet. She nodded vigorously, like she couldn't be paid to make a sound.

Ellis spoke in a bare whisper, more mouthing the words than anything. 'They're going to come down single file,' he said, 'pistols drawn, okay? I need you to do something.'

Her eyes widened.

'When the second guy passes, I want you to reach through the rungs here,' he said, gesturing to the steps in front of them, grimacing at what he was about to ask her to do, 'and I want you to cut across the back of the heel. Nice and hard.'

'W— what?' she stammered. 'I can't do that!'

He looked at the knife. 'You were going to stab me with that, right?'

'Only if I had to. If it was life or death,' she said, almost apologetically.

'You have to,' he replied, his eyes hard and cold. 'This is life or death.'

'What are you going to do?'

He lifted the five-iron. 'I'm going to cave in the skull of the one that comes down first.' Even he was surprised at the calmness with which the words came out of his mouth. But what he'd said to Steph was the truth. This was life or death. And if they were going to get out of this, it was because he was going to have to kill these two men. Two men he'd worked with for years. Two men he'd considered friends, even. But they weren't the kind of men he thought, and they weren't the kind of men that he was.

But what kind of man was he, exactly?

He took one final look at Stephanie Taylor, trying to decide.

But before he could make a decision, the door to the basement opened above them.

Chapter 46

The door opened slowly, silently.

Ellis stood firm, the flare gun tucked in his belt, the golf club in his hands.

He motioned for Steph to take her position behind the stairs as they began to descend. Little motes of dust drifted down as they stepped on the old wood, the whole thing bowing under their collective weight.

Steph's hands were shaking, but Ellis laid one of his on top of them and they stilled. He gave her a slow nod, and then made a swift cutting movement with his hand. Slice deep.

She swallowed and Ellis took a step sideways, slowly moving into the open in their blind spot as they came down. He'd only get one chance at this, and he hoped that he had the stomach for it.

They stepped down, the first – Adams – already near the bottom, while Fitz came down behind him, a little more cautious.

Steph watched him while he watched them. And when Fitz hit the step level with her, Ellis gave the signal.

She grimaced, almost closing her eye as she whipped the knife through the air, right between the steps.

The sound of her blade cutting flesh rang in the darkness, swiftly followed by a pained shriek from Fitz. Blood sprayed across the concrete floor with a dull splatter and

Fitz's knees quaked and gave out, sending him plunging forwards while he grabbed for his ankle.

Adams turned, pistol flying in a circle as he homed in on whatever the fuck was going on behind him. But he didn't get halfway before Ellis was on him, five-iron flashing in the half-light. It came down swiftly, the steel head crunching into his hand.

The snap of bone was audible, reverberating through the shaft of the club as the pistol was torn from his broken hand. Before it left his grasp, though, the weapon discharged, a final convulsion of the trigger finger enough to set it off.

Muzzle flash lit the air, the bullet pinging into the wall to their right before the gun clattered to the ground, Adams yowling.

Fitz landed heavily between them, curling into a ball as he fumbled for his profusely bleeding foot, forcing Ellis back.

Adams let loose with a stream of profanity, all but diving for his spilled weapon while Fitz went on howling and clutching at his heel.

There was a second of stillness in him. Then, as he saw Steph between the treads of the stairs, he locked eyes with her, finally understanding what had happened.

'You fucking—' he roared, spraying flecks of saliva over his legs. The rest of his words were drowned out as he lifted his pistol and fired into the steps.

Steph yelped and dove for cover and Ellis wasted no time in winding up for another swing, coming in low and hard on the back of Fitz's head. It sling-shotted forwards, his chin rebounding off his chest, the heavy thwack of the club against his skull enough to make his skin break out in gooseflesh.

His eyes lolled in his head, his body losing all tension as it folded awkwardly and then flopped to the side, a deep gash visible through his thick hair.

Ellis had no doubt that he was dead before he hit the ground.

Which just left Adams.

Though by the time that Ellis recovered from his last swing, Adams already had his spilled gun in his left hand, his right cradled against his chest, a wild and agonised look in his eye. His mouth moved, braying something vicious, but Ellis didn't hear it, didn't hear anything except the rush of blood in his ears as he turned and threw himself in the opposite direction, a series of inaccurate shots splitting the thick basement air.

He was shooting with his left, which meant he'd struggle to hit a target – but they were no more than ten feet apart and Ellis wasn't exactly a bullseye at a hundred yards. And Adams had seventeen tries.

This had to end. And it had to end now.

Ellis moved right, ducking behind the pillar he'd been bound to a few minutes before, and ripped the flare gun from his belt, twisting into space and taking a knee as more bullets ripped through the space right above his head.

He'd only get one chance at this. But in the same way he was a target at point blank for Adams, the reverse was true, too. So as long as this fucking thing fired, he couldn't miss.

The trigger was stiff, flimsy in his grasp. It felt like the whole thing would shatter if he pulled to hard. But there was no time to be cautious.

Ellis ripped back on the trigger, the thing snapping under the pressure, but not before the hammer fell on the cartridge and the thing exploded in his grasp.

It backfired, spitting flame into his face. He threw his hands out to let go of it and shield himself.

He landed hard on his side. The only signifier that he'd hit his mark was Adams's ear-splitting cry – a long, sustained note of pain.

When Ellis managed to open his eyes, his fellow officer was flat on his back, a burning hole in his chest spitting red-hot flame twelve inches into the air above him. He clawed at it, the flesh on his fingers sizzling and peeling as he tried desperately to dig the thing out.

But it was no good, and a few seconds later his scream faltered and died in his throat, his body convulsing as he went into shock. His face contorted repulsively, his lips peeling back over his teeth, hands locked like claws in the air above him. His back arched upwards, his muscles contracting involuntarily as the life slipped from him. A moment later, he slumped to the ground, the smell of burnt meat filling the basement.

Ellis grimaced, holding the back of his hand to his nose as he righted himself, supressing a gag as he looked at the two men he'd once called friends. 'Steph?' he called gently. 'Steph? We've got to go – the gunshots, neighbours will be calling the station, and—' His words petered out as he moved to the side of the stairs, seeing her sitting against the wall, holding her stomach, her shirt and hands soaked with blood. She looked up at him, blinking slowly.

Ellis fell at her side. 'No, no, no,' he muttered, pulling her hands away.

She winced, hissing in pain.

'Fuck, fuck,' he said, looking at the wound. Gut shot. Below the ribs on her right-hand side. Had to have hit an artery with this much blood. Liver maybe, kidney possibly. Perforated intestine or punctured stomach. Either way, it was fucking bad and the blood was pumping itself free of her body, her heart beating fast and erratic as the pressure dropped.

Ambulance? He had to, didn't he? Fuck! No, if he did, God, how would he explain this? Who would come? Would they even help her?

He turned and launched a punch into the floor, the pain reverberating through his fist and up his arm, tempering him, focusing him.

Steph's hand touched his arm then, grabbing it meekly. 'Hey,' she whispered.

He looked up, saw she was crying.

'Jacob,' she whispered, her voice catching in her throat. 'Find him. Make sure…' She winced again. 'Keep him safe. He needs… someone to…' She sighed, the strain of it too much. 'He needs… you. Please.' She mustered the strength to smile one last time. 'Help him,' she asked.

And then her eyelids fluttered, her breath halting in her chest before Stephanie Taylor fell still.

Ellis didn't need to check her pulse to know.

She was dead.

Chapter 47

As much as Ellis wanted to stay and mourn Stephanie, he knew that there was no time.

The shots would no doubt trigger people to call the police, and when Adams and Fitz didn't check in with the chief, who knew how many people would descend on this place. When that happened, Ellis couldn't be here.

He stood, turning away from the body, pausing before he even made it a single step. This would be swept under the carpet. The bodies gotten rid of, no doubt. The chief would want this cleaned up nicely, which meant that Steph would no doubt just disappear. And if Jacob made it through this, he'd never see her again.

He deserved better. And so did Steph. She'd given her life to save Ellis's, and her dying wish had been for him to help Jacob.

He couldn't leave her.

His truck was still outside, he just needed to get her there.

At this point, appearances didn't really matter. If someone saw him, what were they going to do? Call the cops?

He left the basement quickly, heading into the living room where there he'd seen a throw on the couch earlier that morning. He retrieved it and brought it down, stepping over Adams and Fitzhugh for the second time. He didn't notice it going up, but on the way back, Fitz's blood had spread all over the floor and the stench of Adams's charred torso smelled like barbequed vomit.

He stifled a gag, then went to Steph, pausing only for a second to pick up Fitz's fumbled pistol. He laid the throw on the floor and gently pulled Steph onto it. Her skin was still warm, her body limp and bloodied, her eyes staring at him while he did it. If he tried to close them now, they'd just pop open again. For about an hour after death, they'd do that. Until rigor mortis started setting in, at least.

It was the reason he covered her face first, bundling her up like a mummy before he hoisted her into the air – his head throbbing from the concussion as he did so – and carried her upstairs. He was more out of breath than he expected, his mind clouded by the head trauma. He got to the kitchen, panting, and had to get his bearings before he figured out which way to go. He gently shook his head, fighting the exhaustion that had started creeping in, and headed through the broken back door. The glass had been smashed, the door left ajar, and Ellis managed to hook his foot around it and open it without setting Steph down. Her blood was soaking the throw, and now his arms, but he ignored the cool wetness of it and pressed on, going down the steps and around the house to the front curb.

As he walked across the lawn, blood dripping from his hands, he saw some of the neighbours on their lawns. Others peeking through their windows.

He kept his mouth shut and his eyes fixed on his truck. No one screamed. No one said anything.

They recognised him, he was sure. He was six foot four inches, and one of only two black cops in town. And in one as small as Devils Lake, not many people didn't know every cop, every meter maid, and every bank teller. It helped him some, maybe made them think twice about what they were seeing. But either way, he didn't really give much of a shit.

He carried Stephanie Taylor's body to his truck and opened the back doors, placing her on the bench seat before he closed it and circled to the driver's side.

A woman came forwards from her lawn, wrapped in a dressing gown. 'Officer Ellis?' she called out.

Ellis ignored her.

'What's going on? What happened? Is that...? Is that Stephanie?' Her voice shook as she spoke.

Ellis glanced back at the woman. She was in her sixties, a frightened look on her face. 'Go back inside,' he said, his voice softer than he expected. 'The police are on their way.'

'Aren't...? Aren't *you* the police?' she asked, coming forwards another step.

He stopped, the door handle in his grasp, and looked back at her, then at the other people outside their homes, a look of fear in their faces. 'No,' he said, after a moment. 'I'm not. Not anymore.'

And then he climbed into his truck and started the engine, peeling out of there at speed, just as sirens began to rise in the distance.

Ellis drove quickly through town, not really thinking about where he was going, or what he was going to do next.

But when Steph's phone started ringing in her pocket, he was starkly reminded of the situation at hand. Jacob was out there, with Lily right now. And it was very likely him calling her. Jesus – he probably thought Ellis was still tied up in the basement and his sister was completely fine.

'Fuck!' he yelled, thumping his hand into the wheel. He took it in both hands and pulled at the thing, letting out a low, long shout of frustration.

This fucking town! These fucking people!

He put his foot down, putting as much distance between him and town as possible.

He'd fished a lot as a kid and there was a spot his dad used to take him – one that few people knew about. Even the locals here. A couple of guys in the know moored their boats there or pulled them up onto the beach. It was a quiet spot to figure out his next move.

His eyes were heavy as he drove, sleep licking at the corners of his vision. And when he refocused them, he was already there. Shit. He'd lost the last ten minutes of his life. That wasn't a good sign.

Gingerly, he lifted a hand and touched it to the top of his head, hissing at the pain. Fuck, how hard did Steph hit him?

The truck jostled into the dusty lot and he parked with the nose up against the trees nestled at the far end, laying his head back against the seat.

Think, Ellis. Think. How do you get out of this?

But the answer didn't come, just darkness instead.

And when he opened his eyes again, Steph's phone was ringing once more, and he had no idea how long he'd been asleep.

Chapter 48

Back in high school, if he'd got a blow to the head, they'd have tried to keep him awake. Told him not to sleep.

Now, he knew better. Sleeping off a concussion was the best way to heal.

Though he was far from that. His drowsiness had now turned into a pounding headache and mild disorientation. When he came to, he didn't know where he was. He looked around, expecting to see the inside of Stephanie Taylor's house. It was the last thing he remembered clearly – walking around there looking for Jacob… And then…

'Shit,' he said, blinking and rubbing his eyes. He pressed them into his skull with the heels of his hands. Why couldn't he remember? It played for him then like a slideshow. Jacob in the cupboard. Pain. Darkness. Coming to in the basement. A conversation with Stephanie. A sandwich. Hammering at the door. Fear. Adams and Fitzhugh. Upstairs. Jacob was free. Golf clubs. Fishing toolbox. A knife. A flare gun. He could see it in his hands. Steph Taylor under the stairs. Fitz and Adams coming down. The noise the five-iron made as it caved in Fitz's skull. Ellis shuddered. Adams shooting. Ellis shooting back. The flare burning in his chest. The ringing cry of pain he let out as he died.

Blood. His. Fitz's. Stephanie's. *Steph!* He sucked in a sharp breath, almost gagging on the smell.

He turned in the chair, the blood-soaked blanket in the back seat no more than a mass of crimson. The stench coming off it was thick, palpable. It was emanating in waves. The car was hot, the day was hot, and Stephanie's corpse was already turning, the body letting out everything inside it. Gas. Urine. Effluence.

Ellis gagged, putting his hand to his mouth. No. It was coming up. No stopping it.

He opened the door and emptied his stomach on the ground, choking on the smell in his nostrils.

'God,' he coughed. 'God fucking dammit!'

He slid from the driver's seat and collapsed to the floor, the tears coming before he could stop them.

He remembered now. What had happened. How it happened. What she'd said to him. What she'd asked him.

Ellis stayed there, letting out gentle sobs, his head in his hands, puke dripping down his chin.

The ringing in the cab stopped and Ellis looked up. Jacob calling. He couldn't ignore it forever, could he? No, he owned the man that. He had to know the truth. But it had to be face to face. He deserved that much.

Ellis lifted himself off the ground, sweating in the summer heat, and turned back to the open door. His uniform and badge were folded on the passenger seat. When he'd gone to the station last night, he hadn't known if he'd need them.

Now he didn't think he'd ever need them again.

The phone started ringing for a second time and Ellis opened the back door, gently unfurling Steph until he could get at her jeans.

He pulled her phone free and waited for it to ring off.

Grimly, he turned the screen towards her, then slid the device into her hand, moving her thumb until it triggered the sensor and unlocked it. Hopefully that was the first and last time he'd ever need to do that.

He opened her messages and typed one out quickly: *All ok. Meet me here.*

He hit send and then navigated to the map app, grabbing his location and pinging it across to Jacob. What the hell he was going to say when the man arrived, he didn't know.

The truth, he guessed. It was all he could say.

Adams and Fitz had come to the house. He'd done his best to save them both, but Steph had got shot.

And there wasn't a scratch on him from the exchange.

Jesus, he hated this. It wasn't the first time he'd had to tell a family member that a loved one was dead, but it never got easier. That was part of the job when he'd done that. But this was different. This was harder. This time, he could have done better, could have stopped it. God, he *should* have done better. Never should have made Steph use the knife. He should have let her hide. And he should have dealt with it.

But it was done now, and the only thing he could do was uphold Steph's dying wish. Help Jacob. And Lily, he guessed. Help them... expose the farm? He didn't even know. But whatever it was, he'd do it.

This madness, this violence, this death? It had to stop.

And he would stop it.

But first... he needed to get Steph out of the truck. He couldn't just leave her in there. No, he needed to find a good spot. Somewhere calm, somewhere pretty so that when Jacob saw her, she wasn't just wrapped in a bloody rag in the back seat of a 2006 Tacoma.

He steadied himself and tugged Steph towards him by the ankles, feeling the stiffness in her body. He couldn't have been out more than an hour or two, but rigor mortis set in pretty quick and would last for almost a day. He'd have to be careful sitting her up. Careful not to break any of her bones.

With that thought in mind, he carried her, stiff as a board, down to the water, letting the throw fall from her body, and waded in up to his knees.

The water was cool and clear, a gentle green hue to it this morning. Ellis stared down at Stephanie Taylor and then gently lowered her into the lapping waves, letting the water wash over her body, her arms, her hands. He sat backwards so that she was across his lap, and carefully cleaned the blood from her as best he could, a painful ache throbbing in the back of his throat as more tears threatened to come.

'You deserved better,' he muttered. 'Better than me.' He closed his eyes, feeling the sun hot on his neck and Stephanie's body heavy in his arms. 'I'm sorry,' he whispered. 'I'm sorry for everything.'

Chapter 49

Ellis set Steph against a tree overlooking the lake and headed back towards the truck, wiping his knuckles across his cheeks. The salty water stung his eyes, but he didn't care. He deserved the hurt.

He got halfway before a dusty Subaru turned into the dirt lot of the fishing spot.

Ellis froze and ducked into the trees about ten feet shy of his front bumper, crouching out of sight behind the scrub. He wasn't absolutely sure it was Jacob – he never texted back and Ellis had no way of knowing if the chief or anyone else had caught up with him.

The car stopped next to his truck and the engine died. Ellis held his breath.

Jacob Taylor stepped out and went to his Tacoma, cupping his eyes against the window to look in the front.

'Steph?' he called out, walking away.

Ellis stayed quiet, mustering what little strength he had left.

He was about to reply when Lily Graham got out of the passenger seat and followed Jacob.

He called out again. 'Steph?'

The longer Ellis left it, the worse it would be. He drew one last breath and came out of the bushes, hands raised to show he meant no harm. He'd gone back to the truck before putting Steph to rest, left Adams's pistol in the cab, taken another long look at his badge and uniform.

Now, he was unarmed, walking towards Jacob.

He heard the brush crack under Ellis's feet and turned. 'Steph!'

Seeing Ellis, his face dropped.

'Where's Steph?' he asked.

Ellis swallowed the lump in his throat. 'Let me explain, okay?' he said, trying to calm the situation before it escalated.

'Where's my sister?' Jacob demanded.

Ellis felt his fingers begin to tremble. 'I'm so sorry, Jacob,' he said. 'I didn't mean to...' *Get her killed*, he wanted to say. But the words wouldn't come. 'I didn't mean to... Okay? I didn't mean to—'

'Didn't mean to *what*?' Jacob snapped. 'Where is Steph? Where is my sister?'

All his words left him. The pain in Jacob's face was so stark, even before Ellis said anything. He already knew. 'She's... She's dead,' he said, finally.

Silence fell like a curtain around them. The lake seemed to hold its breath, the gentle lap of the waves stopping, the breeze halting, the trees falling still all around them.

Jacob just stood there, staring at him.

'Please,' Ellis said, tears forming at the corners of his eyes. 'Say something...'

Jacob's mouth opened but no words came.

Lily, who'd been standing, facing the other way the entire time, turned and stepped next to him, leaning over his shoulder on her tip toes until her lips were a few inches from his ear. She said something, but Ellis didn't hear. Couldn't hear. He was transfixed by her – not by her beauty or anything as human as that. But by the cold fucking look in her eye. Like a viper lying in wait for an unsuspecting rat. And those eyes were homed in on Ellis. Zeroed on him. He could already feel her fangs in his skin.

She whispered something else. He didn't hear what, he just watched. Could only watch. Watch as she put a hand behind her back and pulled a pistol free – *his* pistol – and pushed it into Jacob's hand. Her fingers closed around his knuckles and guided the weapon upwards until it was aimed right at him, her eyes never leaving his. A flicker of something in them sent a shockwave through his system. Fear. The rat seeing the viper for the first time. He'd seen that look once before, and it wasn't during the course of his career. It was the two days earlier. At the farm. The same flash he'd seen in David Hall's eyes he was seeing in Lily Graham's now. A look that told him one thing: they didn't see themselves as the same species that Jacob and Ellis were. No. They were nothing but prey. Not to be cared about, or cried over. Just animals to be slaughtered when the time came.

Ellis swallowed, staring into the chasm of his own demise. 'I...' he tried to say, but the word died in his mouth. Ground out under the heavy bootheel of Lily's gaze. There was nothing he could say. Nothing that would change what happened next.

He caught snatches of her whispers to Jacob.

'He did it,' she said. 'He killed her.'

Jacob closed his eyes.

'Look at him!'

Jacob's eyes opened.

'Do it,' Lily said. 'He deserves it. Pull the trigger, Jacob. Kill him.'

Jacob was shaking.

'Do it! Do it!'

Ellis didn't hear the shot.

Just saw the flash and felt the blow.

It hit him in the middle of the chest, staggering him.

All the air left his lungs at once and he let out a sharp heaving whine as he toppled backwards, the only thing crossing his mind as he did was relief. Relief that he no longer had to look Lily Graham in the eye.

He saw the canopy above, light splintering through the trees, white and pure as he'd ever seen.

There was peace in him for a moment. Everything was still.

And then he hit the ground, raking in little, gasping breaths, the pain radiating from the centre of his chest in great, sharp waves.

There was a deep ringing in his ears, the heavy beating of his heart punctuating it.

He just watched the light, trying not to think about it. Think about what just happened.

Distantly, he heard voices, indistinct. Someone yelled. Ellis flinched a little.

Then footsteps, a car door. A car engine. The rumble of tires on stones, a car turning, then driving away.

It faded to nothing and the ringing returned, filling his ears, his mind, his whole world, building to a rushing crescendo that felt like it was going to burst his ear drums.

And that's how he stayed, drowned by the dappled summer light on the shore of Devils Lake.

Chapter 50

When Jacob Taylor finally peeled himself out of the dirt, he was alone.

Lily was long gone, and Todd Ellis was lying on his back fifteen feet away.

Jacob looked at Ellis, and grimaced. A few days ago, Jacob had never so much as been in a fight in his life. And now he'd claimed one – no, *two* lives. He was fairly sure that the man he'd tackled down the stairs at the farm had died then and there. And maybe it was even three, if the guy he'd shot in the fields hadn't made it. That thought turned him sick.

But the thing that was crushing him was the thought that Steph was gone. He didn't know how, or where, but he knew she was dead. And even though he'd exacted his revenge, it made him feel no better. If anything, he felt worse.

He'd claimed another life, and for what? He thought of Lily. Of how twisted she'd gotten him. How, from the moment she'd seen him, she'd manipulated him. Going home with him, the bathroom door staying open as she stripped off, crawling into bed with him, seducing him? All while she knew what he was to her. Jacob shuddered. It may have been chance that brought them together, but he was nothing more than a mark to her – someone to con to get what she wanted. And didn't she have it in spades? She wanted carnage, death, destruction, for this town, for the farm to rip itself apart. Well, she was well on her way. Jacob was just glad he was out of it now. Out of her clutches and...

He looked around. Alone. No Lily. No Steph. No one.

He was more alone than he'd ever been in his life, and he had no idea what to do.

Miles from town, the only thing he could do was take Ellis's truck. The keys must be on him, Jacob surmised. He sighed, tired of grimacing, and walked over slowly, kneeling next to Ellis and feeling his pockets for them.

Suddenly, Ellis's hand shot out and grabbed Jacob's arm.

He let out a strangled squeak and fell backwards as Ellis keeled onto his side and groaned.

'What the fuck!?' Jacob yelled, clutching his chest, his heart pounding.

Ellis coughed and raked in a few shallow breaths.

'You're fucking alive?' Jacob asked, though the question seemed a little moot. He grabbed Ellis by the shoulder and pulled him onto his back, searching for the bullet-hole.

Ellis's shirt had a hole in it, right in the middle of the chest, but Jacob could see now that it wasn't bare skin beneath it. He was wearing a ballistic vest.

Jacob had seen him on duty wearing it before. But he wasn't in his uniform now – still, he had the good sense to put it on. He was both relieved and livid at the revelation, but Ellis was coming around, already muttering, already saying something.

Jacob didn't want to hear it, whatever it was.

'—didn't do it,' he coughed. 'I didn't kill Steph.' He hacked, and then pulled himself upright, catching his breath.

'What did you say?'

'I didn't kill her,' Ellis muttered, spitting between his knees. A long strand of saliva clung to his lips. 'It was Adams. Or Fitzhugh.' His breath was laboured, wheezing. Though Jacob figured that getting shot in the chest would do that to you. Ellis looked up at him then. 'I tried to save her,' he said. 'I'm sorry. I'm so sorry.'

Jacob searched his face for any hint of a lie, but found none.

'I saved you in that cell,' he said, rubbing his sternum. 'Left the door open, tossed our phones out so you could get away... You know I did.'

Jacob stared at him. Did he know that?

'Your sister cut me free to help stop Adams and Fitz. I should have done more, but I couldn't...'

Jacob swallowed the bile rising in his throat. 'Where is she?' he asked, his voice thin and harsh.

Ellis turned his head, looking down the shore, and lifted a hand.

Before he'd said anything, Jacob was up and running. His apology could wait.

He found Steph a moment later, sitting against the trunk of a tree, looking out at the water. It looked like she was sleeping and he couldn't help but collapse to his knees next to her and shake her. 'Steph?' he asked. 'Steph? Wake up.'

She was cold and stiff under his hands.

Ellis managed to walk over, but he didn't say it. Didn't say the obvious.

Jacob knew she was dead.

He held her hands, folded on her lap, and leaned forwards until he hunched over, head resting on her knuckles. He remained there for a while, sobbing gently as Ellis stood by, watching.

Why was he even there?

Jacob looked around, seeing the man standing with his hands clasped in front of him, like he was paying his respects.

The reality of it dawned on Jacob then. 'What are we going to do with her?' He looked at his sister. Calling the cops or an ambulance would only lead them right to Jacob and Ellis. And he was *not* leaving her.

'What do you want to do with her?' Ellis asked.

Jacob's brow crumpled. 'Why are you even still here?'

'Your sister asked me to make sure you made it out of this. She asked me to keep you safe. It was the last thing she asked.'

Jacob clenched his teeth together to stop his lip from quivering. He swallowed painfully and cleared his throat. 'I don't know what to do,' he said.

'We should bury her,' Ellis said after a moment. 'Is that okay?'

Jacob looked at his sister, thinking about it. Then he nodded.

'Do you know somewhere you'd like to do that?'

He thought for a second, then nodded. 'Yeah, I do.' His eyes traced the shoreline to the skiffs pulled onto the beach. 'Can we get any of those boats going?'

'Why?' Ellis asked.

Jacob looked out across the water. 'My parents' place is out there,' he said. 'And our place is, too.' He glanced back at Steph, and then up at Ellis. 'Will you help?'

Ellis stared down at him. 'Yeah, I'll help. You want to stay with her while I get a boat?'

Jacob nodded, watching the man go. Wondering whether he was telling the truth, whether he could trust him.

He squeezed his sister's cold hand. Steph had trusted him, and it got her killed.

But did he have another choice?

He wouldn't make it on his own, and he didn't want to spend his life running.

As much as it frightened him, he knew one thing: that he'd have to finish this. Some way, somehow. For himself. For Steph. For his mother.

And for all the girls the farm and that freak in the bedroom had claimed over the years.

As the dim chug of an outboard rang in the air, a fire kindled deep in the pit of Jacob's stomach, stoking itself to life.

He was so sick and tired of being scared.

For once in his life he wanted to do something. To make all of this, all the pain, all the hurt, mean something.

Just once.

'You ready?' Ellis asked, coming back over.

Jacob took a final look at his sister, his hand leaving hers for the last time, and stood up. 'Yeah,' he said, turning to Ellis and drawing a deep breath. 'I'm ready.'

Chapter 51

The breeze on the water helped to move some of the smell away from them. Steph was lying in the bottom of the craft, arms folded, knees tucked gently to her chest. Like a child, asleep. At least that was how Jacob forced himself to think of it every time he glanced back at her. He sat at the front of the boat, looking forwards while Ellis was at the back, manning the motor.

Ellis had grown up on the water, and had learned to fix outboards pretty early. And that kind of knowledge came with the knack to get them going without keys if it came to it. Whose boat this was, neither of them knew. But they were a little past caring about something as petty as boat theft.

The lake was expansive and everyone else was out, either enjoying their Sunday afternoon fishing or water skiing, or just generally lounging in the sun, and had no idea what was going on right under their noses. That the skiff skimming across the lake right now wasn't a pleasure craft, but a water-bound hearse.

Every now and then, Jacob looked back and gestured for Ellis to course correct one way or the other.

Neither talked much, but as they cruised closer to shore, Ellis let the motor settle and their speed drop a little.

'What happens after, Jacob?' he called over the din of the engine.

Jacob turned back slowly. 'What do you mean?'

'Steph told me to make sure you were safe. I want to talk about what that looks like. If you'll excuse the pun – we're in the same boat right now.'

'How do you figure?' It was everything he had not to look at his sister.

'What I did to Adams and Fitz… Freeing you… I've crossed the chief once to many, I think.' He let that sink in for a moment. 'I'm going to leave town. You should come, too.'

'No,' was the only thing he said, turning back to the lake.

'I don't think you understand what's at stake here. Your sister told me to—'

'But she's dead, isn't she?' He looked at Ellis again and he eased off the motor all together. The boat rocked gently, slowing in the salty water. 'If you want to go, then go. I'm not stopping you.'

'But you're not coming with me?'

'No.'

'Why not?'

'Can you just drive the boat, please?' Jacob asked curtly. He was keen to get this done and not sit here in the middle of the lake arguing over his sister's dead body.

'Not until you give me a good reason. Or I'm going to have to handcuff you and take you with me anyway.'

Jacob growled under his breath and turned back. 'Because this whole thing is fucked, alright? My entire life's been set on fire, and for what? So some wiry old fuck with a Viagra addiction can get his rocks off any time he pleases? Have you been up there? Have you *seen* what they're doing? What *he's* doing? To them?'

Ellis looked him dead in the eyes. 'Tell me — what happened? With Lily? What did you see?'

He looked back at Ellis. 'Drive the boat and I will.'

Ellis took the deal, cranking up the outboard once more.

Jacob switched seats, moving back a bench so that he was sitting next to Steph. As much as he wanted to avoid this, he couldn't. And she was a good reminder of why he was so angry, of what he needed to do.

'Lily isn't who I thought she was,' Jacob started.

'What do you mean?'

He wasn't about to tell Ellis the truth — not the whole truth, anyway. 'She lived there. At the farm. As a kid. She escaped with her mother, but her mother died. They killed her. And she's been plotting her revenge ever since.'

Ellis kept his eyes on Jacob but said nothing.

'I went to find her this morning, and someone from the farm had trashed her motel room. I thought they might have taken her, so I went out there to find her, and...'

'And what?' Ellis seemed to sense how hard it was for Jacob to say. He spoke softly, not rushing him.

'And it's fucked.' Jacob shook his head. 'They've got girls chained up in the barns, and they were doing this fucking... ritual in the house. God, I don't fucking know, alright?' He was gesticulating now, too. 'All I know is that it's all fucked up and those goddamn people... That fucking guy, the one in charge, the one I saw... He... They just can't keep getting away with it. I can't just turn my back on this.'

Ellis's keen eyes didn't miss anything. 'Why is this so important to you? What stake do you have in this? Lily abandoned you on the beach. It didn't seem—'

'You don't know what happened. Not today, not twenty-five years ago. You don't know shit.'

'Twenty-five years ago?' Ellis looked deep in thought for a second. 'This have something to do with your mother?'

'What do you know about that?' Jacob snapped.

'Only what I looked up after we arrested you. I looked into you, your sister, your family. Father, deceased. Mother reported missing, never found, declared dead three years later.' Ellis chewed his lip. 'Was she there? At the farm?'

Jacob tried not to flush but he couldn't help it. Ellis was smart, and he was erring dangerously close to the truth.

'I don't know. I think so,' he said quickly. 'But even if she wasn't, then I'd still want to do something about it.'

'You don't need to be a hero, Jacob.'

'If not me, then who? I don't see people lining up to do something about it.'

Ellis sighed. 'What about Lily? What's she liable to do?'

'Burn it to the ground.'

'Metaphorically?'

Jacob shook his head.

'That's what I was afraid of,' Ellis said. 'If she doesn't get herself killed, she's going to hurt a lot of people.'

'Good riddance,' Jacob muttered.

Ellis seemed less keen on the idea of wanton destruction and death. 'You said they had women locked up there? Prisoners?'

'Yeah, there was a woman in the field, she asked for my help...' Jacob's face contorted in shame. 'I couldn't help her.'

Ellis took that in slowly. He looked conflicted. 'What do you suggest? What's your plan?'

He could only shrug. 'Save them. Many as I can, I guess.'

'And what about Lily?'

'What about her?'

'Do you care what happens to her?'

'She's my—' Jacob cut himself off before he finished that. 'She's… on her own path. She's not right. You heard her on the beach, right?'

He was searching for reassurance.

'I heard. I saw,' Ellis said. 'Would you have pulled that trigger if she wasn't there?'

Jacob didn't answer right away. 'You didn't kill Steph. I was wrong to shoot you.'

Ellis seemed to accept that in lieu of an apology, smiling briefly before he spoke again. 'I still stand for something, Jacob. The badge. Justice. Whether the others do or not. It means something to me. I can't stand by and let Lily kill people. Not if I can help it at least. But I also can't stand by and let the farm, the chief, carry on like this, doing what they're doing. You say there are women being imprisoned there, then we'll free them. But as for the others… If I can, I'll bring them in. Make them pay for their crimes the right way. No one dies if they don't have to.'

Jacob turned back to the water, taking in the growing shore. 'Three people. Three different plans. Lily wants to kill them. I want to save them. And you… You just don't want anyone to get hurt.' He tutted and shook his head.

'What is it?' Ellis called from the back of the boat, guiding them towards the edge of the lake.

'Nothing,' Jacob replied, laughing sardonically. 'It's just…' He turned back to Ellis, seeing a fool at the wheel. 'You're a bit fucking late.'

Chapter 52

They buried Steph where the water meets the sky.

It was the clearing in the trees that bordered the water they'd played in as kids. That he'd met Lily in. That he and Steph had always treasured as their own special place. And it felt right. Jacob gave Ellis directions to get to his place through the woods, and sent him to fetch a couple of shovels.

By the time Ellis got back, Jacob had already selected a spot and brought Steph over. Jacob also asked Ellis to get something to wrap her in, and Ellis had grabbed the only thing he could, the padded blanket Jacob kept in the car port for when he was working on his truck.

They carefully bundled Steph in it and set to work, the afternoon wearing on as they worked, their sweat dotting the dry earth. The shovels made light work of it, and when they finally had the hole done, they carried Steph over and laid her there together.

'Look,' Ellis said, pointing out to the water.

Jacob turned, knowing what it was before he even saw.

The lake had turned peaceful, as it often did in the afternoon, and as the sun sank lower, you couldn't tell where the water ended and the clouds began, the mirror image of sky and lake melded into one. 'Yeah,' he said, smiling a little, feeling Steph's warmth once more. 'I know.'

They carefully filled the hole in, covering Steph over and gently patting the earth flat.

'Do you want to say something, or—'

'No,' Jacob replied, leaning on his shovel. 'I'll come back and say something when we're done.'

'What if you don't make it back?' Ellis asked, eyeing him.

'Then I'll tell her in person.' Jacob leaned his shovel against a nearby tree and headed back towards the boat.

Ellis let out a long sigh and followed him. 'You even have a plan? You're walking like a man who doesn't care if he lives or dies,' he said, still trying to convince Jacob to rethink this.

'I got in once, I'll get in again,' Jacob said.

'You think they won't see you coming a second time?'

'I don't really care, I have to do something.'

'Wait!' Ellis grabbed his shoulder and Jacob turned, swatting his arm away. Ellis lifted his hands to show he meant no harm. 'I've been thinking – if we bust in there, then there's no hope of arresting anyone.'

'That's your problem, not mine.'

'What I'm saying is that if we can lure them away from the farm – or if I can – you'll have a better shot of saving the people locked up there.'

Jacob narrowed his eyes. 'What are you suggesting?'

'Jeff Harris, Devils Lake police chief. No doubt in my mind he wants my head on a spike. If I tell him where to find me, he'll come. And when he does…'

'I slip in the back?'

Ellis nodded.

Jacob had to admit, it didn't sound like a terrible idea. Ellis got to assume more of the risk and it'd give him the chance to do what he needed to. He didn't rightly care whether Ellis lived or died. Jacob stared at him and felt nothing. It was like someone had scooped everything out of him and dumped it into that grave with his sister. He was completely numb. He'd taken lives, and felt nothing. He looked at the ground, feeling the weight of it on top of him, suddenly. Like he was in a grave, too. Did he even care if *he* lived or died? He didn't think so. Before the night was out, blood would be spilled. His. Others. He didn't know. He didn't care.

'Guns,' he said then. 'Bolt cutters, too.' He looked up at Ellis. 'You have them?'

'I have Adams's pistol, a .38 special, at home. A .338 Win Mag, Kimber 8400. And a Remington .870 Express. For turkeys.'

Jacob listened to the list. He wasn't a hunter himself. Hadn't ever much liked the idea of killing things. But now he wondered if it was enough. It'd have to be, he supposed. 'Okay. Let's go.'

Ellis folded his arms. 'They'll be watching my place, no doubt.'

'Then we should be careful.' With that, he strode past Ellis and climbed back into the boat. 'Come on, it's a big fucking lake, and it's getting late.'

Ellis huffed a little and then pushed the boat back off the shore, hopping in as it hit the water, causing it to rock heavily. He didn't seem wholly pleased about his armoury being raided, but Jacob didn't really care. He wasn't going in there unarmed.

'What about Lily Graham?' Ellis asked as he brought the motor to life and guided them towards open water.

'What about her?'

'What happens if we run into her?'

Jacob had been wondering that himself.

'Is she included in your list of people to save?' Ellis said, twisting the handle and opening the throttle. The boat dipped backwards and moved through the water, picking up speed.

Jacob didn't have an answer to that.

'You said she grew up there, and coming back, wanting to do what she's gearing up for... She needs as much help as anyone else. Just because she's not chained up in the barn, doesn't mean she's not still a prisoner of that place.'

'Thanks, Freud,' Jacob said, deflecting the question.

'So what are you going to do?'

'Jesus, I don't fucking know, alright? If you're so concerned, why don't you arrest her, too, huh?'

'She has already killed two people,' Ellis reminded him.

'They had it coming.'

'Still... she's dangerous. If you see her, watch your back.'

'Thanks for the advice,' Jacob replied, as sarcastically as he could. But the truth was that Ellis was right. Lily had given Jacob a choice – with her, or against her. And he'd pretty well made his choice. If he did cross her path at the farm, was she liable to shoot first and ask questions second? Jacob didn't know what he wanted to happen to her – she'd killed two men, sure. But if she was going to kill more, and if she succeeded, what then? Just let her go on her merry way?

Ellis was right about that, too. She did need help. And as much as Jacob wanted to just drink the memory of her out of his mind forever, he knew he couldn't. And if she really was his sister, then she was the only family he had left in the world. He couldn't see a future where they spent Christmas together, but, hell, she did need help. Real help. In a place where she could be kept safe, and other people could be kept safe from her. She was unhinged. He knew that much. So what would he do if he saw her? He doubted he could talk her off the ledge she was on, and letting her get herself killed seemed like a neat ending, but one he didn't know if he could live with.

'You look like you're wrestling with something,' Ellis offered, watching Jacob closely.

Jacob looked up at him, sick of the attention, sick of Ellis's prodding, prying questions. 'Just drive the fucking boat,' he growled, turning his back on the man.

But, no matter how much he focused his eyes on the distant shore, he could still feel Ellis's eyes on his back, and Lily's claws sunk deep into his brain.

He had no idea how the night ahead was going to unfold, but there was one truth he couldn't ignore. Before the sun rose tomorrow morning, blood would be spilled. And lots of it.

The question was: whose blood would it be?

Chapter 53

When they finally got back to shore, the day was fading into evening.

The landscape was flat and expansive, and it took a long time for night to fall. They still had hours of light left, but the sun was already sinking lower, taking on a dimmer, warmer hue. It was glowing orange in the west, the air thickening with the humidity that came around this time every day. Any wind that had been blowing across the water had now died and the chittering of bugs became incessant.

They drove out of the lot by the lake in Ellis's Tacoma, and swarmed across the fields to their flanks, wheeling mindlessly, hurling themselves against the windscreen and grille.

The little pattering of their bodies against the glass was the only sound in the cab.

Ellis drove the speed limit, not keen on drawing attention to them. Or, maybe he just hoped the longer it took for them to get there, the longer Jacob would have to second guess his choices. There was little chance of that, though.

He was reflecting on it a lot. How he was likely walking to his own demise, and how that didn't seem to frighten him at all. There'd always been a part of him morbidly curious about what it'd be like to die. Losing both parents, never marrying, never having kids… he was going through the motions of life, not working towards anything. He never felt like there was that much to lose. He'd never put a gun in his mouth, never really thought about it, but he'd wondered what it'd be like if he just… went. If he just deleted himself from the earth, how far would those ripples reach? Now? Nowhere, he thought. Steph was the only one who would have cared, and now, she was gone. So what did it even matter if he died?

Especially if he did *one* thing that actually mattered. Saved someone. A few someones, if he was lucky.

He thought about that as he dug the dirt from Steph's grave out from under his fingernails and flicked it into the footwell of Ellis's truck.

They headed back into town, and although Ellis had his head on a swivel, Jacob felt almost relaxed. He watched the world go by, seeing Devils Lake in a new way. Like he was driving through it for the first time. He'd never really thought about how pretty it was, how quaint. How the tree-lined streets felt homely and welcoming. How the kids played hockey on the streets with their pull-out nets and rollerblades. How it felt like one of those places you might drive through on the way somewhere and think, you know what? I could live here.

Ellis guided them onwards until the houses just sort of *stopped* and gave way to the flat, open farmland, and straight roads that dwindled all the way to the horizon.

They drove another half mile until Ellis pulled off the road and slowed. They were on a dirt track that seemed to lead nowhere.

The trees closed in a little and Ellis pulled them up onto the grass so the truck was nestled gently off the track.

'You live here?' Jacob asked, looking around.

'No,' Ellis said, pulling his pistol from the space next to his seat and checking the magazine. 'I live about five hundred yards that way.' He nodded through the driver's window. 'My grandparents place – it's small, but it sits on a few acres.'

Jacob thought back to what Ellis had said. He thought there could be someone waiting for him there.

'We're going on foot,' he said. 'This is an access road to some farmland that borders the property. We can skirt it and get around behind the house. There's not many places for them to hide and I want to get a look at it before we go in. There are some trees on the driveway they could tuck behind, that'd give them the drop on anyone driving in the front. That's where I'd sit if I wanted to ambush someone.'

Jacob nodded slowly. Ellis had the training, but he was also smart. And he seemed to be more intent on getting out of this alive.

'You want to wait here?' Ellis asked. 'I'll get the guns and come back if you'd prefer?'

'No, I'll come with you,' Jacob said. 'Don't really want to be caught here unarmed if they have the same idea you did.'

'Okay, then.' Ellis chambered a round in the pistol and climbed from the cab.

Jacob did the same, looking around.

They were a good way from town, the building just rising in the distance, hazy and mottled by the humidity.

Ellis gave a low whistle, called Jacob with him, motioning him to crouch a little and stay close.

Jacob obliged and they followed the road on foot. Exposed to the sun, Jacob couldn't help but sweat, the heat of it licking at his skin as it trickled down his neck and back. When the wind died, the summer heat here really was oppressive.

Ellis skirted the boundary of his property, easing down into the trees beside the road and crossing into what had to be the outer edge of his land. They made a wide circle until they left the cover of the trees altogether and moved into the long grass and wildflower that bordered the farmed fields to the north of the couple of acres his house occupied.

Ellis lowered himself even more, skulking through the undergrowth until he drew level with the house. It was about two hundred yards straight across open ground, a modest two-bedroom with a set of glass doors leading out onto a deck facing the setting sun. Behind it were a separate garage and tractor shed. Its wooden exterior was faded, the shingles on the roof tattered with age. But Jacob could see it was taken care of – the lawn mown, the vegetable beds full with life, runner beans and tomatoes, what looked like garlic and onions. Ellis was the last person Jacob expected to have a green thumb, but as he looked at him, he realised he didn't really know a damn thing about the man other than he'd saved his life.

As Jacob rolled the incident in the cell over and over in his mind, he came to accept that fact. Ellis had risked his own life to do that, and despite everything else that'd happened, he thought he was probably the only man in the world he could trust in that moment.

Chapter 54

'There,' Ellis said quietly, lifting a hand and pointing across the land.

Jacob followed, spotting what Ellis had rightly predicted. An old F100 pick-up was parked with the bed against a wall of trees that blocked the view of the house from the road. The driveway swept past it, and Jacob thought you'd completely miss the truck until you'd already passed it. Which was why they picked it.

'Can you see how many guys?' Jacob asked.

'Uh-uh,' Ellis replied. 'But it's a single-cab, so I'd guess two, three at the most. But they'll be cosy if it's three. Shit!' Ellis lowered himself quickly and Jacob followed suit as a figure appeared from behind the house.

A tall guy in a faded cream cowboy hat sidled into the open, a hunting rifle over his shoulder, and stopped, looking around.

Jacob dared to lift his head a little to look. The guy'd been doing a lap of the house, it looked like. And though Jacob'd never met him, he recognised him right away. It was Aaron, the guy who'd greeted Lily at the gate her first time to the farm. And the guy that was apparently watching over the girl chained up in the barn.

He stared around, his eyes sweeping the perimeter before he spat on the ground and started another lap, heading out to the perimeter to their right, and then moving left towards the truck.

He neared it, and then approached, leaning on the open driver's windowsill. A man inside handed him a cigarette and lit it, and they both remained there, smoking for a few minutes.

There was no cover from where they were crouched to the house, except for the vegetable plot and an old planter that looked to be filled with blueberries.

'We've got to make a break for it,' Ellis said then.

'What?' Jacob questioned. It was a lot of open ground to cover, and whether he was non-plussed by the idea of not making it through the night, he didn't want to invite death on himself. And that seemed like what Ellis was suggesting.

'We've got to go now. We run for the garden, if they fire, we'll return it, and then we break for the house. Ready?'

'No,' Jacob said.

But Ellis didn't seem to hear him. Or care about the answer.

He took off before Jacob could say anything else, running full pelt across the grass.

Jacob went after him, immediately regretting not staying in the truck now.

A shout echoed from across the lawn and Jacob turned his head to see Aaron cursing and swinging his rifle off his shoulder.

He levelled it and fired, the bullet ripping through the air above Jacob's head.

Instinctively, he ducked and stumbled, clawing his way forwards as Ellis slid into cover behind the planter and drew his own pistol.

Aaron chambered another round, kneeling and shouldering the rifle a second time as the other guy climbed from the truck and drew it, firing through the gap between the frame and the door.

Jacob swore, diving forwards now as little spurts of dirt erupted around him, the bullets finding the ground at his feet as they tried to bring him down.

More shots echoed, then – sparks dancing off the hood of the truck as Ellis fired back.

The guy with the pistol ducked behind the door and Aaron scrambled sideways behind a tree, giving Jacob enough time to crawl behind the planter, too.

He was out of breath, panting, reminded starkly that he'd let his cardio go to shit.

Ellis was already sizing up the house.

It was about fifty feet away, no more, but with two people firing at you fifty feet would feel like five hundred.

The two men were yelling at each other now, chastising one another for not seeing them sooner, not being prepared.

They were a good hundred feet away, and from that range, a pistol wouldn't be too effective, and the driver clearly didn't have much faith in Aaron. The car door slammed closed as he climbed back into the cab and cranked the engine, spraying dirt into the trees behind him as he stomped on the gas.

Jacob watched him come, Aaron breaking from cover and running behind the truck as it came closer.

'Fuck,' Ellis growled. 'Take this – cover me.' He shoved the pistol into Jacob's hands before he could say anything and pushed himself to his feet.

'But—'

'Shoot!' Ellis ordered him, leaping into space and sprinting towards the house.

He turned, resting his elbows on the planter and started firing. One, two, three bullets into the front of the truck. Steam started hissing from the grille. He hit the radiator but it wouldn't do much to stop him.

He blinked, the sweat from his brow running into his eyes, stinging them as he sighted up the driver through the windscreen and fired again, another two bullets. They punched through, spider's webs lancing through the glass around the holes.

The truck swerved and the driver hammered on the brakes, forcing it to slide and turn sideways, no more than twenty feet from them.

The driver didn't seem to be hit or dead, however, and a few seconds later was out of the cab once more, resting his arms on the hood of the truck, putting bullets into the planter.

Jacob ducked back behind it, feeling it shudder with each hit, the blueberry bush shedding berries with every round.

There was a louder shot then, the rifle. The heavier calibre punched a hole right through the bush, spraying Jacob with leaves. He swore, twisting and squirming down onto his back as another rifle round ploughed through the planter six inches outside his shoulder. It blew a hole straight through the wood, spraying the ground with soil and splinters.

'Fucking hell!' Jacob yelled, holding the gun over his head and firing blindly back.

The onslaught ceased for a moment, but no more before the shooting kicked up again.

He looked towards the house, seeing no sign of Ellis. God damn it, had he abandoned him? Left him there to die? Just run off and—

Before he could finish the thought, the patio doors exploded in a shower of shards and a heavy boom echoed across the fields.

Shouts of alarm flew from the two men at the truck and Ellis stepped through the doorway and onto the deck, the .870 Express in his hands. It looked small, but Jacob knew it packed a hell of a punch, and from twenty-five feet, it'd put a big fucking hole in whatever he aimed at.

He pumped the weapon and let another set of shot fly, blowing out the fat off-road tyre on the truck.

It sagged heavily, losing six inches, exposing the top of the driver's head over the other wheel.

He turned just in time to watch Ellis pull the trigger for a third time.

The buckshot ripped across the hood, digging into the steel and punching two-dozen steel ball bearings into his skull.

He let out a sharp, curtailed scream and spun to the ground out of sight.

Aaron had to know he was outgunned and outmanned now. His rifle was a big gun, but in tight quarters like this he'd have to stand out of cover, bring the rifle up, sight Ellis, and fire. And he'd only have one chance.

Ellis on the other hand might as well have been wielding a fire-hose of death as he strode across the deck with the gun shouldered.

He wasn't going to wait for Aaron to grow a pair, and he put another dose of buckshot into the cab of the truck, bursting the passenger window and frightening the shit out of the man.

Jacob heard the words 'Fuck this!' echo from behind the F100 as Aaron turned and made a break for it. He launched himself into open space and started running, headed for the main road, and freedom. Ellis stopped, watching Aaron go, and lowered the shotgun.

He's going to let him go, Jacob thought, watching him.

Ellis seemed to consider it and took a breath, the distance stretching out. And then he decided, brought the gun to his shoulder and pulled the trigger.

Fire lanced from the muzzle. The shotgun ejected the spent casing over Ellis's shoulder while the shot tore the summer air in two and buried itself in Aaron's back, flinging him forwards off his feet, sending his cowboy hat spinning in the air.

He landed heavily, sliding to a halt on the grass, and lay still.

From that range, no more than fifty feet, getting hit with a dose of buckshot was lethal. If it was 00 buckshot then each ball bearing was over 8mm in diameter. The spread was tight, especially off an .870. Enough to take Aaron off his feet. Enough to punch a big fucking hole through his spine and ribcage. If he wasn't dead already, he would be soon.

Buckshot was designed to take down a buck at forty yards.

Aaron didn't stand a chance.

Ellis lowered the shotgun and scanned the area for anyone else. When silence returned to the fields, he turned and headed towards Jacob, offering a hand and pulling him up from behind his destroyed planter.

'I thought you wanted to arrest them?' Jacob asked, dusting himself off.

Ellis grumbled. 'I did. But then they fucked up my blueberries.'

Jacob couldn't help but laugh, a single bright spot in an otherwise endless day.

'What do we do now?' He looked around at the steaming truck, the two dead bodies.

Ellis seemed to think on that for a while. 'First I'm going to eat,' he said, sighing. 'And then we're going to finish this.'

Chapter 55

Jacob stepped through the broken patio door of Ellis's house and into an interior not unfamiliar to him.

Ellis said he'd inherited the place from his grandparents – and, like Jacob's own house, the place was a time capsule, just with a little more taxidermy. Hunting was obviously a big deal in the family. In the middle of the living room was an elk's head, its antlers all but touching the ceiling.

'Shot that when I was twelve,' Ellis said. 'With my grandpa.' He paused to look at it wistfully. It told Jacob that they were no longer around, that he missed them. And that Ellis was a crack shot.

'You still hunt a lot?' Jacob asked.

'Not so much since my grandpa died,' Ellis replied, moving on towards the kitchen. He stopped, looking back. 'But I can still shoot. If that's what you were worried about.'

'I gathered,' Jacob said, following him.

Ellis fixed some leftovers from the fridge, some roasted meat. And they ate in silence, both of them thinking about what was to come. Jacob watched Ellis, chewing slowly. He didn't seem too fazed by what was coming. But Jacob couldn't stop thinking about it. The reckless abandon he'd felt earlier had somewhat faded. Bullets flying past your head would do that to you, he thought. But he still felt the undeniable pull of the farm. The deep-seated desire to return there, to liberate those who were trapped. His mother had been just a few miles from him for years – a decade after Jacob thought she was dead. And what had he done? Drank and smoked his twenties away, living in their house, wallowing in misery. He didn't so something then, but he would now. It wouldn't make up for it. But it was something. And something was better than nothing.

'You can take my truck,' Ellis said, then.

Jacob looked at him.

'I'll call the chief once you're gone.'

'Thanks,' Jacob said. 'You think he'll come alone?'

'I doubt it,' Ellis said.

'How're you going to do it? Arrest him, I mean.'

'Hopefully without firing a shot.'

'You think it'll go down that way?'

Ellis put down his knife and fork, looking like he'd lost his appetite. 'I don't know. I doubt it.'

'You want me to stick around? We could face them together.'

A flicker of a smile played across Ellis's face. 'No, but I appreciate it. You've got your own war to fight, right?'

Jacob nodded. 'I guess so.'

They finished their meals in silence and then stood up. It was getting dark now, the sun split in two by the horizon, a deep, bloody glow spread over the land.

Ellis disappeared into the attached garage for a second and then reappeared with his hunting rifle over his shoulder, motioning Jacob out onto the deck. 'Here,' Ellis said, picking up the Remington .870 Express from its position against the wall and handing it to him.

Jacob took it, the shotgun heavy in his grasp. 'You sure?'

'Yeah,' Ellis said. 'And keep hold of the .9, too. Take these.' He handed him a box of 9mm ammunition. 'You know how to load it?'

Jacob nodded, pocketing the small box of rounds, the pistol tucked in the back of his belt already.

'You should get going,' Ellis said then, looking up at the sky.

'I guess I should.' He lingered a little, building up to say something. 'I just want to say thanks.'

'For what?'

Jacob shrugged.

Ellis looked at him for a moment, then nodded.

They didn't need to say it, they both knew.

Ellis offered his hand and Jacob took it, the pair of them shaking like they'd likely never see each other again.

'Look after yourself,' Ellis said then, taking his truck keys from his pocket and tossing them in the air for Jacob. 'And try not to scratch the paint, eh?'

He afforded a small smile. 'I'll do my best. Bullet holes buff out though, right?'

Ellis smiled back and clapped him on the shoulder.

Without another word or look, Jacob turned and walked down off the deck, heading across the field towards Ellis's truck.

As he got to the trees, he knew he'd lose sight of Ellis, so he looked back once more, but the big man was gone.

Jacob let his eyes linger for a second longer, hoping to catch another glimpse of him. But it wasn't to be. This was now Jacob's task, and his alone. And with that thought weighing heavily in his mind, he turned to the shadow of the trees in front of him, and plunged into the darkness.

Chapter 56

Ellis turned back to the house and walked inside, pulling his phone from his pocket.

He took a deep breath and then called the chief.

He was surprised the chief hadn't been calling him. The reason for that, he wasn't sure. But either way, after the first ring, he answered.

'Ellis,' he said gruffly. He sounded tired, and pissed off. Losing two officers would do that.

Ellis needed to set him straight, feed him the story he wanted him to believe, and hope that he choked it down. 'Chief,' Ellis replied, 'sorry I haven't been in touch – I've been on Taylor's trail all day, hunting him down after what he did to Adams and Fitz.'

There was a long pause. 'You know about that?' the chief asked.

Ellis turned back to the deck, stepping slowly onto it, feeling the warmth of the sun on his face. Jacob was already out of sight and would be at the truck by now. 'Yeah,' Ellis said, hoping the neighbours hadn't ratted on him. 'I cruised by there, saw the lights, ambulances, saw them wheeling two body bags out. Saw Adams's car. I put two and two together.'

He harrumphed. 'Thought you went by there this morning to check if Taylor was there.' It wasn't even a question.

'I did,' he replied. 'Spoke to Steph Taylor, searched the house. There was no sign of him. He must have come back after I left.'

'Or you're just that fucking incompetent,' the chief replied.

Ellis gritted his teeth. 'What do you want me to do with Taylor? Put a bullet in him?'

'No,' the chief replied. 'Hold him. He killed Adams and Fitz. I want this to hurt.'

He hung up then and Ellis lowered the phone, sighing with relief as he looked out across his property. There were two bodies, along with the F100 that he should definitely move. The truck had a popped tire but it'd still roll. He'd stash it around back, throw the bodies in the bed, and—

A sudden flash caught his eye in a field off to his right.

He picked up his head, his brain not working fast enough to compute what it was before something hit him in the leg.

The force was enough to take him off his feet, sending him spinning to the ground. The sound came next, the pain third.

The report of a single rifle shot cut the air, reverberating in the thick air.

From the sound of it, he knew the calibre, knew it was a big fucking round. Big enough to put a serious hole in him.

He didn't need to look to see that, but he did anyway, and only saw red. His fingers were dug into his thigh, blood spilling through them. Ellis let out a low, sustained groan, forcing his mind to focus, for his eyes to focus. You've been shot, he told himself. Which means someone shot you. Which means you need to get the fuck up and move. You can't stay here. You need to get inside, you need to stop this bleeding, and you need to defend yourself.

Defend yourself.

Your rifle. Where's your rifle?

He looked round, lying flat on his back, and saw it off to his right, just out of arm's reach.

He stretched for it, fingers grazing the stock, the pain coming in waves now. It radiated up his leg like bolts of electricity, making his vision pulse black, his stomach turn nauseous.

'Come on!' he hissed, looking back at his leg, trying to use his other one to shimmy backwards, closer to the gun. The deck was soaked now. How much blood he'd lost, he didn't know. Too much, he thought.

'Fuck!' he spat flecks of saliva into the air as he reached for the gun once more, his fingers now closing around the wooden stock. A flood of relief hit him, but was quashed just as quickly as a boot appeared, standing on his rest, pressing down hard enough that his hand opened involuntarily.

Ellis looked up, seeing Chief Jeff Harris standing over him, hands on shoulders, his pudgy build and bald head shining in the sun. He had sweat on his forehead and was a little out of breath, like he'd been all but running to get there. He probably had. The shot had come from far enough away that Ellis saw the flash before he was hit. A few hundred yards, at least.

Ellis doubted Harris was the trigger man but had scarpered over here the second he'd gone down to have his revenge.

'You really think I'm that fucking stupid, *boy*?' Harris laughed, pressing harder on Ellis's arm.

He groaned in pain as Harris luxuriated in his victory. The man stooped and then crouched awkwardly, getting closer to Ellis.

'You've got balls, I'll give you that.' He laughed. 'And I expect it was you who killed Adams and Fitz, huh? Your brothers in blue.' He tutted. 'You can think I'd let that just slide, huh? I knew Taylor didn't have the spine or skills to pull something like that off. Hell, you shot Adams with a goddamn flare gun.' He laughed, bordering on impressed. 'Took a golf club to Fitz's skull. Jesus, that's some cold shit. It's a shame, really,' he said with a sigh. 'Could have used you – really used you, you know? You're big, you're fast, you're smart – okay, maybe not that smart, all things considered – but with a little guidance.' He made a fist and shook it gently. 'We could have had this town in the palm of our hand. Not meant to be, I guess.'

'If you're going to kill me,' Ellis spat, 'then just get it over with. I really don't want to keep listening to you talk.'

The chief squeezed his boot down harder and Ellis let out a sharp exhale of air. 'I ain't gonna kill you. Not here, not now at least. That'd be a waste, don't ya think?'

Ellis just stared up at him.

'No, you're coming for a ride,' he went on, removing his boot and kicking the rifle out of reach. He then dug the toe of his boot under Ellis's ribs and rolled him onto his front, roughly patting him down and stripping him of the .38 Special tucked in his belt.

Harris stood up labouredly and then called out to a second man, presumably the shooter, who'd now arrived. 'Get him up and in the truck,' he said gruffly. 'And make sure he doesn't bleed out before we get there – David's got big plans for him.' He laughed heartily, sadistically, even.

Ellis just closed his eyes and released the pressure he was putting on his wound, hoping, grimly, that he'd bleed out before that happened.

Chapter 57

Night was on him by the time Jacob rolled up the access road to the farm, his headlights off. He'd considered going through the woods again but figured they'd be on high alert regardless.

He wasn't quite sure what his plan was, but he knew that if he had any hope of liberating any of the people imprisoned at the farm, he wouldn't get very far without some sort of escape plan. And driving away seemed a hell of a lot better than running.

With Ellis's pistol in his lap and the shotgun on the seat next to him, he eased up the road, barely idling forwards in drive, searching the gate and the farm itself for signs of movement. Lights fixed to the barns threw a dim light on the courtyard, but nothing moved there. There was also a light at the front gate, but that seemed unmanned as well.

There'd be no one working the fields right now, but he still expected to see people outside. It was a warm summer evening, after all.

Jacob stared up at the farmhouse. A light was burning on the porch but otherwise it was dark.

His heart beat a little harder. If he could see people, he knew what he was walking into but there was nothing and no one to indicate what awaited him.

He couldn't drive any slower, but he was still making ground up on the gate, searching frantically for any hint of what the hell was going on.

By the time he got there, his heart was in his throat, the pistol in his hand, and his hand rested just below the sill of the window, ready to lift and fire at a moment's notice.

But there was no one at the gate.

There was no one *anywhere*.

Jacob let the engine idle for a moment before he got out, standing in the pool of light coming off the lamp positioned on a pole next to the gate post. The sign hanging on the pole said 'Welcome to Hall Farm – The only thing sweeter than our produce are our people!'

Jacob grimaced and stepped forwards to the gate. Hell, it wasn't even locked.

Gently, he unlatched it and swung it open, expecting at any moment to hear shouts and screams, footsteps, gunshots.

But there was nothing.

As he climbed back into the truck and started up the driveway, the stones crunching under the tires seemed deafening to him. Had everyone left? Had they vacated the entire property? Lily had killed two, Jacob one, Ellis four... Had they just cut their losses and moved on somewhere? Run before the state police or FBI showed up?

The thought kept cropping up in his mind, the eerie stillness of the place as oppressive as the summer heat.

He circled the farmyard and pulled up in front of the metal barn, the back of the truck pointed towards the doors. This is where Lily had said they were kept. Where the rest of them would be.

Jacob pulled the shotgun with him and held it in his hands as he walked across the empty yard towards the great double doors, unsure what he'd find, and unsure whether he was ready to find it.

Hello! Don't be scared, I'm here to save you. Is that the best he had? *Everyone, run towards the gate, I'll protect you?* Jesus, he had not thought this through.

He reached for the handle, his hand shaking, the distinct lack of any kind of chain or padlock making him even more uneasy. There was a thick latch, but it was open, hanging loosely.

The steel was cool to his touch as he took hold of the door, pulling to the right.

The slab moved on greased runners shifting easily and rolling away from its partner, exposing a dark, silent interior.

'Hello?' Jacob risked, keeping his voice low.

No response came.

He swallowed, gripping the shotgun tighter, and pushed the doors as wide as they'd go to let some light in, the dim lamps behind him casting a glow through the cavernous space.

Before him was a layout that looked more like a camp bunkhouse than anything else. Down the centre and along the walls there were bunk beds. Rows and rows of them with little bedside tables in between. Some had photographs or little ornaments on, others had clothing folded up, little pieces of jewellery, and some of them just stones or dried flowers.

Down the left-hand wall there was a makeshift block of showers, separated by painted boards with curtains on rails for privacy. Shower heads hung from a long copper pipe running the length of them, and at the far end, it looked like a few toilets were fitted in small cubicles. Along the back wall was a long unit with sinks and mirrors, and on the right-hand side, two refrigerators and a kitchenette. Even from here Jacob could see the massive pots and pans stacked up, the sort you'd find in a commercial kitchen.

But despite beds enough to sleep thirty and a kitchen designed to feed them, too, the place was entirely empty.

Jacob walked forwards, flabbergasted by what he was looking at, the shotgun still in his hands. This is where they lived. Where they were kept. Where they slept, and showered, and ate their meals. This place was their whole world.

He stumbled a little struck by the smell of it, of women. Of their skin, and their sweat, and their pain. Was this... Was this where Lily grew up? Was this where his mother lived? For ten goddamn years?

The thought nearly bowled him over and he had to hold on to one of the bunk beds for support, the metal frame swaying and squeaking as he put his weight on it, the food that Ellis had given him threatening to claw its way up his throat and spill out of his mouth.

'Awful, isn't it?'

Jacob turned, pulling the shotgun to attention. But the only person between the sights was Lily.

She stood there in the open doorway, hands in her pockets, her eyes sparkling in the half-light as she looked into the barn.

'I took my first steps there,' she said, pointing to the alley between the bunk beds to Jacob's left. 'Lost my first tooth over there.' She nodded to the showers now. 'I ate some bread before we'd said grace and got the worst beating of my life at the end there behind you.' She lifted her chin. 'I was seven.'

'Lily...' Jacob started, his voice choked.

'This place was my whole world,' she said. 'I don't remember going outside until I was I don't know how old. Old enough to know that this was home and that was all there was to it, I suppose.' She smiled at him, her face the picture of sadness.

Jacob didn't know what to say.

'You like it?'

'It's...' Jacob said. 'I'm so sorry. Sorry that you had to—'

She lifted a hand. 'It's not your fault, is it?'

'No, but—'

She shrugged then. 'So don't worry about it. It'll all be over soon.'

'What will? What's going on?' Jacob asked, taking a step forwards. 'Where are they?'

'Uh-uh,' she said, the pistol she had tucked in her belt suddenly in her hand, levelled right at him, not a hint of a waver in her grip. 'Don't move.'

Jacob held his hands up, the shotgun in one, the other empty. 'Lily,' he said, 'just tell me what's going on, and—'

She shook her head. 'No. You can't help. So just shut up and do what you've always done – nothing.'

Lily moved quickly and before Jacob realised what she was doing, the door was already sliding closed.

'No!' He charged forwards, but he was too deep in the barn and she already had hold of the other door, sliding that closed, too.

They met in the middle with a clang a half-second before Jacob's hands hit the metal. He was plunged into darkness suddenly, totally blind. He fumbled for the handles but found none – the door was completely smooth from the inside.

As he searched for the seam, trying to dig his fingers into it, pry the thing open, there was a clang from the other side. The latch snapping shut.

Fuck. Fuck. Fuck. No. No. No.

'Don't try to escape,' Lily said through the door. 'Don't try to stop me. It'll be over soon.'

'Lily?' he asked, near frantic. He beat on the door with his fists, shaking them. But there was no breaking through. He surely wasn't the first to try. 'Open the doors!' he yelled, his voice ringing off the cold steel. 'Lily? Lily!'

But there was no response.

There was nothing but silence beyond the door, because Jacob knew she wasn't there anymore.

Lily was gone.

And he was alone.

Trapped.

In the dark.

With no way out.

Chapter 58

Jacob had no idea how he was going to get out, but he knew he needed to. And fast.

Lily had been more human than he'd seen her since he'd first met her. But her words had still rung cold in the night. She was going to 'finish' this, and whatever that looked like, Jacob had no doubts that it would involve something violent, something final... Something deadly.

He turned, fumbling his way forwards in the dark. He kicked a bedside table, knocked into a bunk bed, swearing as he did.

Quickly, he pulled his phone from his pocket and opened it, turning on the torch. A thin, pale light threw itself across the room, the place suddenly frightening, haunted even.

Jacob shuddered, moving through the space. He didn't see any lights hanging up, no switches anywhere. Did the women here simply live in darkness when the sun went down? Were they ushered inside and then locked in, forced into blackness at the whim of whoever was fortunate to exist on the outside of this massive metal box?

The thought followed him as he traced his way along the corridor between the beds, looking for another way out, for some sort of chance at getting out before Lily did whatever it was she was planning.

He reached the very back of the room and checked the wall, finding it solid. He went right to the kitchen, then left, seeing the toilets ahead of him. The smell reached him before he got there, but where there were toilets there were pipes. This construction was done by the men here, and certainly wasn't up to code. The concrete floor he was walking on had cracks running through it — not footed properly. So he doubted that the drainage would be up to the legal requirement, either.

When he reached the toilet, he found what he was looking for. The pipe ran backwards through the wall, mercifully. It looked like a big chunk of the metal exterior had been removed, and a thinner sheet put in place with holes cut for the waste pipe.

This might be his chance. His only chance. Climbing through a hole made for a shit pipe.

He grimaced, finding purchase on the bowl of the toilet seat and the wall. He swung his foot back and then launched his heel into it.

The metal clanged but didn't budge.

He tried again, throwing his heel into the panel.

It buckled a little, denting but not moving.

Fuck, it wasn't going to give.

He looked at how it was fixed to the actual building. Flat rivets. Jesus, this thing was going to be tough. But it was thin. Not thin enough to break, not by his force alone. But he did have another option.

Jacob stood back and lifted the shotgun, pumping it to chamber a slug, lining up the corner of the panel. It wasn't fixed to the ground, just the cladding of the building, and if he could blow some of those rivets out, he could bend it upwards, slide out under it.

Couldn't he?

He didn't wait to doubt himself, just unloaded a dose of buckshot into the metal.

The sound was deafening, the light blinding. Sparks danced and the ball bearings ricocheted and scattered across the floor. The metal was dented mostly, but a few pellets punched through. If he could send the next one right at the rivet, it might...

He held the muzzle closer, lining it up perfectly, then turned his head away and squeezed his eyes shut.

He pulled the trigger, the muzzle flash fierce enough to dazzle him through his closed eyes.

When he opened them, he saw stars, but when they cleared, the light coming from the phone in his hand showed him a hole, the rivet gone.

He let a smile play on his lips for just a moment before lined up the next one, turned away, and fired.

Jacob repeated once more, not thinking of the noise, not thinking of anyone hearing him. He was single-minded. He had to stop Lily. It was the only thing that mattered now.

The sound of the shotgun rang in his ears, a terrible, pained whine, but when he saw what had been achieved, he couldn't help but let out a sharp burst of air. A huff of triumph and relief.

Not thinking about what was on the other side, he took hold of the toilet seat once more and launched his heel into the plate. He kicked, kicked, kicked again until it bent outwards, groaning under the force until it was at a ninety-degree angle, a sixteen-inch space left below it.

He pushed the shotgun through the hole and then got down onto the ground, sliding his feet through the gap, shimmying out into the open air.

The ground beneath him was sloppy and damp, the stench palpable, but he didn't care. Jacob was free, and he was out, and that was all that mattered.

He rolled onto his side and grabbed the shotgun, getting to his feet, suddenly aware of the noise he must have made during his escape. Killing the light on his phone he lifted the shotgun and swung it in a circle. But there was no one around, and no one seemed to be coming for him.

Catching his breath was tough, his heart hammering as his eyes adjusted to the darkness.

He was so unnerved by the quiet of the place. But there was nothing to suggest a max exodus – everyone's belongings were still here; there were trucks and vehicles parked next to the house.

So what the fuck was going on?

He swallowed, looking around, the high-pitched note in his ears subsiding slowly.

Faintly, in the distance, he heard it. Voices? Singing? He turned on his heel, homing in on the sound drifting in the air. Distant, but definitely not in his imagination.

He looked down towards the back of the farm, towards the treeline there beyond the fields. His eyes drifted upwards, unsure what they were seeing. What is that? There were tiny flickers of light in the sky above the trees.

He stared at them. Were they stars? No, he was definitely seeing something else. Tiny embers flickering and burning out as they drifted upwards over the tops of the trees.

A fire? Jacob thought. People? Lily?

Only one way to find out.

He swallowed, pumping the shotgun to chamber another round.

And then he set off down the hill.

Chapter 59

Jacob started down the slope, breath ragged as he ran.

He plunged into the crops and they slapped his elbows as he moved through them, not even sure what they were. Not really caring.

When he emerged, he was on the well-worn perimeter path, but ahead of him there was a gap in the fence, the ground walked to bare earth, another trail leading into the trees. Towards the voices. He'd thought singing, but it sounded too repetitive, too choppy.

He went into the darkness, following the almost hypnotic rhythm of the voices, of the chanting.

The deeper he went, the heavier his legs seemed to grow. The air was thicker in here and he was aching, exhausted. But he had to press on, raking breaths into his body. He'd barely slept in the last two days, barely eaten, and spent more time running and fighting for his life than he'd thought himself capable of. The fact he was still standing was miraculous to him.

As he ran, that thought went around and around his head, but then seemed to muddle and lose itself, his brain growing foggy and slow. He shook his head, wondering if his body was just finally giving out, if he was crashing. But then he detected a familiar, musty smell. A smell that took him somewhere else, back to the farmhouse, to the corridor outside the bedroom. To that moment, to that strange sexual ritual he bore witness to.

He stifled a cough, feeling the choke of that smoke. Jacob slowed, seeing the path in front of him, previously lit only by starlight, now bathed in a warm, indistinct glow. There was smoke floating before him like mist, curling gently around the trunks of the trees to his flanks like phantom snakes.

He squinted through it, at the source of the light, fire dancing through the trees in front of him. He hadn't realised until that moment, but the chanting was louder now, clear and deep. He could feel it in his chest.

His hand lifted to his heart and it felt like it was vibrating instead of beating, a deep sense of dread festering beneath his fingers all of a sudden.

He wanted to run. To turn and run away. But he couldn't. He knew he couldn't.

Shoving his fear down, he pressed onwards, lowering himself closer to the ground, veering off the path to the fire as he got closer.

There were people all around it, dozens. Men, women... *God* – children. Babies and children in the arms of the women, all positioned around the great bonfire.

All positioned around... him.

Jacob froze, shielded by the trees, and looked onwards, no more than ten feet from the backs of the unsuspecting crowd.

David Hall stood before his audience and raised his hands.

The people hushed, their rhythmic chanting quelling immediately like he was the conductor to their orchestra.

He stood there, tall and thin in a pair of linen trousers turned up to the mid-calf, his feet bare and dark with dirt.

He was shirtless, his tanned skin leathery like the wing of a bat.

Though there was no wind, his white hair billowed softly in the current of the flame at his back. He seemed to be standing close enough that a fire of that size should be burning him. But he was unfazed. Jacob could feel the gentle heat of it on his face from where he was standing. How was the old man doing it?

'Life. Death,' David Hall said, looking at the faces of his disciples. He reached to his throat and closed his fist around the crucifix hanging there, squeezing hard. 'It's a part of the natural cycle of the world, isn't it?'

The people nodded in response, entranced by him.

Jacob found that he was, too.

The herbs, the plants responsible for the smoke, crackled softly at the foot of the fire, their fumes slithering their way into the air as they smouldered.

'We know that as much as life is in His plan, so is death. He gives, he takes. We accept that. It is in everything he does. The day gives light, the night takes it. The sky gives water, the earth absorbs it. The trees give air, we breathe it. The body... gives life. The fire takes it.'

A shiver ran down Jacob's spine.

'That's natural, isn't it?' He turned to the fire so quickly Jacob jolted a little. 'There is nothing so glorious, so pure, so *purifying* as the fire. We know this. We accept this. It is the truth he provides us, and it is the truth we accept.'

Murmurs of agreement rolled through the crowd.

David turned back to them. 'We are here to create, to recreate in His image. That's why I'm here, and it's why He brought you to me. Wayward souls lost in this tragic, terrible world. You were searching for something, for a home. For a purpose. And He guided you to me for *that*.

For *this*.' He paused, looking around the faces once more, a seriousness about him that made Jacob hold his breath. 'My dear,' he said then, fixing his eyes on someone in the crowd. 'Come to me.' He extended a hand and a young woman, waifish and small, rose to her feet and walked forwards.

Jacob looked on, watching as she walked into the light, recognising her at once as the girl from the barn. The one who was chained up. The one who was being punished.

She walked into David's arms and he encircled her in his grasp, kissing her head, smoothing her hair.

'My dear,' he said. 'It is not your fault. You know that.'

She remained still in his arms.

'It is His plan. This is what is meant for you.' He held the girl at arm's length. 'You know that, don't you? We all walk different paths. And yours has led you here. To this moment. To this place.'

She nodded, arms at her sides.

'You know what He wants you to do, don't you?'

She nodded again.

'You know that He loves you, don't you?'

She nodded a third time.

'You know that *I* love you. Don't you?'

She was shaking a little.

David leaned forwards, kissing her on the mouth. Softly. A lingering kiss that turned Jacob sick. Made him want to look away.

But he couldn't.

David stepped back, releasing the girl.

'It's alright,' he said, his voice barely a whisper. 'You can go now.'

She sighed, her shoulders falling. A great weight lifted from her. A great relief washing over her, all of her worries, her fears taken away in an instant.

She let out a single note, a sob of utter joy.

Jacob grinned despite it all, feeling it with her. Feeling an overwhelming sense of awe, of hope. Of happiness.

David smiled at her and Jacob smiled back.

Then he stepped to the side and offered her the fire.

And the girl simply walked into it.

Chapter 60

At first there was no sound save for the gentle crunch of the wood as the girl fell into the flames.

She didn't scream at first, but after a second or two, it began. A vile and chilling shriek that exploded from the pyre, sending a column of sparks and embers skywards as she began to flail.

Everything in Jacob told him to leap out and pull her free, try to save her. But he knew it was already too late.

David stood just a few feet away from her and watched, as all the others did, too. Watched. Listened as she burned to death.

Mercifully, the screaming stopped after just a few seconds, her body going into shock, her mind shutting down. Jacob hoped it wasn't too agonising, that it didn't go on too long, but he knew a few seconds in there would feel like an eternity.

He buried his face in his shoulder, not wanting to look at it, her darkening body now as much a part of the fire as the fire itself.

Jacob steadied himself, willing the after-image of it to fade, and then opened his eyes once more, homing in on David who was still just standing there.

A dark desire took hold of him then. David was just twenty feet away. And Jacob held a shotgun in his hands.

Slowly, he raised it up until the barrel was braced against the trunk of the tree to stop it shaking, the sights trained on the old man's back.

He fingered the trigger, licking his lips, readying himself to do it. This wasn't the plan – it wasn't stopping Lily, and it wasn't saving them. It was very likely killing himself, if anything. The moment he pulled that trigger, carnage would ensue. Jacob counted six men in the audience, and he had no doubt they were all armed, and if their leader had a hole put in him, they'd not waste any time returning fire.

But the chance to wipe a man like David Hall from the earth forever? Send him to the God he so loved? Was that worth it?

Before he could decide, Jacob heard footsteps, grunting, harsh voices ordering someone to move, to get up.

The gallery parted and a man was thrown through the gap and into the firelight.

Jacob gave a little gasp, lowering the shotgun slightly, watching over the top of it as Todd Ellis slumped to the ground and then got to his knees painfully, his right leg tightly wrapped in fabric soaked with blood.

Jacob looked at him, a shell of himself, as he got upright, hands rested on his thighs, and stared at David Hall.

Hall turned to him, briefly glancing at Chief Jeff Harris of the Devils Lake PD and another man he didn't recognise, a long hunting rifle slung over his shoulder. He smiled briefly at the two men, who nodded in reverence and then backed away wordless and got down onto the ground like the others around them.

'Ah,' David said, clasping his hands together gently like there wasn't a burning body right behind him. 'I've been waiting for you. I'm glad you're here,' he said to Ellis. He looked at the others in the crowd. 'You remember the story of Job, don't you?' he asked them. 'Of Eve and the Garden of Eden? Of Daniel in the lion's den? Of Shadrach, Meshach, and Abednego? Of Jesus's temptations by the devil in the wilderness?' He lifted his hand and drummed his index finger in the air. 'All of these stories have one thing in common, don't they? A test of faith.' He gently banged a closed right fist into his open left palm like a judge's gavel. 'This man... This man...' he went on, pointing at Ellis. 'He has been a test of your faith, of our faith. I tried to welcome him into our home, into our community, and he spat in our faces. Chose not to do the lord's work, to help us hunt down those who trespass against us, who try to destroy what we have here. Those serpents that lurk in the grass, waiting to poison our minds, our souls.'

Did he mean him? Lily? Jacob tightened his grip on the shotgun, watching, promising himself that if David offered Ellis the fire he'd shoot, no questions asked.

'This man was sent here to test us, and he failed. Failed in the face of our unwavering faith.' David now interlocked his fingers in front of him to show strength. 'We will resist, and we will endure whatever we must to prevail. We know this is his plan, and that all of this is just a reminder of what we have been through, and what's yet to come.'

Jacob cast around the faces in the crowd as nods of agreement rippled through it, homing in on a familiar face. The woman from the field who'd pled for help. She was nodding, forcing a smile, but the terror in her eyes was stark.

'But – one thing is certain,' David continued. 'That justice will be visited upon those who deserve it. That it will be swift. And it will be definitive.' His hand cut the air like a guillotine. 'God works through us, and in his name, in his image, we will defend our faith against those who seek to break it.' His eyes swept the people once more and then came to rest on Chief Jeff Harris. He gave one, almost imperceptible nod and the chief scrambled forwards like a dog, getting to his feet before he took hold of Ellis's hair, grabbing a rough fistful, and pulled his head back, exposing his throat.

A blade glinted in the light of the fire, twisting through the air in Harris's other hand before it came to gently rest on Ellis's jugular. It paused there, anticipating the slash, the arterial spray of blood.

David Hall looked at him. 'This is your chance. Your one and only chance – repent. Give yourself to God, fully, and in His grace, you will be spared. In His love, you will be saved.'

Ellis's lips twisted into an ugly sneer and he spat right at David, the chunk of spittle hitting him square in the chest.

His eyes unflinching, he wiped the viscous liquid from his skin and held it up, his fingers glistening for a second before he lowered them to his mouth and pushed them between his lips. He sucked them clean, moving Ellis's spit around his own mouth before expelling it onto the ground. 'Sour,' he announced. 'Like snake venom. There is no saving you, my son.'

Now, it had to be now, Jacob thought, the muzzle moving from David to the chief and back. Who should he shoot? The chief and save Ellis? Or David and put an end to all of this?

He'd only get one shot, he thought. One clean shot. But he couldn't decide.

There was someone next to him then, a hand on his shoulder, the other on the top of the shotgun, not pressing it down, but just laid there, stopping it from shaking.

Lily leaned into his ear. 'Don't do it,' she said, her words soft, making his skin break out in gooseflesh. 'Shoot him, and you'll achieve nothing. If he dies, this doesn't end. You'll only make a martyr of him, and this all just goes on.'

Jacob turned his head to look at her.

'But if you don't shoot… I can end it. Right now,' she promised, turning her eyes to the women, the children before them. 'I can save them all.'

Chapter 61

Jacob stared at her, searching her face for any hint that she was lying, or telling the truth.

She just smiled back at him.

'How?' was all he could asked. 'How can you save them?'

'Like this,' she said.

The pain was instant, blinding. Like someone had shoved a red-hot poker into his lower back. He cried out. Couldn't help it. Loud and pained.

She shoved him then – with strength he didn't think her capable of – forwards and into the open, into the clearing and the light.

He stumbled, tried to put a foot down, but it buckled, numb and lame, unable to take his weight. He pitched instead, tumbling between two women and onto the ground, turning in the air, to see Lily standing there, a bloodied knife in her hand, pulled from the spot where she'd stabbed him, paralysed him, it felt like. He couldn't feel his left leg at all. It didn't belong to him anymore and it flopped limply as he landed hard, the wind knocked from his lungs.

He gasped, spilling the shotgun onto the floor, the women next to him screaming in shock, scrambling to get out of his way.

But Jacob wasn't looking at them, he was looking at Lily. At her other hand. At the lighter she was holding, that she was sparking.

A little lick of flame leapt from the metal and she turned her knuckles over, opening her fingers, letting it fall from her grasp and twist towards the ground.

It landed with a soft thud and flames spewed from the dried brush all at once, consuming the forest floor. They rose and spread, faster than he could have imagined, like she'd poured a ring of gasoline all around the gathering, ripping through the forest with a sinister hiss until the whole place was fenced in.

The heat was unbearable, the air filled with noxious, choking fumes.

Is this what she meant? Save them all? Free them all? Free them from their lives?

Jacob groaned, trying to roll over, dragging his leg behind him. Ahead, the chief looked on in horror at what was happening. David's face didn't change, his eyes fixed on Lily, snatches of her still visible through the flames as she stood and watched the chaos.

All the women and children leapt to their feet, moving inwards away from the flames, protecting their faces from the heat while the men yelled and searched for a way out they wouldn't find.

A strangled grunt sounded behind him and Jacob looked over his shoulder to see Ellis, his elbow thrown into the groin of the chief. The man folded up, and Ellis wrestled the knife from his neck, taking the opportunity of the distraction to make a final bid. He threw himself towards Jacob and crawled as fast as he could towards him, towards the shotgun.

The chief steadied himself and came forwards, loping balefully, the knife raised in his grasp.

Jacob reacted, kicking himself towards the weapon, his hand settling about the stock, throwing it towards Ellis with everything it had.

It bounced, twisted, and Ellis grabbed, it, swinging it in a wide arc as he rolled onto his back, letting go with a blast of steel shot right into the advancing chief.

The force blew him clean off his feet, his chest dismantling itself in a flurry of gore as he sailed through the air, landing with a loud thud, a few choked, drowning gasps escaping him as his chest cavity filled with blood.

David looked down at the man, seemingly unfazed as he fell still, before turning his attention back to Lily.

Jacob followed his gaze, expecting her to be gone.

But she wasn't.

She was just standing there, eyes locked on the man who stole her world.

And the man whose world she was burning down.

She moved in and out of focus, clouded by the smoke, so thick it felt like someone's boot on his chest. He hacked and coughed, the pain from his back lancing up his spine and into his skull. He blinked, trying to focus, verging on unconsciousness as the pain radiated through him. All around people ran in circles, the women protecting their children, everyone choking on the smoke. The terrified wailing of the children filled the air.

A thought ran through his head – something he'd heard or read once. That in the vast majority of cases it wasn't the flames or heat that killed in a fire, it was smoke inhalation. The carbon monoxide that built up in the lungs and the blood. It put you to sleep, and that was it.

Painless. Clean.

The thought brought him little solace, little comfort. For him, or the others.

Next to the pyre, still burning bright, David slowly raised his hands to the sky, tilting his head back and staring towards his maker like this was some sort of divine act, retribution, or another test.

He breathed deeply, filling himself with the smoke.

No. No. Not for him. He doesn't deserve that. Not a peaceful end. Not an easy one.

'Ellis!' Jacob yelled, voice hoarse and torn up.

Ellis looked back at him.

'Can you stand?'

'Not on my own,' he said.

Neither could Jacob. His left leg was useless. And Ellis's right leg was, too.

But… together?

Jacob extended a hand.

Ellis looked at it and then gripped tightly, the two men pulling themselves together.

To their right, two of Jacob's disciples, less keen on dying than him, tried to make a leap through the flames, but only succeeded in setting themselves alight.

They wheeled backwards and forwards, falling into the brush, setting more of the ground ablaze as Jacob and Ellis pulled themselves to their hips, then to their knees. Ellis managed his feet first, and then pulled Jacob up, each of them standing on one foot, using the other for balance.

'What now?' Ellis asked, holding Jacob so tightly he thought his knuckles might shatter.

Jacob battled through the pain in his hand, in his back, and turned his attention to David, stood there facing the fire, hands aloft, welcoming his end.

Ellis understood, looking back at Jacob. He nodded.

'We're not getting out of this,' Jacob said.

'I know,' Ellis replied.

A tree, engulfed in flames beyond the ring of fire groaned and began to fall, landing outside the fire. It kicked up a plume of earth, dousing a narrow channel in the flames.

A woman pointed to it and a few ran that way, skipping through the gap and to safety.

Jacob smiled. *Good*, he thought. *Go. Run. As far as you can away from this place.*

When he turned back to Ellis, the other man was smiling too.

'Ready?' Jacob asked.

'I'm ready,' Ellis replied.

'Thank you,' Jacob said, clutching Ellis's hand with both of his. 'For trying to save Steph.'

'You'll see her soon.' Ellis replied. 'You're a good man, Jacob.'

'You too.'

'I'm sorry I couldn't do more.'

'You've done enough.'

And with that, they turned to David once more, still clutching each other for support, and started forwards. The first step was awkward, painful, but they gained momentum, gained strength with each stride.

A low, long, guttural, primal roar cut through the crackle of the flames and David turned, eyes widening as they reached for him, grabbed him, held him – pushing him backwards, driving him into the flames.

Unlike his ward, he shrieked immediately, writhing as the fire consumed him, not his God or his faith protecting him from his end.

Jacob and Ellis rocked and staggered backwards, falling to the ground, unable to breathe or move, the last expenditure of their energy too much for either of them.

He felt Ellis's hand squeeze his, and knew they'd hold on until it was over.

With his last ounce of strength, Jacob craned his head backwards, looking for her, looking for Lily.

He found her standing there, eyes on him.

He wasn't sure, but he could have sworn she nodded to him, just the smallest hint of a smile on her face.

But it didn't matter anymore.

Jacob just closed his eyes, breathing deeply.

And went into the darkness, thinking of Steph.

Chapter 62

It was eight in the morning when Lily Prescott pulled into the driveway of a beautiful two-storey home to the north of Sacramento. It was in a small cul-de-sac in the suburbs, on the rich side of upmarket with trees lining the streets and Mercedes and Lexus parked in the driveways.

She killed the engine in her Porsche Cayman – new model; fresh off the showroom floor just a few months earlier – and stared up at the house.

She let out a little sigh, rubbing her tired eyes, and opened the door.

Lily stepped out, straightening her smart, black dress, and walked up the concrete driveway, heels clipping on the hard surface. The sun wasn't high yet, but it was already hot.

Still, Lily wasn't sweating.

She let herself into the house and stepped slowly, silently across the hardwood floor, listening for any sounds coming from within.

When she crossed into the living room from the hallway, she spied a tall man standing at the kitchen island. He was reading something on a tablet, sipping coffee. He had a Tag Heuer on his wrist, his tailored trousers hugging his long legs, his two-hundred-dollar haircut accentuating his already rugged features.

He seemed to sense someone there and looked up, surprised at first. But then he smiled. 'Oh, hello,' he said, putting down the tablet.

Lily walked closer, could see the curves of stocks on the screen.

'I didn't expect you this morning,' he said.

'I caught an earlier flight,' Lily replied, pausing short of him.

'Work finished up early?'

'Uh-huh,' she said.

'Head office finally released you then.' He laughed. 'Thought you'd never come home.'

'There were things only I could deal with,' she replied coolly, shrugging a little. 'But it's all done now. And I won't have to go back.'

'That's a relief,' he said. 'They work you too hard.'

'It has its perks.'

Just then, a little girl, no more than three or four, ran from around the island and charged towards her. 'Mommy!' she cried before Lily scooped her up and cradled her against her ribs.

'Hey, baby,' she said, kissing the girl's cheek and nuzzling her neck.

The girl threw her arms around her mother's head and squealed with joy.

'She's missed you,' the man said, folding his arms and leaning against the counter. 'We both have.'

'I missed you, too,' Lily said, coming forwards and kissing him.

He leaned in, gave her a peck, then immediately came back for a longer, more concerted kiss, his hand finding the small of her back as he pulled her closer.

'I really did miss you,' he said.

'Then it's a good thing I'm home.'

'Can I get you some coffee? Guess you've been on the go all night.'

'Yeah, desperate to get back,' she admitted.

'I bet,' he said, walking around the island towards the coffee machine. As he fixed her a cup he looked up at the TV on the opposite wall, the news playing on mute, subtitles running across the bottom.

He always had it on, usually the financial stuff, but this morning it was mainstream media.

'You seen what's going on?' he asked, lifting his chin towards it.

Lily turned to look, holding the girl tightly in her arms. 'No, I've been on the road, what's happening?'

He put down a cup for her, running his fingers up the back of her arm with affection. 'Bunch of people dead up north.'

'Oh.'

'Yeah, it's everywhere,' he said, shaking his head. 'Sixteen confirmed, but they're still finding them. Big forest fire, but they're saying it's more than that – that they burned to death during some ritual.'

She looked at him, grip tightening on the little girl. 'A ritual? What do you mean?'

'Don't know – they said it's some kind of weird cult or something. Way out in the country. A place called Devils Lake in North Dakota.' He stuck out his bottom lip, perplexed by it all. 'Didn't you grow up out that way somewhere? You ever hear about that place?'

'Devils Lake?' Lily asked, kissing her daughter on the cheek, grinning at her. 'No – I've never heard of it.'

Her husband looked at her for a second longer and then shrugged. 'I've gotta head off in a few. I didn't expect you

293

to be back this morning, so the sitter's on the way – you want me to cancel?'

'No, it's alright,' Lily said, putting her daughter down. The girl hugged her leg like a monkey. 'I'm exhausted from travelling, and I have to head out this morning, too. I need to see her.'

The man looked at her, his brow crumpling apologetically. 'I didn't get to call in while you were away, but I spoke to the hospital, they said she's still hanging in there.'

'It's alright,' Lily replied. 'I don't like going to that place either, but she's my mother, not yours. I didn't expect you to.'

He came forwards and kissed her on the forehead. 'Alright, well, give her my love.'

'I will,' Lily replied, clasping gently at his hand before he pulled away and gave his daughter a squeeze.

He waved them both goodbye and headed out the door, leaving Lily and her daughter there together.

'Are you going somewhere, mommy?' the little girl asked.

'Yeah, sweetie,' Lily said, stooping to look her in the eye. 'I'm going to see your grandma.'

'Is she sick?'

'Yeah, honey. She is.' Lily smiled softly at the girl.

'Can I come with you?' she asked, her eyes full.

'No, not today,' Lily replied, hugging her gently. 'I need to see grandma on my own. We have some things to talk about.' She held her at arm's length, smiling at her again. 'Grown-up things.'

Chapter 63

Lily drove through the hills, winding higher, further out of town towards the private care facility that housed her mother.

She was sixty-four, and life hadn't been kind to her.

Lily slowed at the gate to Sycamore Grove, a long, white wall that was ten feet high and curved backwards on the inside so that it couldn't be scaled. There were trees lining the outside, making it look less prison-like, but the branches had all been trimmed so there was no overhang.

The electric gate was manned at all times by a guard in a blue uniform, and he checked Lily's ID against the approved visitors list and buzzed her through.

She drove up the long, winding road to the main house, a twenty-two-bedroom private, secure hospital that offered around-the-clock medical and psychiatric care. The only kind of place that had what her mother needed. She hadn't spent most of the last decade in a place like this, but this was where she was now, and that made Lily feel a little better. A little less guilty. There's nothing she wouldn't do for her mother. The woman had given her everything. And she'd paid the price for it.

Lily parked in a row of expensive cars. She couldn't have said who was richer, the doctors working here or the families of the patients.

She climbed out of her Porsche, her Louboutins getting dusty as she headed for the front door. She always thought how uncomfortable they were, that they'd never feel right on her feet.

She paused on the stone steps, looking up at the sprawling building in front of her, purpose-built and gorgeous, twenty-five grand a month to keep her mother here. It'd taken her a while to find someone that could afford that. And Keith wasn't all that bad. He came from old money, but once you got past his self-important exterior, he wasn't all that bad. And getting better every day with training. He didn't care what she did, and wasn't particularly interested. So long as she was pretty on his arm when he needed her and made him feel like a man, things were good. It was a small price to pay for all this.

She cast a final eye around the manicured gardens, a few of the patients walking the lawns or picking flowers under supervision.

Lily walked inside and approached the front desk, the foyer more akin to a boutique hotel than a mental institution. Which is what this was – no matter how it was dressed up. They all had the same stench, the same feel. She knew it well, had spent her teenage years bussing from her foster homes to the state one where her mom was kept.

She pulled her Gucci sunglasses from her face and smiled at the woman behind the counter.

'Good morning, Mrs Anderson,' the woman said. 'Here to see your mother?'

'I am,' Lily replied. 'How is she?'

The woman smiled sadly. 'She's had a tough few days. She's been asking for you.'

Lily just nodded. She knew why it'd been tough. She knew why she'd been asking.

'You can go through,' the receptionist said, directing her to the left.

Lily walked that way, approaching the magnetic door. She was let through and headed down a long corridor lined with doors. Some were bedrooms, others sitting or reading rooms. At the far end was the main study, a large room with a grand piano and comfortable sofas, a large dining table with jigsaw puzzles on it, and a Bluetooth speaker system playing soft classical music.

There were a few patients dotted around, interacting with their carers or simply staring into space.

Her mother was at the far end of the room, positioned at the window, staring out blankly. As Lily approached, a middle-aged man stood up to greet her. Michael had been her mother's care provider for a little over two years now and helped her with everything. He bathed her, fed her, helped her into and out of bed, with her medications, everything. He beamed at Lily, and she gave a little smile back. It was harder to fake it when she saw her mom.

'Lily,' Michael said quietly. 'She'll be so glad you're here.' He clasped his hands together in front of him. 'She's been struggling a little – so the doctor decided to increase her dosage until she levels out. She's going to be a little in and out of it.'

'Thank you,' Lily replied, looking around the room. 'It's so lovely out, do you think I might take her for a little walk around the gardens? There are a few things I'd like to chat to her about – private family things,' Lily added. 'I'll sign the waiver, of course,' she added.

Michael looked a little apprehensive, but then gave in. 'Sure, I'll get the form, and you can take her around the grounds.'

'Thank you,' I said, feigning another smile. The second Michael turned away, she let it fall from her face and then took the handles of her mother's wheelchair and began steering her towards the exit.

Chapter 64

The sunlight was dappled through the trees, but warm on Lily's face as she made a slow loop around the perimeter of the garden with her mother. She glanced back at Michael who was standing on the porch, watching them the whole way. And that was fine, it was just what Lily was going to say that she didn't want overheard.

She took her mother to the little pergola that sat under the willow tree in the corner of the grounds, a pair of curved stone benches looking back up towards the house. If Lily didn't know exactly what it was, she might have thought the place was pretty, even.

She positioned her mother so that she had her back to Michael, and then sat on one of the benches facing her. She didn't want the man to see her mother cry. And she knew she would.

Her mother looked at her vacantly. The medication was strong, but she knew her mother was in there, and that she'd hear what she had to say.

'I know they don't show you the news in here...' Lily began slowly, picking at a nail in her lap. 'But if they did, they'd have been showing Devils Lake.'

Her mother's mouth twitched a little and her eyes turned to fall on her daughter.

Lily stared at her. 'There you are,' she whispered. She steadied herself. She'd been waiting so long for this moment. To deliver this news. 'He's dead,' she said after a long time. 'David is dead.'

Her mother's lips parted to speak, but the disconnect between her mouth and brain was too much.

'Shh, shh,' Lily said. 'It's okay. I know you...' She sighed. This was always the thing she hated most to acknowledge. The thing that felt like poison on her tongue. 'I know you loved him. But... But he deserved to die.'

Her mother began to shake.

'I know you wanted to stay there,' Lily went on. 'I know you wanted to keep me there. To give me to him, to the others.' Her voice began to break. 'But I couldn't let that happen. You know that, don't you? What I did to you...' Lily looked at her mother's stomach. At the place she knew there was a scar from the bullet she'd put in her belly. The one she'd had to put there to stop her mother from running back to them. 'I had to. I had to get us out. And I know you never forgave me for that. Or for telling the police you were crazy. For what they did after...' The memories flashed in her mind. Lily's story to the police that next morning after she'd driven all night, barely tall enough to see over the steering wheel, her mother bleeding out on the passenger seat. The way she'd told them that her mother was unhinged, that she'd kept her prisoner in their home. The way she spun that story, and cried, and pled for them to help her. The way she'd kept the farm a secret and not told them about it. Because she wanted it for herself. The revenge. The satisfaction of dismantling that place herself, brick by brick... And it'd taken more than a decade for her to do it. But now she had.

She watched the fury glow in her mother's eyes. And Lily knew if she'd been able to she would have launched herself at her daughter. Scratched her eyes out for doing it. Her mother was unwell – that wasn't a lie. She had loved David. She had loved that place, that farm. When her husband had died, she'd gone there seeking some kind of solace, some kind of escape. And she'd found it.

All it cost her was her unborn daughter. And it was a price she'd been willing to pay.

But Lily hadn't. And the eleven years she'd spent there had been stolen from her. She'd lain awake every night from the time she was old enough thinking about it, how much she wanted to get away from that place, from those men. The cries of the other girls, whimpering, weeping softly into their pillows in the big barn... they still haunted her. Fuelled her.

'He burned to death,' Lily said then, not making any attempt to hide her smile. 'It hurt. A lot. And his God, or his followers, didn't save him. No one did. And I stood and I watched as he burned.' She let that sit with her mother, the frail old woman clutching at the arms of her wheelchair so hard her frail fingers had turned white. 'My only regret,' Lily went on, 'was that it was over so quickly for him. And I know...' She lowered her head to catch her mother's eyes. 'I know that you wanted to be with him. And you probably want to be with him now, don't you? For this all to be over? You want me to kill you, don't you?' Her lips curled into an ugly grimace. She felt disgust for the woman in front of her. 'Well you don't get to die. You get to suffer.' She reached out and laid a hand on her mother's arm. It was so thin. 'You get to live, knowing that David is dead. That Steph is dead.'

Her mother's eyes flashed to hers.

'That Jacob is *dead*.'

Her mother bared her teeth, thin streams of spittle spilling over her lips, her face contorted in pure rage at the news.

'You abandoned your children,' Lily said. 'You let people hurt me. And this is your punishment. You took everything from me. And now,' Lily said, standing slowly so she towered over her mother, 'I've taken everything from you.'

She walked away, a weight that she'd been carrying her whole life lifted, and let her hand drop from her mother's arm.

Lily let out a shaking breath, dragging her knuckles across her cheeks as she walked back towards the building, finding a smile as she reached the steps, looking up at Michael.

'She's in pain,' Lily said to him. 'And she's upset about something. I don't know what, but I hate to see her suffer. I give my permission to up her medication.'

Michael stared out towards the wheelchair in the distance and then looked down at Lily.

'She's always emotional after your visits,' Michael said. 'And her delusions seem to flare, too. But it's good you come to see her. She needs it.'

'She does,' Lily said, not a hint of a lie in her words. 'I just want her to be comfortable, and to make sure she doesn't try to hurt herself. I fear she might, considering her history...'

'We'll take good care of her, don't worry,' Michael said, stepping down off the porch and offering Lily his hand. 'She'll be around for a long, long time. Don't you worry.'

'You know, Michael,' Lily said with a little sigh, turning to look at her mother once more. 'That's exactly what I wanted to hear.'

CANELO CRIME

Do you love crime fiction and are always on the lookout for brilliant authors?

Canelo Crime is home to some of the most exciting novels around. Thousands of readers are already enjoying our compulsive stories. Are you ready to find your new favourite writer?

Find out more and sign up to our newsletter at canelocrime.com